ZERO AT THE BONE

David Whish-Wilson lives in Fremantle, Western Australia, where he teaches creative writing at Curtin University. He is the author of short stories and the novels *The Summons* (2006) and *Line of Sight* (2010).

davidwhish-wilson.com
@davewhishwilson

Praise for David Whish-Wilson's *Line of Sight*

'Beautifully crafted. The characterisation is flawless and economical, the plot has a creeping intensity that grows greater and greater as it progresses to the unexpected conclusion.'
WEST AUSTRALIAN

'First-rate crime noir.'
Ross Southernwood, SUN HERALD

'One of the best things to come out of Australia in a very long time . . . Well written and meticulously researched, it's a wonderful piece of hard-boiled writing and an incisive analysis of the changing nature of corruption in Western Australia.'
crimefictionlover.com

'Briskly paced and the mood is unadulterated crime noir.'
Stephen Pollock, FREMANTLE HERALD

'This is hard-boiled and riveting writing, with a sense of place and urgency . . . A notable addition to Australia's crime-writing canon.'
CRIME FACTORY

'Gripping and well constructed . . . A satisfying twist to the end of the tale.'
Katharine England, ADELAIDE ADVERTISER

'An outstanding book . . . There is a realness about the story, an edgy sorrow-filled inevitability . . . that compels you on.'
crimedownunder.com

'Terrific . . . A great book with a terrific sense of place and time, a palpable sense of tension, and a cast of characters that you can really get a connection with.'
AUSTRALIAN CRIME FICTION DATABASE

'A great story . . . It's tough and strong but also has heart.'
Liz Byrski

David Whish-Wilson

ZERO AT THE BONE

VIKING
an imprint of
PENGUIN BOOKS

Dee Whish-Wilson
04/07/13

VIKING

Published by the Penguin Group
Penguin Group (Australia)
707 Collins Street, Melbourne, Victoria 3008, Australia
(a division of Pearson Australia Group Pty Ltd)
Penguin Group (USA) Inc.
375 Hudson Street, New York, New York 10014, USA
Penguin Group (Canada)
90 Eglinton Avenue East, Suite 700, Toronto, Canada ON M4P 2Y3
(a division of Pearson Penguin Canada Inc.)
Penguin Books Ltd
80 Strand, London WC2R 0RL England
Penguin Ireland
25 St Stephen's Green, Dublin 2, Ireland
(a division of Penguin Books Ltd)
Penguin Books India Pvt Ltd
11 Community Centre, Panchsheel Park, New Delhi 110 017, India
Penguin Group (NZ)
67 Apollo Drive, Rosedale, Auckland 0632, New Zealand
(a division of Pearson New Zealand Ltd)
Penguin Books (South Africa) (Pty) Ltd
Rosebank Office Park, Block D, 181 Jan Smuts Avenue, Parktown North, Johannesburg 2196, South Africa
Penguin (Beijing) Ltd
7F, Tower B, Jiaming Center, 27 East Third Ring Road North, Chaoyang District, Beijing 100020, China

Penguin Books Ltd, Registered Offices: 80 Strand, London WC2R 0RL, England

First published by Penguin Group (Australia), 2013

1 3 5 7 9 10 8 6 4 2

Text copyright © David Whish-Wilson 2013

Design by John Canty © Penguin Group (Australia)
Cover images: Image of Perth provided courtesy of Kinder & Scott Stevenson/SLWA;
Whiskey in glass image TS Photography/Getty Images; Ingot wording: Nomurasa/Getty Images
Typeset in 12/17 Adobe Garamond
Printed and bound in Australia by McPherson's Printing Group, Maryborough, Victoria

National Library of Australia
Cataloguing-in-Publication data:

Whish-Wilson, David.
Zero at the bone/David Whish-Wilson.
9780670077533 (paperback)

A823.4

penguin.com.au

for Fairlie Rose

Prologue

Max Henderson pushed Geraldine, his red cloud kelpie, gently with his ankle. She whined to get to the fridge, unlike Bill, who sat with his tongue lolling.

'Go on, get,' said Max again, although his heart wasn't in it. Geraldine never knew when to stop, whereas Bill the pup was always bug-eyed and happy.

Max opened the fridge and felt the cold air on his tanned legs. He nudged Geraldine again, who barked with pleasure. Inside was the goat given to him by another Vietnam veteran, self-sufficient in milk, meat and vegies from his extensive garden. Once a year, his friend culled the boy goats and gifted Max the hacksawed legs, ribs and forequarters in bloodied shopping bags.

Besides the goat, there was nothing in the laundry fridge but his drink, protected from the summer heat. Moselle and claret and burgundy. Max Henderson was a wealthy man, but he'd always refused Jennifer's demands to install the air-conditioning that would make their lives more tolerable.

'Dries the seed in a man . . .' he quoted, before realising he'd spoken aloud.

Geraldine caught something in his voice, ceased her whining, cocked her head. Max blinked, and the tears welled up. It had been like that these past months.

He pushed away a bottle of Lagavulin, rolled it against a Highland Park. On a normal evening, Jennifer would take out his whisky a half-hour before he returned home, to let the temperature settle. He would warm the spirit further in the tumbler in his hand, while Jennifer served his dinner. Bringing the spirit to his nose, he'd gauge whether it had opened up, then add a frond of water over the back of a spoon, releasing the old-country flavours of peat and granite. Jennifer would place his dinner on the coffee table before the record player, set the needle on some Beethoven, Schubert or Bach. He would eat quickly and without pleasure, then politely thank his wife for the meal, lying to her that it was delicious. He could see the trouble that she'd gone to.

Then he would drink more whisky and listen to music, feel himself relax into his chair, sink further from the thoughts of his day. When the bottle was finished and Jennifer was in bed, the needle crackling over the record's end, he would sleep in the armchair. When he got this jumpy it was dangerous for Jennifer, lying in bed beside him. She only had to touch him during the night and he would strike out, or commando roll out of bed, into the wall. Safer that she slept alone.

He pushed the fridge door shut and carried the chunks of goat into the cool night air. The sea breeze sloughed in the needles of the casuarina that circled the patio. His favourite tree, the casuarina, reminding him of childhood holidays, the property on the banks of the Donnelly River where his uncle farmed potatoes and apples and cherries, cattle on the fringes where the fences were strong.

Nothing grew beneath a casuarina, in its carpet of thin brown needles, but there was shade enough for a boy to stare across the valley, to read Commando comics, books of travel and adventure, the iodine-tinted river snagging on islands of rock and branch, running down to the sea.

Max tipped the bundles of meat onto the needle carpet and watched as the dogs began to chomp and tear, only Geraldine turning to catch his eye, suspicious at his silence, his liquid eyes in the darkness.

He carried the bloody bags over to the rubbish bin and pried off the lid, feeling the humidity of bacterial decay over his hand as he dropped the bags inside. He didn't replace the lid right away. Instead, as he had done as a child, he slipped his fingers inside the lid handle and held it up like a shield; the stick and stone battles he had fought against his cousins, and the pellet gun too, fired across the paddock, the shield protecting his face, his eyes.

He took up the .22 rifle that leaned against the nearest casuarina, a semi-automatic that fitted easily into his other hand. He stood as he had done as a child, shield in one hand, weapon in the other; Ned Kelly or a Trojan warrior, he could never decide – the armour of the one crude and heavy, the other beautifully sculpted.

Max Henderson walked behind Geraldine first, held the bin-lid shield above her head, protecting him from her eyes. He fired into the back of her skull, turned his wrist and aimed at Bill, who'd leapt at the ugly sound, his eyes running wet between Max and the twitching body of his elder sister.

'Sorry, old mate,' Max said, although his words didn't come, and he fired and caught Bill in the cleft above the eyes, dropping him.

Max Henderson sat against the warm trunk of a casuarina, the resin scent and the whispering branches and twitching shadows enclosing him as he turned the .22 upon himself, the toes of his bare feet clenching up needles, his trigger finger tightening, and his eyes upon Jennifer as he imagined her tonight, slapping mahjong tiles and reaching for her chablis, the faces of her friends warm in the candle glow, and then his muscles were tense against the coming bark of light, and he put the barrel into his right eye until the spasms of red covered the filaments of dark, and he said it one last time, 'Sorry, old mate,' and then it was done.

1

Swann tilted the page against the moonlight and tried to follow the map of wiring that described, in red and blue and green, the fine print of the manufacturer's instructions. Specifically, how a home enthusiast might install the wireless box of the ERA2012, the latest and greatest in covert surveillance devices – 'perfect for the professional and amateur alike'. The working parts of the bugging system were standard – a radio transmitter and a microphone – but the electronics were a bastard to the amateur eye.

Swann folded the manual and tossed it onto the passenger floor pan, where it rested on iced-coffee cartons and old newspapers, and the piss bottle that he would soon need to use.

The EK Holden was backed under some swamp paperbarks, not a few feet from the lapping waterline. Before Swann set his lair, he'd parked on the roadside verge and stripped sheets off the paperbarks, laid them over willow branches where he intended to hide. It was summer, but the earth was still damp where the edge of the swamp retreated inland. In winter, both Swann and his Holden would be underwater. The cracked bed of dried mud allowed him to wait within sight of the housing subdivision, while remaining concealed beneath the low branches of the modong and flooded gum that circled the swamp, or what they were now calling Bibra Lake, one of the chain of swamps that started in Fremantle and spread across the coastal plain like the beads of a necklace.

There was a burst of static from the CB radio under the dash, then an eager voice: 'Charlie 66 – transporting Detective Sergeant Farquarson and Detective Inspector Hogan from Bentley to Fremantle – estimate thirty minutes. Over.'

'Roger that, 66.'

'More like heading from the Raffles to the National, by way of the Leopold,' Swann said aloud, because everybody talked to themselves on a stake-out. He lit a cigarette and slumped on the bench seat, closed his eyes. He could see the uniformed driver behind the wheel of Charlie 66, closing his nose to the stink of stale beer and sweat and cigars, but keen and polite to the two plain-clothes detectives, pleased to have been trusted as their rostered driver for the night. Being night driver for senior Ds as they trawled around and collected their takings was the first step to making detective, everyone knew that – as long as you cleaned up their vomit, dropped them to their doors, didn't listen to their conversation and kept your mouth shut.

Same as it ever was.

Swann cracked his wrist and looked at the time – gone eleven. He thought about the bottle of Grant's lying in the floor-pan rubbish, then put it out of his mind. He'd need it to sleep, later – whenever that might be.

He dropped his cigarette into an iced-coffee carton and slapped at a mosquito on his wrist. The subdivision was quiet. Every third or fourth house was occupied, naked bulbs pooling yellow on the front verandahs, but the rest lay dark and vacant, waiting for the grand auction to be held next week – the reason Swann was on the job. The developer who'd built the Lego-land houses and the council who'd put in the infrastructure had suffered building site thefts, as was to be expected, but with the auction so near they weren't taking any chances.

Someone was nicking the turf lawns off the front yards during the night. Rolling them up the evening after they'd been laid, before they even had time to sink tentative roots into the grey sand. It wasn't only the lawns of the vacant houses, either. Families were going to bed, only to wake up and discover that the neat green lawn they'd spent the day watering in was gone. Wind kicking up the dirt and filling the house with grit and dust. The place looked more like a child's sandpit than a slice of suburban paradise, ready to go under the hammer.

It would be funny if Swann wasn't so desperate for work. He had bills to pay. All three of his daughters lived at home, though they did their bit with part-time jobs. Blonny was still at school. Sarah was pregnant, ready to marry a bloke Swann didn't really know. Louise was studying law at the sandstone university north of the river, the first in their extended family to go on from high school. Marion had returned to her original job as a community nurse, and was working full-time in the brothels and homes of the elderly in the local area.

Swann relented and reached over and drew up the bottle of Grant's, filled his mouth and let it drain. Felt the immediate warmth in his belly radiate into his limbs. He'd rather be drinking whisky that came with a cork instead of a cap, but the blend would do. He'd put in twenty-six hours of surveillance over the past three nights and would bill the developers for the enquiries he'd made, the time spent trawling through the papers looking for blokes flogging lawn, of which there were many.

Payday next week. Some crayfish on the table and summer wine for Marion. Maybe some desserts from the Italian place around the corner.

A fox pranced over the dried mud to his right, paused to stare at him, skipped away and dove into a storm drain built into the kerbing that fronted the estate. An hour ago a couple of teenagers had scoped out the occupied houses, peering over the front fences to see what they could lift, and had gone away empty-handed.

A new suburb was like a new frontier, edging out into the banksia woodland, and those who lived there were naturally wary – he could see that. Unlike his street in South Freo, where kids left their bikes and toys scattered across the front yards, the lawns here were tidied up, stuff packed away behind garage roller doors. Cars the same. Not even any pot plants on the porches.

Swann saw them coming from his left, three men with wheelbarrows. They didn't muck around. Parked their barrows on the street and started rolling up the lawn, placing them in the wheelbarrows then returning for more.

Swann took up his binoculars and focused. Had to laugh. He thought he'd recognised the eldest from his slope-shouldered gait, the knotty legs and arms. Stan Farmer, wearing the blue terry-towelling hat he always wore, the same grotty white singlet and ball-tight stubbies, barefoot.

It was Stan who had the contract to lay the lawn. Now he was taking it back, recycling. The three men looked pissed – all day laying the lawn, then all night pinching it back; only the pub session in between. His two sons as offsiders.

Swann knew Farmer from his childhood – he was one of his step-father Brian's workmates. Took compo for an injury on the docks, then set up his own gardening business.

Sell something, nick it back, sell it again. Oldest scam in the book. When Swann had asked about the company laying the grass he'd been told by the developer not to worry, it was being done by a mate. Stan was everybody's mate.

Swann put away his binoculars and relaxed into his seat. Took the cap off the bottle of Grant's and allowed himself a good slug. They'd be at it for some time, and he wasn't tasked with arresting the culprits, just identifying them. What he had to decide was whether he would.

Swann's stepfather had plenty of dodgy stevedore mates, but Stan was one of the best. An old leftie, but genuine about it. Part of that ethos meant stealing whatever wasn't nailed down, from those who could afford it. Swann knew the rules, he'd grown up with them – never nick anything from someone worse off than you.

Stan Farmer had often brought food when Swann was a kid and Brian was on the drink, gone for days with his pay packet, coming home when it was spent. Stan would slip Swann's mother a few coins. The children of drunks and gamblers were often looked after by people like Stan, whose own father had been a drunk. Stan knew what it was like to be hungry.

Stan had obviously decided that the developer was either a dickhead or could afford to be ripped off, or both. The trick for Swann was to make sure Stan didn't thieve the lawns again. Only then would Swann get paid. He thought about it for a while, the whisky helping to pass the time.

By four o'clock, Farmer & Sons had taken up each of the lawns on the new street and had wheeled them around the corner. Swann waited for the ignition of Stan's old Bedford truck before starting up the Holden. He followed the Bedford with his headlights off. The truck was fully laden, a tarp thrown over the turf that was ready to be relaid come the dawn.

Stan didn't live too far away, on a quiet street in Coolbellup. Swann parked down from Stan's house, watched the three tired men enter the fibro home, no lights coming on. He lit a cigarette and took up the CB handpiece. It was a crime to impersonate a police officer but Swann knew the codes – there was little chance of being caught. He put on his most youthful voice, pretending to be a uniformed constable from Kwinana station and giving a fake name. He told them about the speeding car he'd followed up the coast to a quiet Coobie street. Described how he'd peered through the kitchen window, seen the table laden with drugs and cash. Mounds of it, just sitting there. He was awaiting further orders.

Swann cut himself off before he started laughing. He wouldn't have long to wait. Sure enough, ten minutes later, they came from both ends of the street. Paddy wagons and unmarkeds, no sirens. He saw Charlie 66 and some of the other nightshift Ds, uniformed from Freo and stations beyond, skidding around the corner, driving up onto the lawn, taking out the letterbox, spilling out of the car. A dozen or more coppers, pushing each other aside, the door cracking down, all dignity forgotten in the race to the spoils. A fistfight between two Ds from different stations spread to some of the uniformed. Lights went on as the neighbours woke up. Swann reversed around the corner.

The kicked-in door and dramatics would give Stan a fright, and Swann would call him later in the day. Stan would be at home to take his call, no doubt about that. Coolbellup wasn't a good suburb to live in, lacking a front door. Swann would call the developer and tell him he'd chased off the culprits, there was no way they'd be back. Then he would get paid.

It wouldn't matter, though, if he wasn't. Twenty of the state's finest blueing on a Coobie lawn was reward enough.

2

Gary Quinlivan eased the antique hog around a parked Nissan Cedric and pulled in to the kerb. He balanced his weight on booted feet and kicked the stand while he set the gear to idle, slow and steady. His leathers creaked as he climbed out of the saddle, thighs aching.

Born to ride, *my arse*.

He unzipped the leather jacket and felt inside for the stock, pulled it out just enough, looking down Quarry Street as he stood tall. The usual Fremantle crowd. Workers and Abos and deros and Rajneeshees – every third person a nutcase. He didn't mind that they looked at him. Conspicuous and invisible. Another man's Harley. Another man's leathers. Another man's helmet, visor down.

He took a deep breath and stepped back. Made his intentions clear. He was going to walk away and leave the hog running, keys in the ignition. Any other bike and it'd be gone. But not *this* bike. The '46 Harley Knucklehead was well known around town, as was its owner.

Quinlivan turned to the sliding glass doors of the R&I Bank. He wasn't nervous. He had the green light for this one, and the next few, at least. That meant protection from Armed Rob, as long as nobody got hurt. Protection from the toe-cutters too, those bastards who hunted other robbers, assuming any of them were smart enough to hunt him down.

He went straight over to the counter. Sawn-off shottie at present arms, on the trot. Hearing himself shouting. Hogan's words in his ear – *Put the fear into them, son. Frightened people don't remember too good.* He struck a suit who'd stared too long, knocked him on his fat arse, cheek gashed and eye swelling. Adrenalin lifted him, flying along. Christ, he was enjoying this.

The bunnies behind the counter were stashing the canvas tote bag as fast as their arms could move. Marked bills and all, he didn't care. Armed Rob would get him the numbers on those. Still shouting. Each of the bunnies flinching at his every word. One of them crying.

Hang on. I saw that.

One of the tellers, the youngest, a thin chick with permed hair and green eyes, had backed out of view of the security camera. Was stuffing wads down her blouse. Looked him straight in the face. Businesslike.

He'd have to watch that one. She had no fear. She'd *remember*.

He took a mental picture of her face. He'd get her details from Armed Rob, after they'd done the interviews. Visit her one day. Help her spend some of that money, rightfully his. In the meantime, good luck to you, sweetheart. Happy birthday from Gary. Twenty-five years old today.

The bag was full. Time to make his exit, leaping over the whimpering mugs on the way to the door. Still flying. The hog still running. Kickstand tucked. First gear out into the traffic. Up yours to a bus driver.

Three minutes from go to whoa.

3

Swann held the green wire and stripped the end with a pair of long-nosed pliers. He laid the exposed copper onto the contact, placed the soldering iron onto the solder and watched the plug melt over the wire. He blew on the weld and pulled the iron out of the wall socket, laying it on an asbestos mat.

Second time lucky. He placed the plastic hood over the sleeve of the receiver and with his Phillips head worked the screws. Set the tape in the recorder and wound it to the beginning.

There was a creak on the steps of the shed. Marion stood in the doorway, framed by the pale morning light, her face in shadow. His wife kept most of her gardening tools behind the door, but she made no move to enter. The fibro shed was small, and if Marion wanted anything from beneath his workbench he'd have to leave first.

'Someone dropped this on the front verandah, drove away in a hurry.' Marion held up the Monday-morning newspaper. Behind her, the sound of Sarah and her boyfriend playing Twister beneath the sprinkler, cicadas working up a racket.

Swann knew the tone in Marion's voice, felt the butterflies rise in his stomach.

'Here.' Marion passed the paper but didn't leave. Swann spread it over the workbench, tilted the full-page article to the light. There he was, ex-Superintendent Frank Swann in full uniform, coming out of the Royal Commission in 1976, looking guilty and hunted. Like Lee Harvey Oswald before he copped the gut shot. Beside that was a picture of Detective Inspector Donald Casey, corrugated hair and small hard eyes, before he was assassinated at his front door on the final day of the Royal Commission, killer unknown.

The headline read 'BROTHERS-IN-ARMS'. But the devil was in the detail. The caption: 'Three years after the cold-blooded murder of his friend Donald Casey, Detective Inspector Ben Hogan has vowed he will never forget, and he will never forgive'. Hogan's words were reinforced by his photograph beneath the caption, one from the archives, aiming a shotgun over the bonnet of an FJ Holden, necktie slung over one shoulder, rollie burning at his lips: the scene of an early-sixties domestic siege in Lathlain.

Swann remembered it well. He'd been stationed at the back fence when the shotgun went off, killing the twenty-year-old longhair who'd barely cracked the front door, armed with a screwdriver.

Marion's hands were cold on his shoulders.

'Is that what I think it is?'

'Hogan's got his nose in front.'

Detective Inspector Hogan had long coveted the top job in the CIB, and it looked like he'd succeeded. There was no way the Commissioner would have permitted the article unless he was backing Hogan as the new chief, once the incumbent retired in a few weeks.

'I don't like it,' Marion said. 'I didn't hear anything about this.' Marion's father had been a senior detective and her sources were as extensive as Swann's.

The article was a hatchet job, rewriting Swann's involvement in the Royal Commission and his long years of service beforehand.

The caption beneath the photo of Swann read: 'A very close friend of murdered brothel keeper Ruby Devine, forced to retire without pension after Royal Commission'.

Swann didn't know who'd gunned the inspector down, but Hogan had been spreading the rumour ever since that it was Swann's doing, and had sworn to avenge his friend. Now Hogan was nearly a boss, that day was drawing near.

Swann tore out the page of newsprint and crunched it into a ball. His daughters wouldn't have seen the article. The years since his forced retirement had been quiet, all about keeping his head down and looking after his family. He'd made a pact with Marion that he wouldn't drink at home, tried to make their lives feel safer.

On the parched grass, Sarah and her boyfriend were still playing Twister beneath the tacking sprinkler. Sarah sat cross-legged as the sprinkler lobbed out silver beads. She spun the arrow while Cameron tried to get his left leg over his right to reach the line of red dots. Both his hands were twisted beneath him and his arse was in the air, and he was laughing with the effort. There was no dignity in it but the boy wouldn't quit.

'Don't give up, boof!'

Sarah squirted her boyfriend with the hose, who grunted and collapsed in a tangle of limbs.

Swann still hadn't made up his mind about Cameron. Marion and Louise had given him the all-clear, but Swann wanted to be sure that his daughter would be looked after. Sarah was already five months pregnant and had only just turned eighteen.

Swann crossed the lawn and held up the bug and the recorder. 'Test this for me?'

'Oh Dad, really.'

But Cameron was looking at it like an eager child.

'Dad, it's illegal.'

'Highly. But not with your permission. Just continue what you're doing, but don't let the sprinkler near it.'

He attached the bug with Blu-Tack to the underside of the wooden outdoor table that he'd made with Marion's father from old wandoo planks and jarrah offcuts. 'Give me one minute, then start talking.'

Sarah rolled her eyes and Cameron shrugged, took a seat and poured a glass of Cottee's lemon.

Swann walked through the sleep-out where Louise was practising her bass guitar, sprawled over a bean bag, her feet on the amp that fed through to the bulky headphones that made her look like Mickey Mouse. Through the kitchen where Blonny had her nose in a biology textbook, still in her school uniform of jeans and T-shirt, her permed red hair covering her shoulders. She didn't look up as he went by. Out the front of the house, he slid over the bench seat of his Holden, put the recorder on the floor of the car, and waited. Presently, the red light on the receiver flickered and the tape started recording. He waited a couple of minutes, then turned it off. Played it back. A duet. Sarah and Cameron singing 'Pinball Wizard', a parody of Swann in the shower that morning. The boy had a sense of humour at least, even if he couldn't hold a note. And the bastard thing was finally working.

Swann looked up to see Marion on the front porch, fist to her ear in the phone signal. Come hither with her other hand. She didn't look worried. Could only mean a new job.

Swann needed the money, and he needed the distraction.

4

Jennifer Henderson brought Swann a glass of iced water and stood beside him. He was staring at a sepia photograph, trying to place the swathes of mist rolling off granite mountains, paddocks full of Black Angus. Somewhere near the Porongorups, in winter?

'It's Tasmania, my father's old property.'

Jennifer Henderson was a decade younger than Swann, in her early thirties. The first thing he'd noticed was her long black hair, ice-cream skin, pale freckles over the bridge of her nose. High cheekbones and elfin ears, mischief in her dark blue eyes – that Irish look he'd always loved. She stood close to him, closer than was usual for a new client, looking up into his face. Perfume that smelt like honeycomb, white wine on her breath. Sleeveless silk blouse that clung to her shoulders.

'Beautiful piece of land. Does he still work it?'

He'd picked her as a spouse who wanted revenge, the usual story. A little drunk and bold. Soon to be disappointed when he didn't play.

Her smile was sad, and for the first time the moneyed accent dropped away. 'The bank took it when I was a teenager. Poor Dad, broke his heart. It was just a hundred acres of alpine scrub, but *his* father had been granted it as a returned soldier after the Great War. Now, Mr . . . Swann, why I asked you here.'

Stepping away, but her scent not leaving him. She indicated a buttery leather settee that was worth more than Swann's car. Sat beside him, but he didn't turn. Felt her eyes continuing to measure him, a test of some kind. The house was tastefully decorated; nothing shouted attention until you looked closer and saw that everything was interesting, the furniture mostly Japanese lacquered merchant chests and altars; samurai armour and Papuan tribal masks on the walls.

Jennifer Henderson turned the dewy glass in her hands, stared inside the cage of her perfectly groomed fingers, the single gold band on her ring finger gently tapping the glass. Meeting his eyes then looking back at her drink. First sign that he was mistaken, that there was more here than flirtation and revenge.

Unlike most rich women, Jennifer Henderson wasn't composing herself. She wasn't entirely natural, either. But he could see warmth there. The working-class father might explain that, but then he'd met plenty of women from humble backgrounds who'd chipped themselves into stone and ice.

Was it grief?

'I need your help, Mr Swann —'

'It's Frank. Usually just Swann.'

'All right then, Swann . . .'

It was grief. She was no longer tapping her finger against the glass, but the cubes were still trembling.

'Last week, my husband shot himself. In the backyard.'

He hadn't seen this coming, beyond the suspicion that her familiarity was a test of some kind. She'd turned it off now. Her eyes were down, and so was her voice. No other sign of emotion. No tears, or stumbling over words. In control, but feeling it deeply.

'He shot his dogs first. Fed them, shot them. Then shot himself.'

Swann took a deep breath. What he'd assumed was the kind of surveillance job he flicked over to enquiry agents, specialist peepers and creepers, was something else.

'Did your husband —'

'Max.'

'Did Max leave a note?'

'No, no note. No goodbyes. No last meal for me.'

No self-pity in her eyes, just the irony in her voice.

'Where were you at the time?'

'Playing mahjong. My regular Wednesday.'

'Mrs Henderson, I'm sorry for your loss, but —'

'Please don't say no.' Her movement to cut him off was so abrupt that she spilled her drink. Like he'd slapped her. She drew herself up to her full height and stared at him, sadness in her dark blue eyes.

'I'd like to help you, Mrs Henderson, but I'm paid by the hour. There may not be an answer to your husband's suicide. Or not an answer you'd like to hear.'

She laughed ironically. Eyes wide. 'There *is* an answer, Mr Frank Swann. Ex-superintendent of uniformed police. Ex-detective ser-geant. I followed your progress through the Royal Commission. I know who you are, and how you resigned in . . .'

Disgrace. He waited for her to say it.

'. . . disgust. It's why I came to you. To find the answer. You put the murder of a brothel keeper ahead of your own career, the trust of your colleagues. Was she murdered by a policeman?'

'Yes, she was.'

Swann looked into her eyes. Had she read this morning's paper? He drew back, glanced away, sat with his hands on his knees. Drawn into her eyes again. Behind the grief, a fierceness there. Strength. Purpose.

What he was initially wary of – the look a woman gives a man, when *he'll do* – now gone. Made it easier to say yes.

He leant forward, elbows on his knees. 'No promises . . .'

In the upstairs den, he settled into the dead man's seat. Max Henderson's personal effects were placed in tidy folders over the leather-studded desk, evidence that he'd planned his exit.

Henderson was a geologist, and according to Jennifer, one of the most highly regarded in the world. After Vietnam, where Max had served as a decorated chopper pilot, and been involved in resupply to the trapped infantry in the Battle of Long Tan, he had done a Master's of Science. Mining was in the blood, apparently. His father and grandfather were both prospectors, first around Kalgoorlie and Coolgardie then up in the Cosmo Newberry area, the Cue digs, before going bust and heading into the city, young Max in tow. His mother had died out there in tragic circumstances; Jennifer had only sketchy details. The drink got his father and he too had died young. Before Jennifer's time. Max never liked to talk about his childhood.

After graduating, Henderson had been a riverwalker in Papua New Guinea, one of the three fabled geologists who discovered the Ok Tedi El Dorado, a mountain of gold in the remote highlands that was still producing. Ok Tedi had made Henderson's reputation and secured his fortune but it also ruined his health. He'd nearly died of malaria up there, and had suffered recurrent bouts every year.

Three tours of Vietnam and recurrent bad malaria. Growing up without a mother; a father who'd died young. Not a good combination for a man's mental health.

Swann opened the folder labelled 'Memberships'. Swanbourne

RSL and Claremont Rotary. Swan Districts football club. Various geo organisations, where he was a regular guest speaker, according to Jennifer, even as he did less and less practical work.

Didn't need to work much, apparently. The house was paid off. They owned a large portfolio of blue-chip stock. Max was wealthy enough to retire in his forties.

But a year ago Max had started work again, as a consultant to a new stake out in the desert somewhere. In a file labelled 'Rosa Gold' there were aerial photographs of red desert scrub, no roads, borders ruled blue to demarcate the stake, surveyors' markings and a few red crosses towards the left southern border. Beneath that a folded map. Same thing. Activity marked in the left southern border, concentric circles enclosing a rhomboid shape sketched in pencil. An ore map? Swann had no idea. There were a few pages of foolscap, written in neat looping script. What looked like the first draft of a speech, detailing the Rosa Gold stake in the jargon of his field. Discussions of brecciated formations and magmatism from the upper Cretaceous period, but no sign of where or when the speech was delivered. The language matter-of-fact, no trace of enthusiasm in a paper describing what was a 'highly significant find'. Nothing else in the file hinted at Jennifer's suggestion that Henderson was working for some 'very serious people'.

Swann closed the file and leaned back in the chair, put his hands behind his head. Noticed the framed quotation on the wall, the only adornment in the darkened room. *'I and my men suffer from a disease of the heart that can only be cured by gold.'* Hernán Cortés.

Swann took the frame off the wall, turned it over. 'For my son Max, on the occasion of your birthday, 30 April 1948. Clarrie Henderson.'

5

Gary Quinlivan tapped the contents of the bag onto his finger and snorted it up, leant against the porcelain tiles. There was something crudely satisfying about using his own product in the toilets of the Northline house of Tommaso Adamo, a man who wholesaled for a living.

Not many people knew he did, of course, and never would, because Adamo was just like his terrace home: nondescript on the outside but with a surprising interior. Adamo had flown out Calabrian masons and tilers for the sole purpose of renovating the old dump. In the backyard beneath the grapevines was an entertaining area with a wood-fired oven and a Byzantine mosaic floor. Painted on the wall was a vast trompe l'œil of the view from his grandfather's villa over the ocean at San Nicola Arcella. His kitchen was ornate and spacious, with marble-topped benches and a country oven that could bake a whole goat with room left for loaves and fishes.

But it was the toilets of Adamo's home that Quinlivan particularly admired. This had a lot to do with the amount of time he spent in there staring at the flickering wall of black porcelain tiles as he passed in and out of consciousness. The toilet and bathroom were so clean you could almost smell the stone of the granite vanity. The house was kept by Adamo's ancient mother, who lived next door. A vase of roses from Adamo's front garden completed the simple effect.

Quinlivan slumped against the toilet cistern and lit a cigarette. There was a lot he needed to learn from Adamo, certain that one day they would be rivals. Adamo's heroin was brought in by a team of mules from Thailand and Malaysia. It was sold on to wogs and others besides. But it was Quinlivan who had access to the pool of money that went with rich kids going off the rails. Kids who bought regularly by the gram, rather than the heavily cut ten-dollar packets on the street.

Adamo was powerful because he had the local Italian vote in his pocket, and because hundreds of men were regularly in his debt, having run up huge losses at his two illegal casinos. But Gary had advantages that Adamo lacked. The man was an outsider, for a start, even if he was an outsider who played court to businessmen and politicians. When Gary arrived earlier, none other than the Honourable MLA Terry Sullivan, the Minister of Police, had been leaving, his ministerial LTD double-parked in the narrow suburban street. On other occasions, Gary had witnessed councillors and senior public servants waiting in their cars for an audience.

But Gary Quinlivan was not on the outside. His father was a judge. He knew all the right people. Who had dirt on whom. Who could be bought, or blackmailed. Who had paper money, and who had it for real. Still, there was a lot that could be learned from the old Italian, no doubt. Now that Quinlivan had promised Adamo wealth beyond anything he'd made from drugs and casinos.

He dropped the cigarette between his legs, walked over to the granite vanity and threw some water on his face. His legs surged and swayed beneath him. He loved heroin so much that he couldn't imagine life without it. He had always been the restless one, the angry one, the boy with too much energy. In his teen years it had been barbiturates and then valium and now it was the bright white powder. Heroin brought harmony into his world.

Quinlivan washed his hands and wiped them dry. His stomach had settled and he felt he could eat some cassata. Yes, he could drink some wine and eat some cassata and listen to Adamo. He already knew what Adamo was going to say. The old boy was anxious about Max Henderson's suicide, and needed reassuring.

Unless, of course, he was somehow responsible for the geologist's death. It was Adamo, after all, who'd been most insistent early on that they pump the Rosa Gold stock and dump it quick, as they'd done with three other penny dreadfuls. It was Henderson who'd convinced them otherwise, at the board meeting where he'd put his money where his mouth was.

Max Henderson was one remarkable cat, tall and rangy, tanned the deep red of the desert from where he'd just returned. He had given them the presentation that convinced them to stump up the money for on-site drilling, the excitement evident in his voice, his face as lined as the aerial photographs of the contours of the stake. He'd laid it out for them, the geology of the site, brecciated structures that some early prospectors had picked up on but lacked the technology to properly exploit.

Adamo had been the only sceptic amongst them, even after Henderson had finished his pitch. It was Quinlivan who'd brought Henderson in to spruik the operation to Rosa Gold, having seen the geologist speak at a mining conference. They'd gotten talking about gold exploration and financing new ventures, and a week later Henderson had called him with news of a promising find. Henderson had convinced Gary of the site's merits, enough to win

Adamo over, although it hadn't been easy. Yes, it was true they'd make a quick dollar from the pump and dump, as safe a con as had ever been played, but here was potential for *serious* money, legitimate money. The gold ingots Henderson had dug from the abandoned mineshaft of some poor bastard were glittering there on the table. And Henderson's own money, forty thousand in cash, was on the table beside them. The geo wanted in, and that was good enough for the rest. You could see it on Henderson's face. He was a believer.

Adamo had raised his hands in mock surrender, but in his mind Henderson was still an outsider. He would be useful when it came to pitching the prospect to mug punters and institutional investors, should the drilling confirm his early surveys, but unlike all the other directors, Henderson wasn't a criminal.

And why would you trust someone who wasn't a criminal?

But the geo had done his job well. The early drills had contained promising assays, just as he'd said. His presence on the board had generated plenty of respect about town. But now that the mine looked like going into operation, now that they were going to be super-rich, Quinlivan could see how Adamo might want to get rid of Henderson, and close the circle once again.

Quinlivan smiled at his reflection in the mirror. Yes, there was plenty he could still learn from the old Italian. How to play the long game, and work from the shadows, avoid the light.

6

The Bulldogs colts and reserves teams were training in the afternoon heat when Swann arrived. The colts, distinguished by their whippet bodies and mullet haircuts, did circle work around the outside of the reserves, running timed sprints the length of the centre square. The coaches shared a cigarette by the fence where the grass was yellow. The Bulldogs league team had placed third last winter and both the colts and reserves had won their premierships. Things were looking good for the coming season, although Swann didn't envy the players training through the summer heat.

Danny Yates filled Swann's pony glass, and one for himself.

'Fly right.'

They tapped glasses and sipped the best brew in Fremantle. Yates had managed the South Fremantle Bulldogs' members bar for near twenty years, ever since his leg broke in a derby against the Old Easts. It was a total bust, and his day job as a hod carrier was over too. Someone had taken pity on him and set him up behind the wood and he'd never looked back. The tap pipes were flushed twice a day, and considering the boozy weekends the place didn't smell too bad.

'Nother bank robbery. You hear about that?'

Swann nodded and lit a Craven A, exhaled down at the carpet. 'Five in less than a fortnight. Greedy. Or an adrenalin junkie . . .'

'Or the bastard's raising a stake for a knee op. All my doctor needs is the fucken balaclava.'

'You still saving that up?'

'Doc reckons they're gonna have to break my thighbone again, reset it. Why the knee's never come good; the bone's out of whack.'

Swann imagined a band-saw screaming over Yates's leg, made a face.

'Yep,' said Danny. 'And I'm paying for the pleasure.'

Swann and Yates had gone to high school together in the fifties. They'd sparred at the local gym and had even stolen cars and done break-ins together. When Swann became a copper, Yates kept that quiet, something for which Swann was always grateful.

Yates passed the phone and left to serve another customer. Swann didn't have an office, but between public phone booths and the odd bar, he made do. The number he used to advertise his services in the Yellow Pages was his home number, where there was always somebody around.

'Hello?'

'Cameron. Put Marion on?'

Swann could hear laughter in the kitchen, the sound of an egg beater in a steel bowl, more laughter. Rolling Stones on the record player. Marion must be home.

'Frank?'

That tone in her voice. 'All good,' he answered.

'Then it's good you called. Phone's been running hot. You need to get yourself into Perth. Bloke by the name of Percy Dickson. Head of security at Boans. Said you went back a bit. He's got a question for you. And that bikie bloke you know.'

'Gus Riley? Leave a number?'

'Said you'd know where to get him.'

Doesn't rain, it pours. Swann had intended to drive over to the Swanbourne RSL to get some background on Max Henderson, but now it would have to wait. So would Gus Riley, sergeant-at-arms of the Nongs. Percy Dickson wouldn't call him unless he was desperate. Swann hung up and emptied his pony glass. Tapped it on the wood and nodded to Yates, picked up his cigarettes and keys.

'Eyes on the till, Danny. Looks like you're about to be robbed.'

While Swann had been talking to Marion, some men he recognised as coppers from Fremantle station had entered and taken seats at the bar. The eldest, a bloke called Curtis, a Breaks detective who had a pug's nose and a small clenched mouth, casually drew open his suit jacket to reveal his holstered .38, making two of the rookies look down into their beers, nervous.

Swann laughed as he went out into the fading light. The colts were practising their wet-weather pick-ups under the beads of silver hacking out of sprinklers, the coaches smoking and watching, megaphones by their sides.

The Freo Doctor was blowing over the open water where the Swan River joined the Canning. Swann passed the Raffles Hotel, crossed Canning Bridge and swung onto the freeway into the city. This time of year the resin-coloured water was warm, shallow and salty, and the wind carried the smell of stewing algae and guano and baking limestone. The sun was hot on his forearm, the Holden purring as he put his foot down. The EK was seventeen years old and handled more like a truck than a station wagon, but that didn't matter to Swann. His days of car chases were over. With all the souped-up models on the streets these days, he wouldn't stand a chance. Even

Marion's Datsun 120Y would burn him from a start.

Swann patted the dash out of respect. The EK's red paintwork was fading to pink on the bonnet and roof under the force of the sun, but her insides were sound. The perfect car for a man his age, in the job he was in. Plenty like it still around, and plenty of cheap parts to be had. He could park and observe from a distance and not stand out.

The Hay Street Mall was busy with the afternoon crowd, punters keeping to the shaded footpaths and skirting the buskers who worked the pitches between the first shops, a hippie drummer and a Don McLean noodling on a battered guitar, two old Nyungar women selling boronia from yellow plastic buckets.

Down the length of the strip, flags and pennants commemorated 150 years since the birth of the Swan River colony. Strung across the open spaces, their black swans with red and yellow wings fluttered in the breeze. Beneath them, a few skinheads slouched over the benches between the shops, astride massive flowerpots whose plants had mummified in the summer heat.

Louise, who knew about these things, had told him that the skinheads held the prime real estate of the Mall, the Bogs had lower Wellington Street and the Blacks still had large parts of East Perth. But the skinheads didn't look like an occupying army to Swann, more like the GIs stationed in Fremantle he remembered from the war: young, crew-cut, listless and bored, too far from home.

'This goddamn town's a graveyard with lights,' a US sailor had once said, folding the *Mirror* Swann sold him outside a brothel on Bannister Street.

Swann entered the air-conditioned thrum of Boans department store on Wellington Street, the glass doors sliding behind him. In the chilled cavern of the cosmetics section there was a sharp scent of acetone and ambergris. There weren't many customers, and Swann held the stare of a young woman behind a counter, elegant in a white silk shirt and floral choker, flirting with him out of boredom.

Percy Dickson was waiting on the raised floor leading into women's clothing. He was a short, muscled man with close-cropped hair and a disapproving mouth. Swann had known him for close to two decades. Dickson had tried out as a copper after his return from Korea, but was too aloof and hot-tempered, not a team player.

There was no trace of the awkwardness in his eyes that Swann expected. Swann had hit Dickson for a job as soon as he'd resigned his commission, but Dickson hadn't come through. He was head of Boans' security, and also acted as security consultant to most of the banks and the flasher jewellery stores around town. He'd claimed that Swann would become bored with the banality of busting shoplifters and passers of dud cheques.

It looked like he'd done Swann a favour by knocking him back.

Dickson's office was next to the toilets near the stairwell. Small, stuffy, the walls banked with monitors, coffee stains on the threadbare carpet and the strong smell of foot odour, ashtrays and chicken cup-a-soup.

'Welcome to the eyrie. Take a seat. But don't lean back.'

Swann put his haunches on the single office chair, which creaked ominously, the back support broken, the casters stuck with what looked like pie meat.

Dickson began to rummage in the mess. He extracted a video cassette and slotted it into a player covered in paperwork and chip packets. Returned his gaze to Swann. 'Run this by you?'

'Straight to the point, Perce, as always.'

'Force ten hangover, Swann. And I need your help. A matter of trust.'

'You caught a copper on one of your tapes? You need to take it elsewhere.'

'I already made that mistake. Fat lot of good. While one of the Ds was up here viewing it, the other was down the loading bay where they'd parked, helping himself from a rack of suits.'

Dickson didn't see the humour, looked at Swann's smile with distaste. Twitched his beak like an angry rooster.

'Sorry, Perce. How can I help?'

'Just watch this. That's all I ask. Tell me if you recognise any of these jokers. Footage is from last week.'

Dickson pressed play, then stood back and folded his arms, the look of someone about to witness the execution of a loved one.

The black-and-white picture was grainy about the edges but clear in its band of focus – an overhead shot of the menswear floor, fisheye lens taking in the racks of suits and high-end knitwear folded into backlit shelves. A man entered the frame and approached the service desk, where the staffer looked up from sorting neckties and guided him to a display case, just inside the frame.

'Watches. The bastard asked to see the watches. Check this out.'

Into the frame entered three younger men and a woman pushing a pram, who clocked the security camera and turned her face away. Swann could see why Percy Dickson was so angry. Without wasting any time, the three men began stowing shirts, suits and neckties into the pram, smiling as they worked. The woman lay a blanket over the haul as they left.

'Anybody up here at the time, Perce?'

Dickson shook his head. 'Can't be everywhere. Someone started a fire in one of the dunnies, cigarette butt in the wastepaper bin. I was down there, along with —'

'Let me guess, reported by one of these mutts.'

'Yeah, the older gent.'

'No offence, Perce. But it's hardly grand larceny.'

'I was getting to that. Watch the next shot. Taken at Massitoni's jewellers, down in Claremont.'

The camera shot of the menswear floor fizzed to white noise and then a clearer shot, much closer, came into focus. Swann recognised the interior of the jeweller's shop on Bayview Terrace in the rich western suburbs, the most exclusive jeweller in Perth. But that wasn't all he recognised. The older bloke was right in the frame, fronting the counter, the woman at his side, the pram gone but replaced by a large hatbox, blocking the counter staff's view of the three younger men who were peering into a display case containing rings and pearls.

'Recognise the clothes?'

'Suits from your floor.'

'Watch this. Far as technique goes, it's impeccable.'

In the three seconds it took the jeweller to turn and reach for a gold chain in a cabinet behind him, one of the younger men, blocked by the woman with the hatbox, slid to his knees, crept around the counter and reached into a cupboard beneath the till. Waited there a beat until the jeweller was diverted by another question, then joined his colleagues at the display case containing the rings.

'That a master key?'

'Yep. Against my advice, of course.'

While the jeweller was kept busy, the young men emptied the trays of rings and pearl necklaces into the lining of their suit jackets, then when their jackets were full, inside their trousers.

'Customised their trousers, I notice.'

'In a matter of hours. Wondered why they stole jackets one size, and strides one size larger. Now I know.'

Having emptied the whole display cabinet, the thieves left the store.

'Like bloody piranhas. Nothin' left but the bones.'

Swann grunted in agreement, his eyes on the older gent, looking up at the camera now, winking.

'After Massitoni's they hit Jacobson's, then Bartholomew's, then Anderson's. Took a couple of hours off for lunch, then hit Carew's and Cohen's in Fremantle, Gardener and Sons in Cottesloe, finished off the afternoon here in the mall – took out Exclusive Opals and D'Angelo Gold. The grand bloody tour.'

'All your clients, eh?'

'Every *one* of them. Net haul – 'bout a mill gross. On the black market, about a quarter mill. Not a bad day's work.'

'Didn't read about it in the papers.'

'You won't. My clients can do without the embarrassment. And they don't want others getting ideas.'

Dickson's voice had lost its usual volume. The old sergeant major looked newly demobbed, wringing his hands.

'What did the Breaks squad make of it?'

'I told you. They made off with some suits. Wanted to take the tape, but I wouldn't let 'em. You thinking what I'm thinking?'

Swann agreed. 'Looks like a green light. No way they'd allow out-siders to embarrass them like this. And unless you get some of it back, you're out of a job, eh?'

Dickson nodded. 'So . . .'

'What's the reward? My cut for a name?'

Swann saw dollar figures scrolling in Dickson's eyes, each of them rejected.

'For a name, 20 per cent. *If* I get anything back.'

'And if *I* get it back?'

'Over a barrel, Swann. Pants round me bloody ankles.'

'You asked me, Perce.'

'The lot. You can have the lot. Save me getting fired.'

Percy Dickson was lying. He'd never part with more than half of anything, but Swann knew the reward would be substantial.

'The old boy. The smooth-looking bloke. That's Barry Cassidy. Sydney Major Crimes, last I heard. Good mate of various currently serving detectives, as I remember it.'

Dickson kicked the leg of his desk, sending an electronic shiver through the bank of screens, which went sizzling white, then black.

Swann turned the EK off Wellington Street and entered North Perth via Beaufort. He may as well visit Gus, the Nongs' sergeant-at-arms, while he was in the area. In Swann's line of work, being on first-name terms with blokes like Gus Riley was a necessary evil.

Riley's house was at the top end of William Street, just past the lines of Italian restaurants, Asian grocers and travel agents, the mosque built by Afghan camel traders late last century. The house was one of a row of terraces that looked better than when Swann had last seen them. Amazing what a coat of paint can do. Riley sat on his front steps, drinking a Passiona and smoking a cigar butt. He wore greasy jeans and workboots, but his chest was bare. Unlike most of his Nong mates, who had no time for Asians, Riley favoured Japanese tatts, and his long arms were inked from neckline to wrists with dragons, demons and cartoon samurai.

'Looky, looky. Welcome to Chogie-town, Swann. Good to see a white man now and then.'

'If it wasn't for your ugly head, Riley, what with your Asian tough-stickers . . .'

Riley looked at his coloured arms and flexed his biceps, made a dragon lady grimace. 'Fit in or get fucked, Swann, that's what I always say.'

'You going to invite me in?'

Riley led Swann into the cool interior of the terrace house, all polished jarrah boards and rendered limestone, finely detailed architraves and heavy, white-painted doors, carefully restored to its original gold-rush condition. A room off the hallway contained a Japanese futon bed and a giant calligraphic wall hanging. Smoking incense. Sleeping girl with lacquered red toenails, naked.

In the kitchen, Riley took two Emu Exports out of the freezer and placed them on the table. Sat and lit another cigar, huffed until it took. Swann lit a Craven A, cracked his can.

Riley had a pretty face for a bikie, with broad cheekbones and a quiff of red hair, a disadvantage overcome with acts of viciousness famous around the country. Handsome and lean like Charlton Heston amongst his apes.

'Gotta job for you, Swanny. Heard you're doing it hard.' He grinned beneath cold green eyes.

Swann snorted. 'I'm doing all right thanks, Gus.'

'I saw the morning paper. Hogan and his shottie. Get the feeling he's gunnin' for you, Swanny?'

'Get to the point.'

'Backed the right horse, didn't I? First thing our new CIB chief's gonna do, I reckon, after pickin' a pretty secretary and findin' wallpaper that matches his pretty ties, is give me a call. Say, hey Gus, gotta little job for you, involves Swanny and a chainsaw.'

Swann stubbed out his cigarette and stood. Picked up the beer. His part of the game.

'No wait, Swanny. *C'mon*. Nothing meant.'

Swann stopped, but only because he might need Riley later, in the event that he located Dickson's stolen jewels. Taking the silverware off the shoplifting gang would require a team, and the Nongs had hired out muscle for beatings, debt collections and rip-offs for years.

Riley's attitude was also part of the game. A matter of saving face. He was a fizz, but unspoken between them was the memory of the first time they met, when Swann had beaten Riley to his knees. That was in the late fifties, when Swann was a rookie cop. Word had got out about his boxing chops, and his hot temper, and he was called on by some older police to go the bash. Like the job of breaking open a gang of teenage bodgies who were terrorising the owner of a Bayswater pizza parlour, putting the fear into his customers.

The local cop shop staff sergeant had pulled to the kerb, just down the street from the pizza parlour. Patted Swann on the shoulder. Swann was in his civvies, in case it got ugly. The ten or so blokes in the gang leered at the paddy wagon, neon flickering. All of them looked like Swann used to look, not that many years ago – stovepipe jeans and boots and T-shirts beneath duffle coats.

Swann glanced up and down the street and saw that it was empty. 'Who's got the most dash?' he asked.

'That one in the donkey jacket. Pretty-looking bloke, Mr fucken West Side Story. Watch for his knife when he starts to dance. They've got bats, bottles down the alley.'

Swann emerged from the wagon to jeers and catcalls. He locked eyes with Riley as he approached. Didn't take his eyes off him until Riley was down, then turned on the nearest bloke and went at him, took a few limp blows to his back then started on the next. The rest of them took off into the park across the street.

Swann stood over Riley and nudged him with his boot. Riley was smart enough to stay down. No words were necessary.

It was free pizza after that for the Bayswater coppers, not that it was any good to Swann. He was stationed down in Freo, and rarely made it uptown.

'Consider this.'

Riley reached into his boot and threw a roll of cash onto the kitchen table. It landed with a decent thump.

Swann sat back down. 'What happens to be the problem, Gus?'

'Thought you might've heard. These bank robberies over the last couple of weeks, they've been done using my bike. My *stolen* bike. My *favourite* bike. My fucken '46 Knucklehead. In my stolen leathers, too.'

'I heard. Assumed you had a falling out with Ben Hogan.'

'Assume what you want, but that's not why I need you.'

'I can see how a man of your . . . position might have a problem with some bloke pulling armed robs on your bike, but I don't —'

'Listen up, Swanny. I just want my bike back. Like I said —'

'The bank robs. Who's the investigating officer?'

'Farquarson. But the bastard's fucking with me. No witnesses have come through, but he's hit me for three thou just this week. And he'll be back. Claims there's pressure on him, so he's gotta pay to keep bosses sweet. You know the story. I'm already paying Hogan, for —'

'Don't want to hear it, Gus. I'm not going to get between you and Hogan. Sorry, but I can't help.'

'Come on. That's five thou. Near a copper's yearly salary. Using *my* bike for armed robs . . .'

'Makes you look like a fuckwit.'

'Yeah.'

'And you just want the bike back.'

'Too right.'

'Pig's arse.'

Riley laughed through perfect teeth. The guy really was a joker. Came from a good family. Home owner. Hardworking panel beater. Thug. Speed dealer. Murderer.

'I've got my boys out there looking for him, don't you worry about that. He's dead meat, for sure. But this thing between you and me – that's about my bike.'

'Ask Hogan. He's got mates in Armed Rob. Farquarson's one

37

of them. Five hold-ups in less than two weeks? That crim's either greedy, stupid or . . .'

Riley nodded, chuffed on the cigar until it glowed, veiled him in a grey shroud. 'I did ask Hogan. Reckons there's no green light.'

Swann laughed. 'Hogan's word. Rolled gold. Well, I guess that's that.'

Swann drained his can and stubbed out his cigarette. Riley's meatheads might be useful if he located Percy Dickson's jewels, but until then the pain of turning down five grand, well, it hadn't been for nothing. He could see the doubt he'd planted in Riley's eyes blossom loud and bright like the chrysanthemum on his shoulder.

The sun slid across the Indian Ocean, leaving tracer lines of amethyst and orange over the coastal heath that marked the fringes of suburban Swanbourne. Swann passed the Graylands Asylum and the Karrakatta infantry barracks, and headed down to the rifle range nestled amongst the dunes, where the RSL was situated. Perhaps if he was lucky he'd get a swim at Cottesloe before dark, his old trunks and sand-dusted towel on the back seat of the EK, as always.

He'd turned down Riley's cash because he didn't want a murder on his conscience, and Riley would certainly kill whoever had stolen his bike. But what was interesting was that Gus Riley's insider in the police force and the Sydney cop invited to Perth for a shoplifting spree had one person in common – Detective Inspector Ben Hogan, head of the Fraud Squad. The go-to man for those who wanted quick money on the side.

Hogan was notorious for graft, but he was also smart and ambitious. He had a university degree. He dressed well and kept his hair neat. He was precisely the new style of cop that the bosses were looking to promote. It was Hogan who'd pitched to the

Commissioner that the Consorting Squad be used to enforce the Government's new 54B law, which didn't permit more than three citizens to gather in public without permission. The state was in the middle of a mining boom, and the Liberal Government wanted the unions and activist organisations crushed, looked to the police to help out. With the Commissioner's blessing, Hogan and his men had diverted their attention from prostitutes, bikies and criminals to the disruptions of 'commies, ratbags and bludgers' to great effect. As plainclothes, they attended illegal meetings and made arrests, which made the Commissioner, a man in political lock-step with the conservative government, very happy and grateful. Hogan had been promoted to head of the Fraud Squad, where his dubious reputation as a bent cop might be purged on paperwork and quiet service, until he made the next leap.

Once Hogan headed the CIB, he'd have the run of the town. And politically it would be too embarrassing for any government or Police Commissioner to fire him. Percy Dickson's shoplifters were worth looking at, just in case Swann could link them to Hogan, who had to have given the green light.

7

High above the city, Gary Quinlivan held the door of the Revolving Restaurant open for Tommaso Adamo and followed him into the chilled air. Adamo hadn't mentioned the geologist's death at their meeting earlier that day; he'd had another reason for summoning him, and in the silk-lined lift up to the highest floor, Gary had struggled to wipe the smile off his face. With Rosa Gold looking good, Adamo had decided to bring Gary under his wing, make him privy to things useful for the project. What that meant would soon be revealed.

In the meantime it was a beautiful Perth dusk, perfectly matching Gary's buoyant mood. Gary could see along the coast as far as Kwinana, the Marseille clay-tiled rooftops tracing the beach north to Scarborough, veins of clotted traffic through the foothills of Guildford and Greenmount, strung along the cambered ridgeline of the Darling Scarp. From the forecourt of the nearby council buildings the incandescent beams of the wartime searchlights had started up, designed to imitate 150th-anniversary birthday candles, rising as twin columns 10 000 metres into the sky. On Mounts Bay Road the colourful lights of the Swan Brewery flicked on, alternating between a giant colonial sailing ship and the black swan logo, lighting the decks of the Perth City Showboat, an ancient paddle-steamer slogging its way to Barrack Street Jetty.

Gary had dined in the Revolving Restaurant with his mother when he was a child. She'd always liked dining out, and dressing for the occasion. The Tosca and Plaka on James Street. The Kunming for Chinese. Luis' down on the Esplanade, for a splash out. The set menu at the Oyster Bar: dhufish, scallops or squid, oysters done four ways, cheesecake for dessert.

Gary felt a pang for his dead mother, but this was no time for nostalgia.

Adamo, wearing a cream three-piece polyester suit and hand-tooled Italian leather shoes, his hair combed into a side part, was taking in the room. Gary wore his custom two-button jacket, tan with bronze tints and a single back vent, and some flared grey slacks. He had also combed his shoulder-length hair into a side part.

The crowd closed behind Adamo as he sauntered through the sea of conservative blues and greys, everyone sporting a black swan breastpin, towards the Lord Mayor in his full regalia, including the original chain of office and glittering semi-pendant worn by Alexander Forrest the previous century. The Lord Mayor was stiffly polite with Adamo, thanked him for coming, then moved away to converse with another.

Gary expected Adamo to be angry at the snub, but he didn't seem to mind. Adamo didn't drink or smoke, and despite being dwarfed by the large men in the crowded room, he somehow maintained a space around them into which stepped businessmen and civil servants, politicians and journalists. Between one and the next, Adamo gave his summation of their worth, as men, and their worth to his enterprises.

Adamo hadn't introduced Gary, and he hadn't explicitly

mentioned why he'd been invited to the City of Perth function. The formal meet and greet was designed to thank corporate sponsors of forthcoming events celebrating the anniversary – the Heirisson Island community spectacle; the launching of the R&I Bank's reproduction of George Pitt Morison's painting *The Foundation of Perth 1829*, depicting a woman with an axe raised against the first sheoak to fall; the ongoing replacement of the continually stolen flags that lined the Causeway and St Georges Terrace; the forthcoming Miss Universe pageant at the new Entertainment Centre; the distribution of 8500 saplings to primary school children; and the Mardi Gras and fireworks planned for next week.

The atmosphere was one of celebration and self-congratulation; the state was forging ahead. The price of silver and gold was rising, diamond production was up; it seemed the entire north-west was made of iron ore. The price of land in central Perth was rocketing, particularly on the Terrace, bringing hundreds of millions of dollars of new investment in modern buildings. You could feel the optimism and barely veiled opportunism in the air, the performed rituals of banter laced with business enquiries, the genuinely casual way of doing things in a city where everyone who mattered knew everyone else.

Gary had failed badly in his first business venture, gone bankrupt in fact, but his ancestors who had arrived on the *Parmelia* in 1829 had passed down to him an old saying: 'The first word to rhyme with West Australia was failure'. It had been drummed into him as a child how tough things had been for his people, how many had struggled, died, gone mad, risked all and finally succeeded. That there was blood on their hands, too. Before the gold rush of the 1890s, his family's wealth came from running cattle in the Murchison, and secrets were starting to emerge. There were plenty of Aboriginal Quinlivans in the outback, and new stories in academic circles about some of his ancestors and how they'd cleared the land, their dusty realm governed by law .303.

But the fin-de-siècle gold rush had brought everyone back to the city. As long-standing locals, they'd struck up companies and supplied the hundreds of thousands of miners who'd passed through the city, become merchants and insiders in the larger gold-mining enterprises. The story of gold and the story of his family had been linked ever since, something that he'd described in some detail to Adamo as background to his passion for Rosa Gold.

Gary recognised some of the entrepreneurs around him, men not much older than himself who had doubled, tripled and quadrupled their wealth over the past few years, buying old buildings in the city, knocking them down and selling on the land. Most of these young men had lately branched out into the mining game, creating investment banks and quickly altering the political landscape. Both sides of politics now preached the benefit of giving the young entrepreneurs their head, encouraging them to do what they did best – make money. The newly elected Leader of the Opposition, a short man with thick red lips and shrewd dark eyes, was drinking with them, conspicuous with his loud laughter. The man made a point of greeting Adamo warmly.

After his departure, Adamo said, 'He's a good man to cultivate. His time is soon.' When Gary responded that the man seemed surprisingly charming, not what he expected from that side of politics, Adamo snorted that charm was always the best substitute for goodness, something to be mindful of when dealing with politicians, not to mention the entrepreneurs gathered nearby.

Gary wanted to seize the opportunity and introduce himself to them, but he didn't, not yet. The only occasion he attempted to leave Adamo's side, to greet an old friend of his father's, Adamo restrained him with a hand on his arm. 'You stay here.'

Adamo was there for Gary's benefit alone, the gesture seemed to suggest – Adamo didn't need to see and be seen.

The Premier worked the room, wearing a tuxedo, shaking hands and smiling broadly, as did all of his ministers. He glanced at Adamo, but didn't come over.

'Don't worry about him. He finish next year,' Adamo said quietly.

Until this point Gary had listened and said little, but this prophecy seemed too unlikely to pass without comment.

'Can't be true, Mr Adamo. He's in fine health. He's polling well. He'd be crazy to —'

'For this one,' Adamo interrupted. 'Quiet.'

The Minister of Police, Terry Sullivan, planted himself into the space before them and shook Adamo's hand, his eyes gleaming with drink, his necktie loose, talking through his teeth.

It was as if Gary didn't exist. The Minister never looked his way, leaning down to Adamo's ear. The conversation was about Northline, some plans Adamo had for developing the area, the sympathy Sullivan felt for him – anything he could do to help. Some passing concern about the rising crime rate, the number of overdoses, the bank robberies. Didn't look good, in such an important year.

When he'd left, Adamo allowed himself a smile.

'Should we be worried?' Gary asked.

Adamo rocked on his heels. 'No, now they busy keeping up appearances. Any trouble we make, they clean up. And that one – he knows everything.'

'Even about me. The banks?'

Adamo shrugged. 'Perhaps. It's possible. He's Minister for Police. His older brother was police. He knows how it works.'

The rumours about Sullivan were legion. 'So it's all true . . .'

'Yes, he take. And I pay. Just because he ask. But for what I need, he's not a big man. The ones I need most, they're here, but quiet like me. When the time comes, I'll introduce you. I need their help, for my new buildings. We need their help, for Rosa Gold . . .'

'The public servants.'

Adamo looked into Gary's eyes and nodded. 'Yes, some of the senior ones. The politician, he come and go, he take or he don't take, but the public servants have the real power. Some of them, they like presents. Holidays. Boats. Beach house. Mercedes.'

'You don't want to introduce me?'

'They see you here now, with me. They don't know you, but they'll remember. This state is gonna be very rich, Gary, and they gonna make it happen. Them . . . and them . . .'

Contempt in Adamo's voice, as he indicated with a peremptory flick of his hand the loudest group of men, drinking champagne by a baby grand, covered now in cigar ash. Gary's heroes. The entrepreneurs were closest in dress to Gary and Adamo – three-piece rayon suits with high-rise waistcoats, pointed Barrymore collars, wide floral ties and longish hair. Gary knew each of them by reputation. Real estate developers, mining directors, dabblers in finance, rumours of shady pasts, legendary parties, profligacy – bright futures. Already where Gary wanted to be.

'Keep away from them. They gonna make money, then they gonna lose it all. Fucken con men. You stupid, you gonna get conned, lose it all. You smart, you listen, you got balls . . . you gonna be very rich, Gary.'

'Thanks, Mr Adamo.'

Gary stood taller and looked across the crowd, quietening now as the Premier took the stage. For the first time, influential men were meeting his eye, alone in the quiet space beside Tommaso Adamo, and Gary did not look away.

8

Like most West Australian RSLs, which lacked the pokie revenue of their eastern states' branches, the Swanbourne chapter of the Returned Serviceman's League looked like a toilet block on a neglected rural oval: heavily painted besser brick and rusting zinc roof leading to a car park laid over the humped roots of Norfolk Island pine.

Swann parked next to a Kingswood, a Falcon 500, a Chrysler, an identical pair of white Belmonts, one Rover – all in immaculate condition. Not a Mercedes, Datsun or Toyota in sight.

He entered the building through a heavy steel door, into total silence – one minute's silence. It was crowded for a Monday evening, a dozen men holding beers and darts and cigarettes, heads bowed. The sole woman behind a chrome banister that segregated her from the men. Like the others, she didn't look up as Swann entered, stopped in his tracks by the nightly ritual of remembering the dead.

Jennifer Henderson was dressed in jeans and a corduroy jacket, cowboy boots. Swann could only remain still and look. Her hair, so black it looked blue, coiled over her shoulders. Unlit Capstan held in nails bare of polish, zippo in her other hand. Knee pushed into the bar, other leg snaking back. The posture of someone who'd had a few, but knew how to hold it.

A bell trilled and immediately conversations resumed, cigarettes were lit and beers emptied. Jennifer Henderson's dark eyes caught him watching her. None of the men looked squarely at Swann as he moved past them, although they'd taken him in, used to assessing risk at a glance. Swann had sensed their radar on him during the minute's silence, even though their eyes were closed. Most of them were old enough to be WWII veterans, the few younger men would be Korea or Vietnam vets. Couple of father and son teams.

Jennifer Henderson looked him square in the face, comfortable in the all-male environment. Hint of a challenge in her eyes, payback for his secret observation. That cute gap between her front teeth when she smiled. Glossy white teeth, like pearl shell.

'You're late.'

Jennifer nodded to the barman, a tattooed older man wearing Buddy Holly specs who placed a glass of what looked like breakfast juice on the towel.

'Salty Dog. With a crown of salt. By the book.' He lingered, wanting to see Swann drink. 'They'll have to pay me more, Jen, now I do cocktails.'

Swann took a sip. Vodka and grapefruit juice, tart in the gills, much like the look on the barman's face, waiting for his verdict.

Someone down the bar shouted, 'Make us a Sloe Screw, Mick, willya? Nah, a Harvey Wallbanger. Nah, make it a Sloe Screw Against the Wall.'

'Like it,' Swann answered, the moment calling for diplomacy. 'More than a tequila sunrise.'

The barman slung a tea towel over his shoulder. 'My work is done.'

Jennifer waited until the barman was out of earshot. 'Good at the white lie, Swann?'

'More a backhanded compliment, I thought. Either way, years of experience.'

'Your profession?'

Swann took another sip of the Salty Dog, felt it bite again in the gills. 'First thing we're told as police rookies. Everyone lies; all the time. Job's not so much a matter of finding the lie, but catching liars out with the truth.'

Jennifer laughed, rested a hand on his forearm. She shrugged off her jacket, leant across to place it on the bar. Swann could smell her, fresh and cool like the wind through a forest. He watched her straighten the cuffs on her silk shirt, pat herself down, withdraw into secret thoughts. It was the change in her eyes that made him notice this – vivid blue to bruised in a moment – as though her watchfulness was difficult to maintain.

The blue of day; the blue of night.

'Your wife sounded friendly. Marion? What does she do?'

'Community nurse. Part of a new program. Tends to the aged in their homes, visits working girls in the brothels, kids too sick to get to clinics, deros in the dunes. Sometimes ships at the docks, when their last port of call was Asia, and penicillin is required.'

'Must be useful for you, in your profession, a wife who tends to the community.'

'You mean information? Sure. She knows what goes on, more than most.'

'And your face. They've faded, but there are scars. Your nose has been broken . . . Like my father, you were a boxer.'

He let her continue the game. She knew all this, he could tell. She wasn't just killing time, either. She was watching him closely, as he had watched her. But what about him could she tell by observing? Swann was at an age when he no longer needed to pretend. He looked down at her and hid nothing, scanning the creamy skin and freckles, her face tilted upwards.

Like everyone with a cop background, Swann appeared confident, even calm. He was lucky enough to have a face that people liked.

But she was looking deeper than that.

He also had a bad temper, and was practised in violence. Prone to bouts of melancholy and disgust. Proud and reckless, a combination that had brought him trouble.

But for all that he was a father of three daughters, and since his last fiasco with a lover, which had ripped his family apart, a loyal husband.

'Teenage kids?' he said in answer to her question. 'Has its moments. You and Max never . . .?'

She shook her head, withdrew behind her quiet reply. 'Max never wanted them. Went and had the job done on himself in his thirties, before we met.'

'And you?'

'I never wanted them either. Nor dogs. That's why Max took them with him.' She paused, bit her lip. Swann caught the cocked head of the barman, indicating to her a new arrival.

'Ah, here he is. Swann, I thought I'd come down here and make the introduction for you. I don't have Garth's number. Garth doesn't *have* a number.'

Swann turned to look. Found the tall, lanky man with stringy white hair and wary eyes looking at him.

The man made his way through the handshakes and slaps on the shoulder to stand beside them. He stared long into Jennifer's eyes. Turned his head mechanically and gave Swann the same look, neutral and sustained. He had hoops of sweat under his armpits, long wiry arms and large hands, calluses on the knuckles.

'What are you doing here, Jen?' he asked her while still reading Swann.

'I came to introduce you. I heard you were in town. Swann here is going to be asking questions, and I figured if I wasn't here, you wouldn't —'

'You figured right. I don't know him.'

His voice was hoarse. Flat. He barely moved his lips when he spoke. Dry, cracked lips.

'Garth, this is Swann. Frank Swann. He's helping me look into Max's business associates. Thought you might help too.'

'How?'

No curiosity in his voice. Just the monotone. The minimum it took to communicate.

'Garth served with Max in Vietnam. In the SAS, before he got wounded. Garth is . . . was Max's closest friend. He's been drilling out at the Rosa Gold stake.'

Jennifer tried to conceal it, but it was there in her eyes. Her wonderment, confusion, disappointment at this fact. That a man like Max Henderson, who'd done so well in life, had chosen as his confidant a wreck like Garth Oats.

'Max is dead, Jen.'

Nothing added. Just the mechanical switch of his gaze from Swann to Jennifer, whose eyes flooded with tears. She finished her drink, took her cigarette from the ashtray, tapped. 'I'll leave you two alone.'

She didn't look at Swann, but placed a comforting hand on Oats' chest, who stepped back, watching her exit through the silenced drinkers to the door.

'I'm sorry,' he said, to nobody in particular. He fixed his gaze back on Swann, stretched out a hand. 'Garth Oats.'

The handshake was hard and clammy. When Oats released his

grip, Swann had to resist the urge to wipe his hand on his trousers. The barman was hovering with a can of Export cracked and ready. He reached across the wood and placed the beer in Oats' hand, closed his fingers around it. Patted him on the forearm, went away.

Swann had finally witnessed grief in Jennifer Henderson, and all the confusion you'd expect from a suicide's wife, but as he watched her husband's best friend sip on his beer, his eyes dull and his face burned beyond caring, he felt as though he was in the presence of a ghost.

It was an hour past sunset and North Cottesloe Beach was deserted. The moon was rising over the roofline of the Ocean Beach Hotel. The water was colder than he'd expected, and Swann breathed heavily as he stepped into the wash. The sea breeze had dropped and the swell emerged glassy and sheer out of the darkness. There wasn't much traffic on Eric Street, and between the waves Swann could hear the clink of pool balls in the back bar, the odd shout and laugh coming across the water. He swam through the sets that broke over the reef on either side of him, rifling along the hard skeins of beach behind. His breathing had settled, and his skin tingled with the cold, diving down into the darkness and watching the glow on his fingertips as he kicked to the deeper banks of even colder water, the faint suck of swell over his back and shoulders, then closing his eyes and letting go, the air in his lungs drawing him up.

He trod water and ran his hands through his hair, cleared his nose and watched a container ship enter the Fremantle port, drawn into the greater light. Swann saw how far he was from the shadows of the beach. He felt a twinge of fear, but as he'd been doing all day, he ignored it, turned to stare across the black ocean, tipping to sunlit Africa.

His conversation with Oats haunted him. The man wasn't the damaged simpleton he'd first appeared. Perhaps it was the presence of Jennifer Henderson that had unnerved him. Perhaps he was awkward around women. Oats lived in his car, a battered HQ panel van with heavy-duty treads, flanks red with dust.

Swann knew the type. Men who struggled with human company, who lived in the bush by themselves and had the worried and hungry look of the wild dog. There were plenty like him.

Oats had met Max Henderson during a battle in Vietnam. Garth was one of six SAS troopers whose covert surveillance of a Viet Minh company had been surprised by a platoon coming from behind, at the very moment the SAS captain was calling in an artillery strike.

The Viet Minh were stealing Australian mines set in the southern zone and resetting them on the roads nearer to Nui Dat, and had killed plenty of Australians this way. The SAS men tasked with tracking the company were hopelessly outnumbered once the shooting began. They'd started their retreat instantly, running and firing, trying to get out of the vulnerable middle ground, leaving their packs and carrying only the radio and their weapons, taking a position and firing behind, retreating to a new position and repeating the rearguard action, soon low on ammunition.

They were cactus, as Oats described it, the SAS captain calling in their position near a clearing, the sound of the battle and the heavy rain obscuring any radio response, then settling in to fight and die, knowing they'd been outflanked, knowing there was nothing left to lose by throwing an extraction flare into the clearing, the red smoke soon beaten down by the rain, until they heard the chopper circling overhead, coming down improbably large and steady into the clearing, already taking fire, the captain dying before Oats' eyes from a head wound, Oats taking a bullet to his shoulder, then another to his wrist, then another in his thigh. He made it to the clearing, the bird yawing above him, bullets zinging off its undercarriage. Oats climbed aboard despite his shattered wrist, beyond pain now, reaching down to draw up his companions with adrenalin-shaking arms, the last soldier firing from his position on the chopper's broad feet, his entrails spilling out of his shirt like strings of sausage, firing and shouting maniacally as they rose into the clouds, the soldier dying in Oats' arms but smiling madly, not knowing that he was dead.

Once the noise of the battle was gone, there was only the deafness, the ringing silence, soundtrack to the war. Then later, one by one, the words of the pilot, unnaturally calm, deep and assured, calling in their position, not a trace of anything but the matter at hand, the reporting to base that he'd been on a routine journey between Vung Tau and Nui Dat to pick up some officers, but had diverted to extract an SAS squad, to prepare the ambulance and hospital, ten minutes ETA, the nasal Australian voice the most beautiful thing Oats had ever heard, the chopper's deck awash in blood and rain and viscera, the windscreen shot out and rain pouring over the pilot too, Max Henderson calmly checking his instruments, the chopper responding to him like a graceless extension of his long angular body, banking towards the coast now, the pretty lights there in the dusk of Vung Tau, the pilot calling in their position again . . . a man's voice but an angel's voice, Oats had thought to himself, as he began to lose consciousness . . .

9

Swann pulled the EK to the kerb outside his home. He climbed out, still in his wet shorts, shirtless and barefoot, left the damp towel on the back seat and carried his trousers, shirt and shoes, socks stuffed inside, onto the front verandah. Inside, he could hear music he didn't recognise on the record player, loud and insistent, which meant that Louise was home. He could smell devilled chops in the kitchen, and once inside the humid smell of shampoo and soap and steam, the sound of Marion's humming behind the sliding door.

He entered the steam and drew back the shower curtain. Marion looked at him intently and he kissed her, to let her know.

She placed a hot, dripping hand on his shoulder. Swann kissed her again, wiped suds off her cheek, ran a hand down her leg, which was slapped away.

'Dad, is that you?'

He stepped out of the bathroom as Louise emerged from the kitchen, a chop in one hand and a tissue in the other, eating on the run as usual. She was dressed in a leather miniskirt and black stockings and monkey boots, a baggy white sleeveless T-shirt. Her lipstick was crimson and her eyeliner black. Her short hair was spiked up.

'Dadadadadada . . .'

'For a bloke who holds a song, Dad, your Addams Family could do with some work. Sounds like Skippy.'

Swann leant down to her ear, the only place he could land a kiss without disturbing her make-up.

She poked him hard in the belly. 'Nother hard day at the office, I see. Well, you'd better hurry up. We leave in fifteen. It's your turn, don't forget. Mum did it last time.'

Swann stood back and rubbed his belly, looked wounded. 'Missed something, have I?'

'It's dinner you've missed,' Marion said from down the corridor. 'Unless you pick it up a bit. Shower's yours.'

'Hang on,' he said. 'What are we talking about?'

Louise moved towards him and he pretended to flinch, put up his hands. She hugged him anyway. 'C'mon, Dad. You're on the till. We *need* you. Mum's got to study. Sarah's out with the boy, and Blonny's too young. None of my mates can count beyond ten, you know that. Didn't matter for our first few gigs, but tonight we're the main event.'

'All right, I'm ready.'

Swann pretended to sweep sand off his shoulders, scratched his belly again. Looked down at his bare chest and flat stomach. Knobbly knees. Long tanned legs, hairy shins.

Louise grimaced, shook her head. 'Get in the shower, then into some jeans. The Wranglers you've worn to death. An old T-shirt'll do, might be some beer spilt . . .'

She passed him the spicy chop, bone wrapped, and disappeared out the back.

Swann had better get moving. He could see in her eyes that

she was nervous about the gig. Louise was his fearless eldest daughter, and he began to feel nervous too.

There wasn't room for Swann in the kombi that collected Louise; full of amps, guitars and boxes of leads. Swann told Louise he'd meet her at the Shents, but on the way he decided to visit Donovan Andrews, one of his old fizzes, before Andrews left to work the night shift.

The early darkness was warm and grey, and the weather was finally turning. Swann crossed the Fremantle Traffic Bridge and looked beyond the giant gantry cranes at the port to see the next front coming over the ocean. Rottnest Island was hidden behind a veil of ripped white water that hadn't reached the groynes. It was storm season up the coast and a tropical cyclone was due to cross near the Pilbara during the morning, gusting to 250 k's and bringing rain to the goldfields and wheat belt. Swann's EK could do with a wash – dust from the heavy industry down in Kwinana had covered the bonnet with a fine grit, and the windscreen was only clear where he'd worked the wipers.

He turned down Wellington Street and away from the coast. Parked the EK beneath the first of the towers and made sure it was locked. The last time he'd visited Andrews his unlocked car had been raided, his dash radio wrenched out and his parking change nicked. Kids, no doubt. The little smart-arses had popped the bonnet and lifted his battery too.

Donovan Andrews lived on the fifteenth floor of Tower 1, as it was called, to differentiate it from Tower 2, which was identical in every way. Swann wasn't scared of heights but the walk from the lift and stairs around the edge of the building to Andrews' flat always made him nervous. The railing separating him from a hundred-metre fall barely came up to his waist. The cold front hit the coast just as he exited the graffiti-marked lifts, wind swirling over him and creaking in the drainpipes and rusted fittings that clung to the salmon-brick walls. He had seen Andrews' BSA Gold Flash in the car park, sheathed in a canvas hood, so he knew Andrews was somewhere in the complex.

Andrews was Swann's favourite fizz. He worked as a kitchen hand at the European Club, making sandwiches for the upmarket clientele of Little Italy's best illegal casino. On the nights he wasn't there, he did shifts as a glassie at the Zanzibar. He spent his days sleeping and smoking pot and rooting the young mothers that inhabited Tower 1, while their husbands were in jail or at work.

Ben Hogan was a regular at the Zanzibar. As a Fraud Squad copper, he worked regular office hours. Swann had checked with Terry Accardi, his contact in the CIB, and learned that Hogan hadn't taken any leave, which meant that wherever he was hiding Sydneysider Barry Cassidy during the day, the chances were pretty good that he wouldn't bother with concealment at night. In the long tradition of the 'swim-through', where coppers visited one another interstate, the locals supplied all the entertainment – the girls, the grog, the gaming. Hogan would want to show off his influence to Cassidy, whether Cassidy's business in Perth was official or not.

Swann knocked extra loud on the cheap plywood door, which shivered in its aluminium frame. It was raining now, and the concrete walkway that separated him from the long fall was slippery wet, and as always with the first squalls of the season, the rain smelt of limestone dust and gum leaves. He scuffed his shoes on the sisal mat and knocked again, shoulders turned against the wind.

Andrews opened the door naked except for a towel. He had a semi hard-on that he tried to conceal by buckling forward at the waist. 'Jesus, detective, I was expecting someone else.'

'I hope so, Don. You going to ask me in?'

The one-bedroom flat smelt of burnt toast. There was a bong on a coffee table by an old couch that had clearly done its time on a verge. Bare walls, grey carpet worn in a track from bedroom to kitchenette to couch. The rain beat horizontally against the sliding door that gave onto a small balcony. As Andrews went through to the bedroom, Swann flicked on the lounge fluoro, which buzzed, came on, the light marbled by a layer of dead bugs in the fitting.

'Offer you a drink, detective?'

Swann shook his head. He hadn't been a detective for more than a decade but Andrews would never call him anything else. The kid was a loose unit, but Swann had always felt a fatherly affection for him. Had Swann been Andrews' real father he might have felt different, but the boy made a little go a long way, and that was always worth respecting.

'Bong?'

Andrews clapped Swann on the shoulder and giggled, threw himself onto the couch. He'd put on a pair of old jeans and a sleeveless Cardies footy jumper that was covered in grass burrs.

Swann sat on the plastic garden chair alongside the couch and put his hands on his knees. Andrews with that eager expression and cowlick hair, dried spittle at the edges of his mouth, building a White Ox rollie, a regulation prison racehorse, thin and tight out of habit.

'You hear anything about these bank robberies, Don? Anyone been splashing money at the European, or over the bar?'

The R&I Bank done over in Fremantle that morning had used the same MO, the same Harley in the getaway, and the talk amongst the robbers and cops that frequented Don's workplace would be all about the bank jobs. Practically one a day now. Every radio bulletin was leading with the story, and the front pages of both the *West Australian* and *Daily News* were given over to the new face on the scene, predictably dubbed the 'Bikie Bandit'.

Thoroughly stoned, Andrews thought about it, brow knitted as he tried to remember names.

Better to keep it simple.

'How are the Armed Rob boys wearing it? Still showing themselves in public?'

This got the reaction he'd hoped for. 'Yeah,' Andrews replied. 'They are. Getting shit from some of the other coppers, and some of the pollies and lawyers, but they don't seem too worried.'

'Rumours?'

Andrews had just told Swann everything he needed to know, but it was always good to hear the rumours.

'Some blokes reckon it's some kung-fu expert from NT. Another bloke told me it's Hogan himself. Boss at the Zanzibar heard that it's a thirteen-year-old boy, who works with the carnies as a motorcyclist on the Wall of Death.'

'Nobody reckons it's Gus Riley?'

Andrews shrugged, but looked at Swann with a new interest. 'You don't reckon . . .?'

Swann shook his head. 'No, Don, I don't. The Nongs have had a falling out with Ben Hogan, and this is Hogan's way of putting on the squeeze and getting a laugh at the same time. Which leads me to your opinion on those jewellery thefts last week.'

Andrews puffed out his bottom lip. 'Nah. Nope. News to me.'

Percy Dickson and his employers had done a good job keeping it quiet, which meant that Hogan was even more likely to be courting Cassidy in public.

Swann described some of the pieces stolen and the four people involved, especially Cassidy of the Sydney CIB.

'Sounds like the bloke drinking with Hogan last night. Cognac drinker. Likes a good cigar, too. Does he have big puffy eyebrows and a beaky nose? Great bloody big head?'

'That's him. You see him tonight, you call me at home, leave a message. There's a reward in it.'

'I can do that. Like old times.'

'Yeah, Don, like old times.'

There was a gentle knock on the door and Andrews' eyes widened. Swann stood and patted him on the shoulder. 'Best be going then, Don. Call me.'

Swann opened the door and let in a young woman in tracksuit pants and a bikini top, who didn't appear surprised to see him there. He shut the door and waded into the wind.

The Shenton Park Hotel was near the university, but it wasn't a university crowd, not on a Monday night. Swann leant against the doorframe that led off the band room onto the dark street.

The band room was packed, a low, dark smoky hall with no windows, and the small money box that did for a till was stuffed with dollar notes, the cover charge for Louise's band. Not much appeared to have changed since the days when Swann and Marion had gone out to see bands in the era of bare-arsed rock'n'roll. It was just as DIY now as it was then. The hotel garnered what they made over the bar and the band took the door charge, as long as they did their own taking.

There was a buzz in the room, but it wasn't as he remembered it, beer-driven and inflected with aggro. When Swann was a teenager he'd often felt sorry for the musicians. The singer'd be up there bashing out his song and the guitarists would be sweating over their instruments and the drummer'd be smashing away like a monkey but you could see the disappointment in their eyes when the fights inevitably broke out. Perth was a tribal place and the rock'n'roll stomps was where the bodgie and surfie tribes came together, to drink and fight and crack onto one another's women; young things in tight jeans with cool knowing eyes. Some of the best bands had broken up because of the fighting. Nobody would hire them once their followers had a reputation for trouble. The blood and the broken glass and the smashed windows not worth it, even at places like the Snakepit.

Swann was reminded again how lucky he was to have met Marion when he did. It was hard to credit how angry he'd been in his teenage years, how quick to get in someone's face. In those days a kid's character was measured by his dash. How much he could drink. How fast he could drive. How well he could fight. And his friends from those days, where were they now? Some of them had ended up in Freo prison, some had joined the merchant navy and disappeared overseas, some of them had just disappeared.

The drummer was taking her place behind the kit. You could feel the atmosphere in the room change, the volume of chatter dropping as kids started to head down the front, to stand before the black wooden stage, drinks sculled and ciggies put out. A new energy about the place.

Louise stood beside the lead singer, a tall young man who was incredibly thin – in leather strides, the bloke was going to sweat. Swann only knew him as Justin, someone Louise had met at uni, before he dropped out. She said Justin was solid considering his childhood in foster care and borstal.

It was the drummer Swann was worried about. Even Swann could see she was on the gear. Penny was a friend of Louise's from high school, and Swann knew her father, who ran the local deli; seemed like a good man. Marion was also friends with Penny's mum, who'd tried her hardest but according to Marion had given up. Penny had moved out when she was sixteen and never made contact. Her parents didn't even know where their daughter was living now. Had to get information from Marion, by way of Louise. And then there were the things that Marion couldn't tell them: Penny's appetite for intoxication, occasionally paid for by going on the game.

That Louise had friends who were into heroin and worked as prostitutes didn't worry Swann too much. He was proud of the fact that she stuck by her friends, but not in a way that would drag her down.

The other band members looked to Louise and she nodded, led into the first number with a stiff bass solo, coarse and brash, before Justin threw himself onto the mike and began to howl. Penny swamped the sound with savage kick-beats and thrashes on the cymbals, but Louise was the centre of the band, rocking forward and guiding the others. Swann smiled with pride as he heard within the bass line the rock'n'roll signature of the music he'd played Louise as a kid, the Screamin' Jay and Johnny Devlin and Howlin' Wolf just speeded up, what they were calling punk music now, all noise and bad manners, and he *liked* it, and so did the kids on the floor, heaving as one.

Up on stage the first number had tracked seamlessly into the next, slower paced, had that ska beat to it, something that set the skinheads in the crowd nodding, then dancing. Swann focused his attention on his daughter, dandling the low-slung bass on her thighs while she stroked out the deep loops and peered through the smoke over the heads of the dancing kids, finding him by the door, reflecting Swann's proud grin back at him now their eyes met.

10

Gary Quinlivan leaned against the wall and cracked the top off his stubby, folded one ankle over the other. He was dressed to match the occasion, in jeans and cowboy boots. He lit a cigarette and took a sip of the beer which tasted like chemical soup, even chilled. How mug punters managed to drink the stuff was beyond him, but the bar was crowded with rough heads and to ask for a glass of white would have attracted attention. Easier to point at the paw of the shirtless oaf standing next to him.

He told himself that he didn't want to stand out, but there he was, standing out. His lean against the wall was too cool by half, his stillness odd in the flux of movement. The three-piece band was tight, playing originals that didn't sound too derivative. Just when he thought he was hearing the bass-driven shtick of the Gang of Four, the tempo changed and he was lost in an entirely new sound. Then, just when he thought he'd nailed echoes of the Saints or the rock-abilly tones of the Cramps, the sound would trip into something more sophisticated, like early Pere Ubu or the joyous hardcore of the Buzzcocks, only better. The lyrics were better all round. Smart, like those of the Fall, but married to the more energetic beat of that other local band he admired, the Scientists, that had them dancing their heads off. Even the doorman was nodding his head, tapping out on the doorframe.

A slurry of powder and mucous ran down the back of Quinlivan's throat, the last traces of the hammer he'd snorted in the car park. His legs were woozy and he uncrossed his ankles, stood upright. He wasn't much older than the kids around him but he was decades ahead. It pleased him to think that whereas they had most likely dined with their sibling hordes on fish fingers and peas and chips before coming out, he, Gary Quinlivan, had been to a function with the head honcho of the North Perth mafia, where he'd been introduced to the Premier and all the biggest wheels of the city. And from there, to dinner at his father's house in genteel Claremont, although he hadn't eaten at either place, had merely sipped on white wine and smiled and listened. His father could be hard work, but the hammer made things easier between them, made Gary less inclined to argue the point, more likeable all round, more the son his father wanted him to be.

His father was a district court judge, a man defined by his service and now in physical decline. Despite his wealth he lived modestly, even more so since the death of his wife from breast cancer those two years ago. That the shame of Gary's troubles might have contributed to her stress had never been mentioned, although it was implicit in his father's new distance, the matter-of-factness when he enquired as to the nature of Gary's current enterprise, the obvious fact that the young man had wealth beyond his means. Gary would never be forgiven, not by his father nor his father's friends, many of whom had been fleeced in his first youthful incarnation as real estate developer, when the company had gone bust and Gary had been forced to claim bankruptcy.

It didn't matter that real estate was in Gary's blood, just as gold was too. Gary's grandfather had been responsible for the parcelling up of some of Perth's premier suburbs. Places like Mount Lawley and Inglewood and City Beach and Scarborough and Nedlands and Dalkeith had been empty spaces until his grandfather built them in the 1920s. The way Gary looked at it, his father was the aberration. Gary's father saw law as an important service, had never come to terms with the appetite for empire building that his own father had manifested, and which lived on in Gary.

It didn't matter. His father's forgiveness was furthest from his mind. Despite himself, Gary's feet were tapping and he realised that he too had been seduced by the music, drums and bass now working in tandem to produce an industrial grinding that was building to a crescendo, hammer and tongs and anvil, glissading movements on the lead guitar fading in and out.

For the first time he looked closely at the drummer, her shaved head under the spotlight a high-wattage bulb burning into the darkness, and saw her eyes, the familiar dullness there, the black corona around the faintly flickering star. He wondered at the provenance of her high, and understood that once the band was finished he would introduce himself to her, so different from him and yet so alike, one people under the goddess of purest desire . . .

11

The cobbled alley parallel to William Street was full of skips and strewn rubbish, and clumps of bougainvillea that clung to the palings of an old jarrah fence. The creeper vine growing on the backs of the bars and strip clubs was so thick that only the doorways and barred windows were slashed clear. Slabs of asbestos roofing that had caved through had been made into dero hoochies, crusty blankets and plastic bags containing clothes and books inside dwellings just large enough for a drinker to crawl into. Empty bottles of goon wine and Brandavino lay on their sides along the fence line. The alley was where street kids slept, tired of getting rousted from the parks and culverts to the north. It was so dark at night and the piss and sour oil in the drains smelt so bad, not even beat coppers would enter it.

It was headed towards dawn, and the bruised clouds sailing on the nor'-westerly trailed ropes of grey rain. Swann had called home after Louise's gig to retrieve Donovan Andrews' message – 'They're here.' He then called Gus Riley to organise muscle, in return for a cut of the reward and Swann's taking on the job of looking for the Harley. And last he tried to call Percy Dickson, who didn't pick up.

That was four hours ago. Swann dropped a ten-cent piece into the payphone at the edge of the alley. This time Dickson answered on the second ring.

Swann cut to it. 'That bloke we talked about, he's still in town. A fizz of mine's put him at the Zanzibar, with Hogan and a couple of other Ds.'

The news didn't appear to please Dickson. 'I *know* he's still in town. The cocky bastard's travelling under his own name. I've got it from a mate at Qantas that he's off to Honkers tomorrow . . . actually, this morning. Few hours from now. Which can only mean —'

'He's still got your stuff. Going to sell it up there.'

'No good if I don't know where the stuff is. I can't have him arrested at the airport, there's no charge. I've spent the night tooling up. I'm gonna jump the bastards in the airport car park.'

'Cut it out, Perce. They don't know we're onto them. They've been out drinking all night. The stuff will be close to hand – my guess is it's already packed in a suitcase, wherever Hogan's got Cassidy hidden. Cassidy'll be escorted onto the plane by the future head of our CIB. You can forget about a rob.'

'So what's *your* plan, bastard?'

'It's only money, Perce. Leave it to me.'

'It's my friggin' *reputation*, Swanny. You wait for me there, or —'

Swann hung up and went back into the darkened alley behind the Zanzibar. It was turning into a cool clear dawn. He wedged himself into the doorway of a Chinese restaurant, buttoned up his denim jacket and smoked and waited. He could hear mahjong tiles clapping on the formica tabletops inside, the smell of clove cigarettes wafting through the fan exhaust into the alley. From where he was standing he could see the rear door of the Zanzibar, where there was still plenty of activity; chefs in chequered trousers smoking and roadies lugging out speakers and amps. The front of the club opened onto William Street but Swann knew that the police who frequented the place always used the alley entrance.

Already a couple of beat coppers near the end of their shift had come by and been fed by the back door, scarfing down their free lasagne and middies of beer, the tradition of food at the back door for uniformed coppers as old as the club itself. If it was raining they ate on milk crates in the kitchen, but tonight they stood under the stars and joked with the chefs and some young prostitutes from the William Street brothels.

Swann saw one of the coppers put down his plate on top of a bin and reach for his cap. He put it on his head and straightened it, picked up his plate and started eating again. Swann knew what that meant and pushed himself deeper into the doorway. An officer of senior rank was coming, and the uniformed copper had been warned by someone inside. Drinking on duty was one thing, but taking your cap off in public was another.

Sure enough, Hogan and Cassidy came out of the kitchens and looked the uniformed coppers up and down, made them salute, then left with the young prostitutes.

Swann flicked his cigarette and followed.

Hogan's maroon LTD Ford ran the red light on Beaufort and headed north towards Mount Lawley, then down Walcott Street and into the suburbs. Swann sat the Holden behind a white mini that was weaving across both lanes as two people argued in the front. He smoked as he drove and kept an eye out for phone boxes. It wasn't long before the Ford turned right into Glenroyd Street and pulled into the drive of a white weatherboard and cut the lights.

Swann drove on past, noting the address, and circled around until he came to the phone box on Walcott and Forrest. He called Gus Riley first and told him about Hogan's safe house, then rang

Percy Dickson, then returned on foot to the house. Glenroyd was a quiet leafy street and he had no trouble inserting himself into a shadowed garden across the road, where he had a clear line of sight to the weatherboard. The lights had come on, and now the faint sounds of laughter and music. He checked his watch and resisted the urge to smoke; he was too close to the front room of the house.

He didn't have long to wait. The V8 chugged slowly down the hill from Walcott. A Fairmont, by the sound of it, and he watched it cruise, lights off, in neutral, to park outside the house. Four large men climbed out and stretched their limbs, hiding their bats and hammers beneath duffle coats and flannelette shirts. One crept down the side of the weatherboard, ducking beneath the bay windows that gave onto the drive, disappearing into the backyard. Three donned balaclavas and went directly to the front door, in a wedge formation. Gus Riley, the only one Swann recognised, stayed with the vehicle, hunkered low in case of a nervous neighbour or a passing jogger.

The front door crashed open and Swann held his breath. Hogan would be armed with his usual .45 but there were no gunshots in the seconds that followed. The front door swung shut.

Swann clambered out of his garden hide and lit a cigarette. He nodded to Gus Riley and walked up the street towards the banked lights on Walcott.

Little Italy was burning. Even before Swann broached the hill on William Street, he could feel the roasting heat and smell the ashes, the gouts of fire and flickering coals. Along with the rest of the traffic headed into the city, he had to pull over twice to let fire engines past. The fire was burning a whole block of Roe Street across from the train tracks, and part of it had spread up Lake Street and along Parker Street on Russell Square. It was the largest fire Swann had seen in the city, and the air was filled with smoke and embers floating like Chinese lanterns on the wind across the suburbs. The streetlights and traffic lights were out and only red licks of fire and white-hot explosions and roiling black smoke lit by spotlights were visible.

Swann turned on his radio and caught the ABC broadcast. Above the sounds of shattering glass and sirens and more explosions, he heard the ABC journo on location describe the scene where the fires had been put out along Roe. The grocers and the warehouses and the semi-detached houses that used to be brothels had been gutted. The residents had been evacuated to the train tracks across the footbridge. The cause of the blaze unknown, although fanned by the wind from the north-west. Fatalities also unknown. Confusion and anger and fear. Rubbernecks gathering at the train station to get a better view. Fireys concentrating on limiting the blaze from spreading further, leaving buildings to gutter down.

Swann looked at his watch and thought about the quickest route through the city. He had a meeting with Percy Dickson and Gus Riley in the Raffles car park. All the buildings along Roe and most of the block behind were owned by Tommaso Adamo, head of the Northline mafia. If the fire was deliberately set, it was either an act of war or an insurance job.

Down the freeway and over the bridge. Gus Riley's ute was already there, and once Swann had parked, Percy Dickson emerged from the shadows near a skip, carrying a small briefcase and a .25 pistol, trained on Gus Riley. Swann ignored the gun and so did Gus. They got busy in the back of the ute, breaking into the locked and heavy suitcase with a chisel, hammer and crowbar. The lock finally cracked and Swann began running his fingers over the hems and collars and seams of the shirts and trousers inside, while Riley slit the suitcase lining with a bowie knife.

Percy stared with growing excitement at the contents of the

gutted suitcase on the tray, glinting in the half-light. And there was cash, too. Rolls of twenties and fifties. Swann and Gus put these in a separate pile. When they were finished Percy Dickson looked satisfied, running his fingers through the gold chains and the diamond rings and the opal and pearl earrings and pendants.

'No time for an inventory now, Perce. Cassidy wouldn't be stupid enough to try and hock it himself. It'll all be there.'

Percy Dickson sniffed. 'Looks like it. Here's the reward.' He made a point of not passing the briefcase to Gus, who was closest. Swann clicked it open, took out half the bills and slipped them into his jacket. Passed the briefcase to Gus, who added three rolls from the suitcase. He winked at Swann. 'My fucken Knucklehead. Top priority.'

'That was the deal. Unless you're responsible for setting that fire.'

Riley laughed. 'If the price is right, Swanny. But Tommaso's got his own muscle now. Brings the fuckers in from Calabria. That kind of work's their bread and butter.'

The three men watched the flickering cityscape, brown smudge hanging like a question mark over the river.

'Wasn't you, Perce? Smoking out our man Hogan?'

Dickson didn't catch the irony in Swann's voice. 'Your bikie mate's got the right idea. Old Tommaso's been trying to get his Roe Street project through council for months. Guess he got frustrated with those heritage protestors. Urban fucken renewal, Swanny, before our very eyes.'

'And we'll be pushing daisies if we're seen here, with this.' Swann stuffed Cassidy's clothes, papers and passport back into the suitcase. Gave it to Dickson. 'Toss this off Canning Bridge on your way into town. And as far as your clients' dealings with the coppers are concerned, this stuff was never recovered. Otherwise Hogan'll hear, and come looking for you.'

'Word of honour, Swanny.'

Then, something Swann thought he'd never see. Out of nowhere, Percy Dickson smiled. Shuffled awkwardly. Might even have saluted if his hands weren't heavy with loot.

12

Gary Quinlivan woke to the sound of a vacuum cleaner coming through the thin walls. The room was dark but for the light playing around the broken slats of a bamboo screen, and it smelt like dog and cigarette ash. He blinked and rubbed his eyes, remembered waking during the night, his arm dead, manually lifting it as he rolled onto his back, felt the blood pulse into his tingling limb before falling into a deep heroin sleep.

He had no idea what time it was, nor cared. A Tuesday, that's all he needed to know. One day before he got on the plane to Malaysia. And he didn't want to look too closely at his surrounds. The girl was a slob, like most junkies. The mattress on the floor and the blankets and clothes strewn about made it hard to know where the bed ended and the floor began. The vacuum cleaner sucked on and on and on, although it was quaint to think of some hard-faced housewife, vacuuming for the sake of something to do. Cleaning and polishing her shitbox just to feel some small sense of achievement. People and their pitiful lives. Amazing.

One of the good things about heroin was the doors it opened to worlds he would otherwise never know. Like the girl's, for example.

Drummer in a punk band. Wild in the sack, despite the anaesthetic. On hammer, Gary could root for hours and never come. He was raw down there, even after he'd shaved her, and then himself, for a laugh. The sex was good, but most of all he loved to spike a naked girl, himself naked, watch the pleasure come into her eyes.

She was from the other side of town, but a kindred spirit. She was exactly what he was after – a female companion to make a run with. They'd talked it over in detail. She had some ideas of her own, and a wig that hid her baldy head. She dressed up for him, and looked the part. Young couple on holiday to KL. All expenses paid. The hammer in a false-bottomed suitcase. She could be paid in smack. She could deal some for him. Musos and their hangers-on was a good new market for him, outside the rich set he already supplied.

He tried to call her but his throat was dry, croaked instead. He stood up, knees unsteady from the hours of rooting, head cloudy.

She was wrong as soon as he laid eyes on her. Face down under the table, inside the legs of a steel chair, where she'd crawled before hitting the kitchen wall, passing out. Her works on the table. His gram packet, folded neatly beside. A burnt-down cigarette in the ashtray, sickly smell of tar. The room flooded with harsh morning light. Ice cream melted in a tub on the sink.

So she hadn't been able to help herself – while he slept she'd taken the packet from his jeans. It was uncut. He never used cut. She'd have been used to street shit, 10 per cent pure. But this was all pure. She'd hit ten times her usual spike. Amazing she even made it to the floor.

He went to her and felt her carotid; nothing. Her skin was cold and waxy. He closed her blue eyes. He put his hand on her bare shoulders, ran it over her naked rump, rubbed her back. He wanted to embrace her. He wanted to hold her. He wanted . . . to feel something. He knew he should feel something. But he was numb. He was always numb. Apart from his desire.

He stood and pulled out a chair at the table above her. Lit a cigarette and stared at his hands. A spasm of desire took him again. He opened the packet and tipped some onto the back of his wrist. Snorted it up. Tugged hard on the cigarette, pushed knuckles into his eyes. Tried to make himself cry, but couldn't.

13

Swann awoke to the image of Jennifer Henderson, close by him, her smell of rubbed amber fading in the lemony morning light. He couldn't remember why she was in his dream, or what they had been doing. He looked at his nakedness, legs tangled in the sheets, and saw that he was aroused. He closed his eyes again, to see if the dream remained, not wanting to make much of it, but knowing that this was how it had started last time. Conversation, harmless flirting, accidental touching, leading to the gradual possession of his mind.

He was startled by a kiss on his forehead, a whisper in his ear. Marion, kneeling beside the bed. She wouldn't question why he'd flinched. Marion had learned early that she needed to be careful when waking him, especially when he was under strain. Once or twice he had lashed out.

Swann kissed her back, took her hands, tried to draw her beside him.

'Everything all right?' he asked.

The look on her face was apologetic, bemused. 'Cameron found your spare revolver in the broom cupboard.'

'Looking for . . .?'

'Sarah threw out his old undies. He was searching for them.'

'That's my girl.'

'You smell like smoke. Were you at the fire?'

'I watched it, along with thousands of other rubbernecks.'

'You could smell it from here. Like the smuts from the old trains. Plenty of my clients live in those tenements. They'll be on the street now. I'm pulling the night shift later, to help look for them, see if anyone's injured, get them rehoused.'

'You need me to help?'

'Maybe. I'll speak to the Sup.'

He kissed her again, threw off the sheet. He'd had trouble sleeping. By the time he got back, the sun had begun to rise over the blue scarp. 'Give me a minute to get going.'

Swann's cut from the night was $3650, more money than he'd made in the last six months, there in a roll in the pocket of his trousers. He wanted to surprise Marion with a night out, a good meal and a few drinks beforehand.

That Jennifer Henderson had awakened something in him was more reason to end their contract. Beyond that, she was grieving, and he didn't want to take advantage of her wealth. There were a million reasons why a man like Henderson might want to take his life, and that he hadn't left a note wasn't unusual. Barely half of suicides ever did. From what Jennifer had described, he'd quite calmly fed his dogs before killing himself. Not the impulsive action of an enraged drunk. In cases like that, not leaving a letter was usually a message in itself.

Swann was going to terminate their contract this morning, once he'd satisfied his curiosity at the morgue. He'd given it a go, but Jennifer had been vague about her suspicions that Max's suicide was related to his work with Rosa Gold, and she hadn't answered his questions honestly. She was unable to tell him why her husband's consultancy might have been a contributing factor, or whether she believed his suicide was actually a murder. She was clutching at straws, in the way of those who grieve. Trying to make sense of what rarely makes sense.

Swann made his way into the kitchen to find Cameron at the table, sullenly drinking a cup of tea. Sarah sat across from him, eyes puffy from crying. Swann's handgun lay beside the milk and Weetbix. He picked it up and cracked the chamber and saw that it was loaded.

Sarah glared at him and he raised his hands in defence, gun hanging from his pinkie. Swann had grown up with guns, as had Marion, her father having been a detective. Swann's stepfather had slept with a loaded shotgun beside his bed and carried a small-calibre Luger wherever he went, caught up in the docker disputes that plagued the port. Once or twice bullets had been fired through their front window during the night.

Swann had inherited both his stepfather's shotgun and a .303 hunting rifle from Marion's father, which he kept wrapped in oilcloth at the back of his wardrobe. He wore his snub-nosed Smith & Wesson .38 service revolver in a shoulder holster beneath his jacket, and a .32 wedged into his boot. He kept the spare .38 in the broom cupboard where his kids knew not to touch it.

'Well?' Sarah demanded. 'Anything to say?'

Both Swann and Cameron spoke at the same moment, and their eyes met. Swann put the gun on top of the fridge. He leant down and kissed Sarah on the cheek. 'Sorry, sweetheart. I thought it was well hidden.'

'I said I'm sorry,' Cameron piped up, voice reedy. 'I didn't know it was loaded. I was just mucking around.'

Marion put her hands on Cameron's shoulders. 'Any gun in this house, Cameron, you need to assume it's loaded. We forget sometimes, don't we, Frank, that normal for us isn't normal for others.'

'Sure we do,' Swann agreed. He looked through the screen door at the backyard bright with sunshine. He had nothing to do except visit Darren Plant at the morgue, to confirm that Max Henderson's death was a suicide. After that, there was only the awkwardness of meeting Jennifer Henderson, to let her know. 'It's hot. Anyone up for a swim? Let's walk down to South Beach, get some lunch on the way.'

Sarah looked at him suspiciously, and rubbed her eyes, nodded, took Cameron's hand. The boy almost laughed with relief. Their first tiff.

'Your shout?' Marion asked.

Swann took out the roll of cash and tossed it to her. She weighed it in her hand and smiled. 'See what I mean, Cameron? What's normal for us . . .'

In the four years since Swann had last seen him, Darren Plant had put on considerable heft around the midfield. He huffed up the steps to the records room, Swann dropping back so that he wasn't eye level with Plant's exposed crack. Darren was no longer a mortuary assistant, had graduated to his new position as clerk, which got him away from the sights and smells of the morgue floor. Gone was the uniform of white dungarees and gumboots. In its place were a pair of brown nylon pants too small for him and a white short-sleeved office shirt and tie. Sweatbands on his wrists. And thongs.

Darren Plant held the records door open with a single meaty arm, his face puddling red, his chest heaving with the altitude. 'Ch-er-rist! Fuck. Shit.' Plant yanked at the necktie and worked a couple of fingers between his skin and shirt.

'Jesus, Darren. Tie's a choker. Like a noose. The more you pull on it, the tighter it gets.'

Plant worked the tie undone and flung it onto the nearest desk. 'Comes with the new pay grade. Compulsory attire for public servants above shitkicker level. That's me, just.'

'No directives given about footwear, I notice.'

Plant looked down at his thongs, hair falling over his face. 'Not yet. Though these aren't *any* thongs, are they? American. Double-plugged. Not cheap.'

'You get the file?'

Plant pushed the hair back over his ears, wiped his face on the Slazenger wristbands and lit a cigarette, offered one to Swann. 'Anyhow, have a Winfield?'

Swann shook his head. Took up the file that Plant had indicated, on the table beneath his necktie.

'Leave you to it, then. I did have a flick through after you called. There was never any question of a coronial inquest, and the police investigation was cursory, once we established the cause of death. I remember the wife, though – beautiful woman.'

'I'll be sure to pass that on, Darren. How would you describe her mental state when you saw her?'

'As I remember it, she found him. Can't have been pretty. She was here for the formal victim identification. That's still part of my job. We had his body covered, so she didn't see where we'd opened him. Only his face. Good of him to use a .22. Shotgun cases, you know about shotgun cases . . . anyway, we stood her on the opposite side to the wound. We'd had to take out the eyeball. She was calm as you like. She had the coldest hands. She thanked all of us personally. She was able to take the body not long after.'

'Are you waiting on anything for the file?'

'Only some blood analysis. There was nothing we could see in the organs. He seemed perfectly healthy. In body, if not in mind.'

'Thanks, Darren.'

Plant sighed as he descended the stairs, thongs squelching. Heavy steel door clanging shut behind him.

There was nothing in the post-mortem report that suggested anything other than 'death by misadventure' – a single rifle shot to the head. No sign of a struggle. No bruising. Henderson's finger still pressed to the trigger. The bullet taken from his brain the same .22 calibre as the bullets removed from his dogs. The photos showed his face intact but for the powder burns around his exploded eye. He looked peaceful in death, relieved, as so many of them did. Some alcohol in his blood. Not much food. A large, strong man. Not likely to go without a fight.

Swann had already checked with Terry Accardi in Homicide, who confirmed that there was no real investigation, that Jennifer Henderson hadn't pushed for one. When Swann had called to tell her that their next meeting would probably be their last, she sounded agitated, suspicious, confirming what he suspected – that behind the emotional coolness she was vindictive in the usual manner of the wealthy, used to getting her own way.

Now she sat on the expensive leather couch that had been slashed all over, the back, the arms, the plush cushions, and sobbed. All around lay the smashed remains of amphorae and vases and pots that had previously sat upon antique Japanese tables, themselves overturned. Wooden masks had been splintered. Paintings too had been slashed. The room stank of kerosene. Whoever had wrecked the Henderson house had intended to set the place ablaze.

The damage was violent, but also methodical. In the rooms upstairs, the mattresses had been slit and gutted. The master bedroom's walk-in wardrobes had been emptied. Papers and clothes piled in the corridors. Heavy work, requiring strength and patience, and time. In Max Henderson's study, the plasterboard walls had been hacked with a claw hammer or a crowbar, ripped down onto the carpet, which had been taken up in rows, rolled into the corners. Henderson's bureau was splintered and its contents strewn about the room. The smell of kerosene again.

A single point of entry, by the back door. A panel of rose-coloured leadlight smashed in, minor damage compared to the mayhem inside. The contents of the fridge pulled out onto the kitchen floor, the cupboards not only emptied but ripped from the wall, jemmied onto bricks to enable access beneath.

A bottle of cognac had been spared, and Jennifer Henderson had made a good start on it. She drank from the neck, and smoked, crouched over herself, not meeting his eye, not answering him. Was there someone he could call? Somewhere else she could stay? She shook her head, only responding when he told her he was going next door to call the police. He was shocked by the anger in her eyes. Anger and clarity.

He went to the neighbours anyway, an older couple with identical white hair in matching red tracksuits, working out in a home gym. They hadn't heard anything. They hadn't seen anyone. But they would stay with her until the police arrived. The look on their faces when they saw the front room said it all. Swann gathered all the papers he could find in Max Henderson's study, the maps of the Rosa Gold stake, the surveyor's report, the aerial photographs and the primary geological indices.

He left Jennifer and her neighbours amongst the wreckage downstairs. It was mid-afternoon, still time to get to Company House. He wanted to have a closer look at the people behind Rosa Gold.

Swann parked on King Street and walked through the shadows to St Georges Terrace, the traffic stalled from Hamersley House all the way to Kings Park and down to the Esplanade, anniversary flags strung from building to building, snapping in the breeze. The city of Perth had started on this street, a collection of wattle-and-daub huts on a gentle hill overlooking the perfect mirror of Mounts Bay. Now it was a concrete canyon through which the sea breeze poured like floodwater in a gorge. Even so, it was stinging hot in the sun. Lawyers and business types in white shirts stalked the footpath in groups of two and three, clusters of flies on their backs. All around the sounds of construction, the thudding of pile-drivers and the yak-yak of jackhammers biting into the travertine capstone. The smell of diesel, the taste of limestone dust.

It was cool and quiet inside Company House. The old colonial building with its Donnybrook stone colonnades and ornately carved wooden doors, studded with black iron spikes, had been built like everything else from the period with gold-rush money. Inside the entrance was a bronze statue of a malnourished old miner wielding a pick over a lump of rock. The miner's eyes were sightless and his mouth was grim. His ribs showed through his tattered shirt, his hobnail boots cracked and split near the soles. Swann thought again of the quote on Henderson's desk. *I and my men suffer from a disease of the heart that can only be cured by gold.*

Swann had been stationed in Kalgoorlie as a junior detective in charge of Vice, and he had known plenty of miners. Odd breed they were. Some came out of hiding when the price of gold made prospecting worthwhile, while others had dedicated their lives to it. The Kalgoorlie dirt was hard and red and dug by hand. No cool rivers to pan for alluvial gold. Dry-blowing was employed instead, tossing red dirt into the dusty air. The sun was hot and the nights were cold. Flies crawled into your eyes, mouth and nose, just to get a bit of moisture. Most prospectors seemed touched in the head; bushies who came into town only when they had to. The hard-rock miners who worked underground were like miners everywhere else. Worked hard and played hard. Kept the Kal brothels and bars in money but kept the coppers busy too. More than your usual number of shootings and stabbings. Plenty of blokes went missing, as well. Plenty of abandoned mines around the place. Good to drop a body down, where it would never be discovered.

He approached the counter where an old woman in a green serge skirt and jacket looked at him closely, tortoiseshell glasses over neutral grey eyes. Behind her was a bank of walk-in files. He pushed across the sheet of notepaper on which he'd written 'Rosa Gold', and waited while she drew across the concertinaed dividers and entered a corridor of files. She climbed onto a mobile stepladder and pulled down a rectangular cardboard box, peering closely at the label on its spine. She returned and passed the file and indicated with an open palm the carrels set against the opposing wall. She hadn't spoken a word and when he thanked her, the sound of his voice echoed like his footsteps as he crossed the floor.

He lit a cigarette and laid it in the ashtray fixed to the sheoak-veneer desk. He opened the file and saw that there wasn't much inside, just a few sheets in a manila folder. He was looking for one thing in particular. By law, every company incorporated in the state had to list their directors in the file kept at Company House. The first page in the folder told him that Rosa Gold was incorporated in August 1978. The second page told him that the directors had planned to float Rosa Gold as a publically listed company in November 1978, but had not done so. That was curious.

Next was a glossy broker's sheet containing a small aerial photograph of the Rosa Gold stake and its location on a map of Western Australia. In small print beneath the map were a couple of paragraphs detailing promising assay results, naming Max Henderson as the 'world-famous geologist' responsible for the discovery of brecciated formations on the Rosa Gold stake, further exploratory drilling of which, he was confident, 'would reveal considerable gold assets'. A date was given for the public listing, at an initial price of five cents per share. But the spruik sheet had obviously never been sent to private and institutional investors because Rosa Gold, as far as Jennifer Henderson had been aware, was still a privately listed company, all assets owned by the company directors, whom she hadn't been able to name.

The name of the brokering service, however, was familiar to Swann – Capitol Services, of Hay Street, Subiaco, written in gold at the bottom of the page. The name of the individual broker was also given – Dennis Gould. But over the page Swann found what he was looking for. Swann whistled as he read the names of the directors, typed simply on cheap paper, and the sharp sound curled around the ceiling of the large room and made the archivist look over her glasses.

Leo Marrone. Tommaso Adamo. Bradley Farquarson. Ron Bevans. Bernard Isaacs. Benjamin Hogan. A who's who of the North Perth mafia and the bentest of cops, plus two racetrack sharks. He'd had run-ins with all of them, most lately Bernie Isaacs, a horse trainer who'd sold a thoroughbred gelding entrusted to him by one of Swann's clients. And a name he didn't recognise. Gary Quinlivan. And another name crossed out, lost to the smudged black ink.

Swann folded the spruik sheet and slipped it into his pocket. He wrote the names of the company directors on his notepad, flicked it shut. Took up his cigarette and inhaled, watched the blue smoke rise towards the ochre-rendered ceiling.

It was Ben Hogan's name that made Swann feel sick. Hogan was the new leader of the old purple circle. When a bent copper reached that high, he had a finger in everything. The presence of Hogan on the board gave Jennifer Henderson's suspicions about Rosa Gold a deal of credence, not to mention the names of Marrone and Isaacs. Cut-throats, the lot of them.

Swann now had his own reasons for wanting to pursue Rosa Gold, namely the possibility of getting some dirt on Hogan before he made CIB chief, before it was too late. But he wouldn't be telling Jennifer that. She had best keep away from Rosa Gold.

It was there in front of him, on the register sheets, the con that played itself out time and again. The classic penny dreadful, the standard pump and dump. On the day of listing as a public company, each of the directors would invest plenty of their own money by way of third parties. The share price would go up. A buzz would spread. Dodgy brokers would spruik it to gullible fools. The price would keep going north. At a certain point, having tripled or quadrupled their investment, the directors and their mates would sell, the share price would collapse, the conned left with worthless paper.

It was the kind of share-market scam that had made so many Western Australians rich over the years, and had fleeced so many ma and pa investors. Perhaps Max Henderson had baulked at having his name associated with such a venture. Perhaps he'd made threats, causing the public listing to be delayed, or even dropped. Perhaps he wasn't aware how dangerous his employers were, although that seemed unlikely. The state of the Henderson house suggested Max might have kept something in store, potential blackmail. If the men who'd trashed the house hadn't found what they were looking for, then Jennifer was in danger.

Swann approached the woman at the archive desk and pointed to the typed paper in the Rosa Gold portfolio. Specifically at the name that had been crossed out.

'Know how I might follow up on this?' he asked, friendliness in his eyes, although the woman's were empty of expression.

'Might I enquire in what capacity your enquiry is being made?'

She looked him up and down, and even in his best kit he felt cheapened. No point lying. She had clocked him for an investigator. 'I'm working for a client who's doing due diligence on this company, at their invitation. It's my understanding that it's required by law that all directors —'

She cut him off. 'I'm already following up on this. At least, one of our most senior staff is. You're the third such enquirer to make this observation, and I told the other two the same thing. The company will be contacted and asked to amend their record, and make it available. Although, if you're doing due diligence at the invitation of the company, as you've suggested, perhaps you might like to ask them yourself?'

The tortoiseshell glasses rising on her long nose. Her days made of such small triumphs. Caught out in the lie, Swann returned the interest with a quick smile, thanked her politely and left. He would need her again, of that he could be sure.

The sun was bright in the hollow sky outside Company House. The vapour trail of a jet hung like a white feather over the hills to the east. Swann lit a cigarette and knelt to tie his shoelaces. He heard the swarming flies gather around his shoulders and shooed them away.

It was only a short walk to where he was parked across the business district. He looked up at the anodised windows of the towers around him and wondered which of them contained the ghost offices of the shell company Rosa Gold, and whether or not they knew he was coming.

14

Peter Henning took out his stethoscope and put it at the horse's heart. The gelding, Rum Punch, shivered and continued to throw its head. Froths of spit rained on Henning's shoulders. Its heartbeat was suddenly through the roof, then gone, then starting again in slow palpitating spasms, firing beyond what he could count.

The trainer, Bernie Isaacs, stood behind him, too close. Isaacs didn't move when Henning stood back and dropped the stethoscope around his neck. The trainer just stayed there, fingers hooked through his belt, eyes set with childish amusement.

'Your horse is clearly distressed, Isaacs. I'm going to have to swab him.'

Isaacs smirked, cocked his head. 'Course he's distressed, Doc. He's just won a 2400 by three lengths. Bad Boy always goes for broke.'

Henning had watched the race from the steward's box. Three lengths, with the jockey on the brake. A Tuesday meet, so no big stakes to claim. Henning had to assume it was a raid on the bookies, or the tote.

Henning stepped around Isaacs and took a needle out of his

Gladstone bag. Isaac's face dropped all pretence of friendliness. 'When you done that, I got something else to show ya. Something ya might've missed.'

Henning drew blood into the syringe and corked the needle. Dropped it into a plastic specimen bag. Put it safely into the old leather Gladstone.

'Go on.'

Isaacs knelt and clutched the horse's hind leg, worked his way down to the tendons in the fetlock, squeezed so hard that his forearms bunched. The horse threw back its head, tried to step away, its breathing laboured. Isaacs held it fast.

'What do you think you're doing?'

'Look at this, Doc. Tendon's gone in the back legs. Bad Boy run so hard he's done himself in. He's gotta be put down. A gelding's no good to me in the paddock. Look . . .'

Henning calmed the horse before putting himself in harm's way. The poor animal was stamping again, beginning to tremble, kick against the two stablehands. Sensitive beasts, horses, but Rum Punch was genuinely distressed. Its eyes were rolling. Tongue lolling in its mouth. Whatever Isaacs had given it . . .

He knelt and fingered the ropey length of tendon, from hoof to fetlock. 'Nothing wrong with this horse, beyond . . .'

There was no point saying it, not until he got the swab results. He would enjoy reporting Isaacs to the steward. The man was a curse on the game. Terrified his jockeys. Rumours of intimidated stewards. Long-odd betting plunges. In thick with Ron Bevans the bookie.

Rum Punch had been backed from twelve to one to even money, in half an hour of frenzied pre-race betting. Average jockey. Plenty of handicap. No form. Winner by three lengths, and then some.

'He's gotta be put down, Doc. It's inhumane. You can see how much he's hurtin'.'

'Nothing wrong with him, Isaacs. Take him away. The swab'll be back tomorrow, then the steward'll be in touch.'

Isaacs leaned in close. Breath rotten. Eyes black with hatred. 'Never had this kind of problem with old Doc Maloney. *There's* a bloke knew his job.'

'Sure he admires you too, Mr Isaacs. No doubt why he emigrated to Tasmania.'

'*Smart* prick. You won't last. I'll see to that.'

'You threatening me, Isaacs?'

Isaacs broke into a slewed grin. Cocked his head again. Jack Russell without the intelligence.

'Nah, I'm wrong, aren't I. Not so *smart*. Just a prick.' He turned to the two stablehands. 'C'mon, Jimmy, Baz. Get Bad Boy out to the float. We got some celebratin' to do before the eighth.'

Henning patted the horse, stroked its neck. Scratched the nub of bone over its eye socket. Eyes still dilated, rolling. Struggling to focus.

A bell trilled on the wall by the old clock. The speakers crackled as preparations for the next race began, leading the horses out into the crowd noise, bookies touting outside, the build-up of excitement that he remembered so well, standing in the concourse as a child. While his dad watched the pre-race showings, Henning would try to decipher the hieroglyphs in his father's form guide, coded so that if he lost it no other punter would gain. Little chance of that. His dad was a smart man, ran his own chain of salvage and hardware stores, but his 'system', as far as Henning could see, even then, yielded little more than promise. Punting was an act of faith, his father had told him, that gleam in his eye that Henning so loved. 'And one bloke's faith is worth a hundred opinions.' His father standing taller, trilby cocked and rollie burning, watching the bets laid and the cash change hands, looking out for the plunge, what his dad called the *bit of strange*, insurance against his own dubious system.

If only his father had known what Henning knew now, after a month working at the track, schooled on the QT by some of the stewards, each of them cynical when talking about the game. Of late, unless you had the inside word, he'd been told, knew all of the trainers and jockeys, then you were a mug, destined to lose. There was no system or scholarship of form that could beat the inside word, the little arrangements made between owner and trainer and bookie and jockey. Because of men like Isaacs, the game was rigged.

Still, that gleam in his father's eye. He missed it. Looking up from under his father's wing. 'Eyes on the strange, son. I'm relying on you. You're my good luck.'

Henning picked up his Gladstone and made for the internal stairs that would take him up to the steward's box in the stand. Rum Punch had been doped, no question about that. If he could get proof, it was one back for his father, for all the mug punters out there.

'Doc, you gotta come quick. It's Bad Boy – he's gone lame. Please, Doc.'

Henning looked around to Jimmy, Isaacs' stable boy. There were tears in his eyes. His voice was breaking as he pleaded, led Henning out by the sleeve, down to the car park.

He heard the horse long before they arrived at the float. Rum Punch leaned into the walls, unable to back up or lie down. Both its hind legs had been broken, at the fetlock. Clean breaks. Squealing and wheezing its pain. A piece of four-by-two leant casually on the rear wheel.

Henning put down his bag and took out another syringe, drew up a vial of the brown liquid in the clear glass jar.

'Where's Isaacs?' he asked the boy, who still had tears running down his face.

'He's up there.'

Pointing to the rear of the stand, the members bar. Race eight under way now. Nasal caller droning through the speakers. Crowd beginning to shout. Isaacs toasting him with a glass of beer, grinning like a winner.

15

Reggie Mansell was precisely where Swann expected him to be – propped in the front bar of the Great Western Hotel, working on a gin and tonic and cryptic crossword. His short legs dangled off the barstool and his cigarillo released a vertical line of perfumed smoke towards the pressed-tin ceiling. Built during the gold rush of the 1890s, the Great Western once had the city's biggest brothel running upstairs. The brothel was gone now but the pub remained the same, bar a few coats of paint and some European liqueurs in vivid blues and greens.

Reggie's freckled forearms were emaciated, and gave Swann a start. It had been many months since he'd seen his old friend. He placed a hand on Reggie's once plump shoulder and felt the bones, had to hide his reaction.

'*Detective*. Drinkies?'

The first word pronounced too loudly, for the benefit of the barman hovering nearby. Swann nodded, and took a barstool. There was no use pretending. 'Jesus, Reg. You've dropped a lot. What's —'

Reggie cackled, and Swann could hear the wheezing, the shortness of breath. The sudden red flush in his skin, the watering blue eyes. Swann immediately felt ashamed. During the Royal Commission, Reggie had stood by him when so many others walked away. As head of the Civil Liberties Association, his contacts had been crucial. Swann knew he could trust him with his life, that he could come to him with anything. And yet Reggie hadn't come to him with this.

'It's all right, detective. The boozer's trifecta, old mate. Emphysema and lung cancer, some pretty bad cirrhosis in my liver. They reckon it's a matter of a year, if I'm lucky . . .'

Swann's drink arrived but he wouldn't look at it. He caught the eye of the barman, who looked guiltily away. Reggie laughed. 'Thomas here's been trying to slip me Claytons. The cordial you drink when you're not having a drink. Can't fool an old soak like me. No substitute for gin is there, Thomas? Though I suspect he's being light on the nips. Nother double, thanks, Thomas, and I'll be watching.'

Reggie necked the rest of his drink, wiped his lips with the back of his hand, and watched the barman pour the shots into a measure. He took a restorative tug on his cigarillo, put it into the ashtray, where it continued to pulse a ribbon of smoke. He raised his glass in an ironic toast. 'There's none of us getting out of here alive, detective. Although I'm sure you don't need reminding.'

Swann had known a lot of alcoholics over the years, had been there himself. Most had a deep core of sadness in them, a collapsed star of anger. But Reggie wasn't like that. He drank because he liked to drink, liked to be drunk. He never became leery or maudlin or bitter. He remained his own good self, only amplified.

'What's the pain level? And who's looking after you?'

'A gentleman by the name of Dr D'Aeth, would you believe it. Comes highly recommended. A Calvinist. A *real* Calvinist. We get on like a house on fire. Odd that.'

Swann had intended to ask Reggie what he knew about the brokers handling the Rosa Gold float. Reggie knew the establishment inside out, although he had burnt his bridges over the years. Clearly, now was not the time.

But as though Reggie had read his mind, he asked, 'And what are you working on now? Anything I can do to help, of course. Take my mind off things, dear friend.'

They hadn't noticed the barman slip out behind the wood until he blocked the light streaming through the doorway. He was a big man, and cast a bigger shadow. A police siren could be heard in the distance, getting closer. On the pavement a crowd was gathered, looking up the street, eyes shielded from the glare. The barman turned to Swann and Reggie, drew fingers over his stubbled chin. 'Nother bank robbery. The R&I, just over on Francis Street. Bloke on a Harley, they reckon. Shot up William Street a minute ago.'

Cheeky bastard, thought Swann. Robs a bank on Gus Riley's hog and then makes his getaway past Riley's house on William Street. Six banks now, in a fortnight.

Swann took the Capitol Services spruik sheet from his pocket, unfolded it and passed it to Reggie, who squinted. 'Rosa Gold, eh? Incorporated August, scheduled for a float in November. Quick work . . .'

'But not floated. Never listed.'

Reggie nodded thoughtfully. 'That happens. Either investors smell a rat, or occasionally the company decides to go it alone. I haven't heard anything about Rosa Gold, but Capitol . . . they're solid, respectable. My father's brokers. I still have shares bought through them, because of my father. Although nowadays they're strictly institutional. This chap here, the broker in charge . . .' Reggie smiled his smile, the one that concealed an emerging secret. 'No longer works for them. But we're related. Not sure how you'd define our relationship, but he's the nephew of a cousin of mine. You might have read about him. Was badly beaten in a home invasion. Yes, around that date. November last year.'

Reggie picked up his stub of pencil and scribbled down an address. 'He lives in Subiaco. My cousin owns the block of flats, along with half the suburb. Mind if I join you? Get a ride down to Subi? I'll wait for you in the hotel.'

Swann put a hand on Reggie's forearm to steady him. Reggie had once been a solid man, as Swann had found when he'd had to carry him, drunk and unconscious, up a flight of stairs on his shoulder. But now Reggie felt light and frail, all the weight fallen off him, wincing as he settled onto his feet and shuffled towards the door.

Crossing Rokeby Road, Swann slowed while he checked the address against the rows of Deco apartment blocks on his left. He found the Miramar and pulled in to the footpath behind a TR-7 convertible. The sun sat low in the west, and the stucco Miramar was cast with flushes of pink as the light thinned.

He climbed the steps that were shot with kikuyu grass feelers that had spread from the lawn, bore water stains like blood up the flanks of the building. He lit a cigarette and rolled his neck in his shirt collar. He felt grimy and hot despite the cooling air. The urge to call it a day and join Reggie for a beer was strong. As he did every afternoon when the urge to drink was strongest, Swann replaced the image of the bar with the picture of slipping into the ocean at sunset, the water cool against his skin and the sea breeze clearing his head.

Swann knocked on the door of number twelve. As he waited, he looked out across overgrown gardens to the rear of King Edward Memorial Hospital. He knocked again and dropped his butt in the ashtray by the stairs. He could smell mutton chops and apple

sponge from the flats around him. The sound of a radio news broadcast, some jazz saxophone. A tumbler in a lock.

He was only a step away but out of instinct thrust his foot into
the crack between door and jamb, felt the pressure on his insole as
the door was pressed against him. He noticed for the first time the
repainted area around the lock in the doorframe, saw the splits in
the wood where the door had been jemmied open. He leaned in
with his hip.

A metre away was a young man, one hand on a Zimmer frame,
the other holding a Colt .32 aimed at Swann's belly. The blue eyes
were wide, the trembling in his gun hand rising up his arm until he
slumped against the corridor wall, took the gun in both hands, but
still couldn't control his trembling.

Swann held up his palms in mock surrender, took a step away
from the door. It was never a good thing to be on the wrong end of
a pointed gun, especially when held by a terrified novice. 'I'm Frank
Swann. Reggie Mansell gave me your address. I believe he's your —'

'Uncle Reggie?' Dennis Gould dropped the gun to his side, slid
a hand over the Zimmer frame and pushed off the wall. Rolled back
on the frame until he'd left the corridor. Swann followed him into
the lounge, a shadowy mess of dank clothes and beer bottles. He
could smell stale food from the kitchenette. Single bedroom off to
the side. Next to the unmade bed was a steel frame, the kind old
people use to get situated on the toilet.

'Sorry about the mess. My cleaner doesn't come until the
weekend.'

Gould walked with the help of the Zimmer along the windows
and scrolled the venetian blinds. Blocks of afternoon light fell into
the room. On the coffee table next to the leather couch was another
pistol, a long-nosed .38 Special, and a box of scattered shells. Swann
had a picture of Gould, drunk and late at night, passing the pistol

from hand to hand, mulling it over.

Dennis Gould eased himself onto the couch, manually lifting his left leg next to his right. He watched Swann watch him.

'I know who you are. You're the copper from the Royal Commission. Reggie's talked about you.'

Swann took a seat on a rickety old bentwood, leaned forward. 'You close to your uncle?'

Gould nodded. 'Used to be. Haven't seen him for ages. My fault.'

'What happened to your leg?'

Gould grimaced. He still had the Colt .32 in one hand. Didn't look like he ever put it down.

'Three blokes came through that door one night, around this time, just on sunset. Caught me in the shower. They wore balaclavas. One of them had a ballpein hammer. A big one.'

Swann nodded. They'd done one leg, but left the other.

'One of them got me in a chokehold, till I passed out. When I came to, they had me on the kitchen table. Stuffed my mouth with a dirty dishcloth, pinched my nose closed. Smashed my left kneecap with the hammer. Shattered it. Then did my ankle the same way. The pain, I can't begin to —'

'They say anything?'

Gould was young, in his late twenties, but in the fading sunlight he looked like an old man. One patch of bright silver hair over his right temple. A handsome face. The only colour his lips, dabby white tongue. Spoke slowly, like a stroke victim. 'They didn't need to. I knew what it was about.'

'Rosa Gold?'

Gould looked him in the eye for the first time. He was barely hanging on. Disappointed. 'You're not here to help me.'

A statement, not a question.

'Depends what you mean by help.'

'Revenge. I want *revenge*. But this leg. It's fucked. I thought Uncle Reggie might have —'

Swann shook his head. Lit a cigarette and waited, exhaled into the dying light. All that anger, and no place to take it. There was only going to be one ending. 'You know your uncle's sick, maybe terminal?'

He said it quietly, still looking at Gould, who had to look away. 'Can I have one of those?'

Swann passed him the packet of Craven A. It was a fair guess that if the kid was out of cigarettes, it was because he never left the apartment. Had his cleaner shop for him.

'Reggie'd never say it, but he could probably do with your help.'

Gould laughed. 'Me help? What good . . .' He didn't finish the sentence, aware of his self-pity in the light of Swann's news.

'He's going to need a lot of help. He doesn't have any close family. He speaks highly of you.'

Gould looked down at his leg, tugged deeply on the cigarette, nodded. He understood what Swann was trying to do, but said nothing. Looking after Reggie would be good for both of them.

'As for that other thing. Rosa Gold. Perhaps I can help, but not in the way you think. I'm working for Max Henderson's wife. Henderson was Rosa Gold's consulting geo. He killed himself last week . . . with a firearm.'

Gould studied the Colt .32 carefully. Put it gently on the coffee table. 'Go on.'

'She seems to think that he might have killed himself because of something to do with Rosa Gold. I've just come from Company House. I know you were the broker in charge of floating the stock. I know who the directors are, bar one. I want you to tell me who that person is. And I want you to tell me why you were crippled.'

Swann read out the names of the Rosa Gold directors he'd

written down. Gould looked at him strangely, and didn't look away. 'The other director of Rosa Gold. The one missing from the register. It's . . . was . . . Max Henderson. He had an equal share, like all the others. Depending on what's in his will, that place will now be held by his wife.'

'Jennifer Henderson?'

'That's right. I don't imagine she'd be selling her stake in a hurry. From what I've been led to believe, Rosa Gold is going to be enormous. It's why the stock was never floated.'

'Not because of you? Then why were you bashed?'

Swann lit another cigarette and passed it to Gould. At the mention of the bashing, his hands were shaking again. 'Thanks. Do you have anything to drink? My cleaner . . .'

Swann shook his head. He'd save the bottle of Grant's he had in the car for later, when he brought Reggie up to see his nephew. Clearly, they had a lot of catching up to do.

'I wasn't always a broker. It was Uncle Reggie who got me the job. I got boarded out of the Air Force. Drinking. Runs in the family. But Uncle Reggie, he's always been a big influence on me. The things he's done. I was doing well as a broker, built up a strong client base until the senior partners came to me with Rosa Gold. It was obviously just a ramp, something that's happening more and more, now the metal prices are rising. Either way, there was pressure on me to spruik Rosa Gold to my clients. Institutional investors, all of them. Big money. And I flat out refused. It was me who was going to look like an arsehole when the shares dived, after the directors and their mates had taken their profit. I told my boss that I wouldn't do it —'

'And you threatened to go to the regulators if they did.'

Gould nodded. 'They called my bluff. Regulation being something of a bluff itself. But I don't think anybody at Capitol . . .

I don't think it had ever happened before, a junior broker standing up to them.'

'Word got out to the directors of Rosa Gold somehow. How'd they know you were threatening to talk?'

Gould looked him full in the face. His eyes were newly fierce. Swann could see Reggie in him now, the same cherubic features masking a deeper strength. 'I told them myself. I told one of the directors. A young fellow. My father knew his father, Judge Quinlivan. I can't remember his first name. I knew the other directors by reputation. I don't know how to talk to people like that. I thought he'd be most . . . I thought we spoke the same language.'

Swann looked at his notebook. 'Gary Quinlivan?'

Gould nodded, tugged again on his cigarette, exhaled through his nose. Hands still shaking.

Swann stood and tossed Gould the rest of the packet. The sun had sunk below the tree line, taking with it the last rays from the apartment, suddenly in darkness. It didn't look like Swann would get that swim tonight. He scooped up the Colt .32 and the .38 Special from the coffee table, stuffed the shells into his shirt pocket.

Gould said nothing, just leaned forward over his hands.

16

Gary Quinlivan put his nose as low on the cue as possible, sighted along the stick to the corner pocket, the smell of chalk on the rail of his fingers and the tip of his cue. The purple-striped ball was nestled amongst a shield of spot balls, the white three inches off the cushion near the middle pocket. He stabbed at the white ball once, twice, three times before he sent it cannoning off the cushion into a forty-five angle, cuffed the purple stripe and sent it rolling, gently, into the corner pocket.

Leo Marrone cheered and slapped the bar. His two goons smirked, the smaller one with the perfect teeth and inkblot eyes nodded in respect. The bigger one went back to staring at the pin-ball machine he was batting around, his reflection bouncing off the smudged perspex of Barbarella and Conan.

It was Gary's best shot; deliberate, yes, but something of a fluke. A one in ten shot, useful only if it intimidated his opponent, who unfortunately didn't look the kind. Gary didn't know who his opponent was, but he moved with a quiet confidence. He was short and thin, in his forties, one of the many men and women who'd sat on their barstools and watched Marrone win big over the previous three games.

Marrone wasn't playing himself but sending out the small thug with the dead eyes as his proxy. The young Calabrian had a steady hand and a quick brain. He won all of his games, but didn't make it look easy. Gary read his game early. When he wanted to stuff a shot he hit the cue ball with his eyes closed, when he wanted to sink it his eyes remained open. Three games in a row, with five thousand a game at stake. The loser was a lawyer, fresh from a day in court, shirtsleeves rolled up, necktie slung over his shoulder, red wash of drink on his face, stain of failure in his eyes. He lost fifteen thousand cash in fifteen minutes, then shook Marrone's hand and walked out into the night. A gambler. A sucker.

That was when the short man in overalls stepped out of the crowd and put down his coin. He looked like a worker, with muscled forearms and a sharpie mullet, a single tear tattooed under his left eye. He took up a cue and balanced it over the palm of his hand, put it down and chose another, chalked it.

Waited, no expression on his face.

The fifteen thousand cash was on the bar next to Marrone. The pool room of the Zanzibar was crowded with hangers-on and clubbers, but nobody would touch Marrone's money.

It was then that Marrone shouted fifteen thousand, flicked a finger casually to the cash and raised his eyebrows, black and thin like a whip.

The man nodded, began to frame up. No sign that he had any money on him. No sign on Marrone's face that this was a problem. Concerned looks on the faces of some in the crowd, a greedy light in some of the others.

Gary wondered if the man knew what he was getting into, whether he knew who Marrone was. A blow-in from the east perhaps, or a miner from up north. Gary felt for him, admired his quiet determination as he pulled the frame off the arrowed balls and waited.

If he lost, he would owe Marrone fifteen thousand dollars. If he didn't have it, Marrone had plenty of dirty work to set him.

Gary looked to Marrone and saw something new in his eyes. A brightness, but a glaze there too on the surface. Marrone caught him looking, and his eyes hardened, nodded to the goon to pass the cue to Gary.

Marrone had practically forced Gary to come out tonight. He was Tommaso Adamo's main dealer and muscle, and he'd turned up at Gary's apartment flanked by his thugs, all of them reeking of the same cologne. There was no excitement in Marrone's voice when he told Gary that he should come raging. That he should wear what he was wearing and come out to the car. Marrone couldn't help himself. Always that quiet menace beneath everything he said, the need to read his eyes for meaning. Adamo had hinted that he wanted Gary closer, that there was a role for him beyond his Rosa Gold duties and his smack dealing. But even when they'd left Gary's apartment and were in the car park, Gary couldn't tell whether Marrone intended to take him partying or bury him in the hills.

The bloke in the overalls potted three smalls but snookered himself between the cushion and three stripes. He jumped the stripes and made his small but missed the middle pocket.

Gary hadn't let go of his cue. He didn't appreciate playing pool for fifteen thousand dollars a game. That the money wasn't his only made it worse. He didn't want to lose Marrone's money, even if the man spent it like water from a tap.

He had to focus. He ignored the looks of the crowd and the heat in his armpits, his sweaty hands. He chalked his knuckles and cue tip, blew off the dust. Leant across the table and sank an easy shot to the middle pocket. There were six balls left on the table, not

ZERO AT THE BONE

including the black. Four of them were Gary's. He made another down the table, which brought the white back to his cue.

He caught the eye of his opponent, who was clearly trying to vibe him out. That prison tattoo beneath his eye. Looking at Gary with hatred and derision, like he had no right to be in his company. The bloke was obviously an out-of-towner, another wise man from the east, who didn't know how things worked here.

It was true that none of Gary's private school mates would be here tonight, or any other night, but that didn't mean they were cleanskins. Life in the better suburbs was boring, so middle-class boys needed more excitement. Most of Gary's school mates had been into drugs and stealing cars but none had been caught. Gary had taken a promotion with the bank robberies, but he wasn't the only one.

He ignored the derision in the eyes of his opponent, smiled back. It suited him that the man had no respect. Perhaps he thought that men got wealthy because of hard work and nice manners. They all underestimated Gary, and that suited him just fine.

But he stuffed up the shot, white off the cushion on a narrow angle, running down to the end pocket, hit it too hard. The stripe went in and out.

Gary heard the collective sigh and then the silence. Nobody would openly laugh while it was Marrone's money on the table, but many would be secretly glad. The old crim in the overalls bent to his task and pocketed his two smalls, didn't hesitate over the black, looked once and sent it the full length of the table into the corner pocket, the white spinning off and dying clear.

Gary walked slowly to the wall and put his cue on the rack. He didn't want to look at either Marrone or the crim, the handover of the money. Two years' salary for the average secretary, nurse, copper.

But then he remembered how he'd come to be there. A test of some sort. He sought out the crim and shook his calloused hand. Shrugged to Marrone and took his seat beside him. Marrone merely whispered, out of the side of his mouth, 'No hard feelings, Gary. But I don't like to lose.'

He slapped Gary on the shoulder, sniffed and put his hands in his wallet. Drew out a wad of cash. 'No, I don't like to lose. Get your cue, Gary. In for a penny . . .' He rapped his knuckles on the bar. 'Double or nothing, eh, Mr White Bread? Double or nothing.'

17

The clouds were low and smelt of rain. Swann pulled off Salvado Road and drove the short distance to Jennifer Henderson's house near the coast. From a hundred metres he could see the verge piled with her furniture, beneath the streetlights. A couple of beachcombers were parked in front, trailers laden. He pulled into the drive and noticed the silver Karmann Ghia in the carport.

An old man in overalls hoisted a mahogany bookshelf onto the bed of a battered ute and looked at him suspiciously, a potential rival. Swann walked past the expensive furniture and shook his head. Despite the darkness, it was clear that much of it was badly damaged, but some of it looked unmarked. Thousands of dollars' worth of furniture, tossed out like garbage. Some of it was stuff he'd like himself, that he could repair. The antique lacquered Japanese altar, for example. Already claimed by the old man, working fast.

Jennifer Henderson was waiting outside the front door, surrounded by a halo of tiny moths. She held a glass of white in one hand, a cigarette in the other. Had she turfed the entire contents of her home because she could afford to, or for some other reason? Her eyes weren't saying.

Swann followed her inside. The place was bare except for Max Henderson's recliner. Patches of polished board remained where the furniture had been removed, tracked with dusty bootprints.

He trailed her through the darkened house out to the backyard, where the wrought-iron table remained. In the night sky the clouds had fallen lower. The air was still, even as the first drops of warm northern rain began to fall, spattering the dirt and ringing out on the corrugated roof.

She pulled out a chair and sat with him, not meeting his eyes. Both of them aware of the dry place next to them, beneath the casuarina, where Max Henderson had ended his life.

It made sense for Jennifer Henderson to spurn her money. She was grieving. She had no family; no parents, siblings or children. Her home, her sanctuary, had been violated. Except that her eyes were animated by a diamond light, behind the drunkenness.

'You're angry with me.' Her voice feathery with smoke.

'You never mentioned that Max was a partner in Rosa Gold. You knew who he was dealing with?'

'Yes.'

'Then . . .?'

'That's why I need you.'

'If you think I can protect you, you don't know much about Tommaso Adamo, Leo Marrone. Ben Hogan. Bernie Isaacs. All their soldiers. Blokes who kill for promotion. Just to get noticed.'

'I don't intend to provoke them. Just get what Max wanted. What he was owed.'

'Being what?'

'The mining rights to the land. Worth a considerable sum. They were passed from Max to Rosa Gold.'

'You're in a position to take the rights back? You haven't said anything to —'

'I just want what Max was owed. He surveyed the claim, started the whole thing off. Offered Rosa Gold the rights to our very valuable land . . .'

'Wouldn't that make them suspicious? Conflict of interest? The consulting geo selling the mining rights to the land he's supposed to be reporting on?'

'Yes, if he wanted money in return. But he didn't. He wanted an equal share in the company, as one of eight directors. And not only that, he stumped up his own cash, our entire savings, to get the drilling started. To confirm what his initial assays suggested.'

Clouds covered the moon. Jennifer Henderson's eyes were hidden in shadow, black lips around her parted mouth.

'So this is about money. Recovering your . . . Max's investment. Why didn't you tell me earlier?'

The moon came out from behind the clouds. She took her time, tamping something down. Any minute now she would say it – what they all say. *The full details are none of your business. Your job is to investigate, retrieve information.* And for the first time Swann would answer no, in this case, my job would be to stay alive.

'I didn't want you to think . . . less of me. Think that I'm in it for the money. But we mortgaged everything, and —'

Swann took a guess. 'And it's all in your name. Why?'

She didn't miss a beat.

'It's a dangerous job, being a geologist in remote areas. Max was away for months at a time, in PNG, equatorial Africa. The Philippines. Lawless places. He often contracted malaria, nearly died of it many times. Typhoid. Once, cholera. Putting the property, our assets in my name, Max thought that was the sensible thing to do, in case he never came home.'

'You didn't think to change it, after he'd retired?'

'Don't look at me like that. It's why I didn't tell you. It's not about the money. The Rosa Gold stake is going to be one of the biggest mines this nation has *ever* seen. Max saw that the first time he walked the country. It's the kind of stake he'd been looking for ever since PNG. His promised land.'

'And the eighth share – is that in your name too?'

'In a sense. It's owned by Henderson Pty Ltd. A company we registered, some time back, to hold the claims Max had staked over the years. I'm one of the . . . I'm the only director now.'

'So you own the stake in Rosa Gold.'

'Yes.'

'To be clear. Do the other directors of Rosa Gold know this?'

'No. They only knew Max. It's fair to assume he never mentioned my name.'

'Meaning he was aware of the potential danger. But why did you buy in? He's mortgaged all your assets . . .'

Jennifer Henderson laughed. 'You clearly don't know gold men. Money's got nothing to do with it. It's the chase. The promise . . . Our property's nominally in my name, but it came from his hard work. I never stood in his way.'

'Why didn't he develop the mine himself? Take it to one of the big players? The Rosa Gold directors are amateurs. Con men. Fucking heroin importers. If he was serious . . .'

She nodded. Looked at him strangely, almost sadly. 'He'd have been marginalised at a bigger company. It'd happened to him before. He discovered the gold, then watched others reap the profits. Dubious as the Rosa Gold directors are, he thought that as a professional, he'd be able to lead. He needed that challenge. Gold mining is a tough school, and it doesn't hurt to have roughnecks on your board.'

'Max wasn't murdered. He shot *himself*. Your initial approach to me, your concern that his death had something to do with

Rosa Gold . . .'

Swann left it hanging there, and Jennifer didn't take it up. But something passed into her eyes, a flicker of darkness.

'I know I'm out of my depth. I know that you can't possibly protect me. I know it'll be dangerous for you. But I'm not selling my . . . our share.'

'Then you'll wind up where he is.'

Her eyes locked with his. She glared at him, but not enough to mask what lay beneath, a spasm of fear. Swann didn't look away, and she stood, walked to the edge of the paving, her back to him, arms clasped around herself.

'I apologise. I'm struggling. Without Max. I just want to know what's going on with the mine. They weren't returning my calls. And when I kept trying . . . my home was torn apart.'

'We may never know if Max was threatened, before his death. But *you* were threatened, or they were looking for something Max had. Either way, what Max chose to do, leaving you alone like he has . . . It doesn't make sense to continue. My advice is to cut your losses, move away.'

She spoke in a whisper as she turned to him, moonlight illuminating her hands, face in shadow. 'I just want to know what they're thinking. What they're planning. That's your job, isn't it? I'm no threat to them. I just want to see it through, for Max. Crazy, but there it is.'

Swann didn't reply. No other PI would touch the job, once they knew who was involved. Not for any money. He looked at her closely. He could see she was serious. He didn't understand that. There were many things worth dying for, but the vision of a man who'd abandoned you, didn't even leave a note, wasn't one of them.

'And I promise to be more forthright with you. Starting this minute.'

If Swann walked away, Jennifer Henderson was going to get herself killed.

'What was Max's next move? Before he . . .'

The question surprised her, made her smile. 'All I know is that there's a directors' meeting in a few days. In the offices above a gold exchange on James Street, in North Perth.'

'Chisholm Gold. I know it. Across from the Great Western. Chisholm's an ex-copper.'

'Yes, Max described him to me. What are you thinking?'

'You've never met any of the directors? Hogan or Marrone? Adamo or Isaacs?'

She shook her head.

'They don't know anything about you?'

'Only what they might have learned going through my wardrobe, my cupboards, my kitchen drawers.'

'The other directors will offer to buy you out, and you'll agree, which will rule out the possibility of violence against you. But you'll have to put them off. Tell them that Max's will is in probate. That the formal settlement of the estate might take weeks, months. *Then* you're happy to part with your share. And keeping you on as director in the meantime is the easiest course. Agreed?'

'Agreed. And then?'

It was Swann's mission to make sure Jennifer Henderson had the sense to do exactly that, sell her share and take whatever money was offered.

'We'll come to that when we come to it, but we can't be seen together. In the meantime, start from the beginning. Tell me about the first trip to the Rosa Gold stake. Tell me what Max saw there. Tell me what's going on at the stake. Tell me everything.'

'You'll need to speak to Garth Oats about that. He's on the drilling crew Max put together. He's probably back out there now. I was hoping he'd tell you the other day.'

'Man of few words, is Mr Oats. How can I contact him? How did Max contact him?'

'You can't. I'll have to take you to him. The site is remote, and deliberately hidden. Garth comes into town to oversee the delivery of the core samples to the assay lab, down near the Perth Mint. Max spent most of his time on-site these past months, supervising the drilling and the logging of the core, the delivery to the lab.'

I'll have to take you to him.

Hopefulness in her glance, before looking away. The hard-bitten woman of a few minutes ago gone.

The rain had stopped falling, a single star rising to the west. The shed roof glistened. A magpie called in the branches of the casuarina, slow and melodic, but no other magpie answered. Somewhere to the north, a cyclone was flooding the parched inland desert where Rosa Gold had their stake. And Garth Oats was out there too, knelt beside a drill rig, cutting hundreds of metres into the hard rock.

The magpie gave up its calling and swished across the watercolour night sky.

18

Fremantle was loud in the Wednesday-morning heat, the easterly turning rubbish in the gutters and making the seagulls work above the streets, headed to the South Fremantle tip. Swann parked the EK around the corner from Papa Luigi's on Market Street, and made for High Street. He followed a fresh blood trail down the footpath that started with coin-sized spots and ended with a long red stain in a recessed shopfront, evidence of the usual violence on the street after dark. He tossed a coin into the guitar case of some hippie buskers on the footpath outside Culley's Bakery, then entered the shop.

Jennifer Henderson was paying one of her husband's bills in old Miragliotta's, the tailor on the corner of High and Adelaide, and he could watch her from the bakery window. Swann had called to check on her, and she'd told him about the man in the parked car, down the street from her home. After the damage to the Henderson house it would be normal for her to jump at shadows, but there was only one way to be sure. Swann asked her if she had any business in town, and she'd replied yes, she needed to pay Max's tailor in Fremantle. Swann had suggested she go for the drive, to see if she was followed. He would join her there.

Swann ordered a cheese and salad poppyseed horseshoe roll, extra white pepper, and a mug of tea. The traffic on High Street was picking up. He drank the tea while he waited for his roll and watched the footpath. He couldn't see anyone likely. The hippie buskers wailing a Bob Marley song were doing a good job of keeping people away. A couple of old Italian gents sat smoking beneath matching fedoras at a bus stop, and some kids from John Curtin High roller-skated past. From Swann's point of view, it was a good thing that Jennifer was scared – it meant she was seeing things clearly, perhaps as a result of their conversation last night. There was his own safety to consider, too. Now that Hogan and Adamo were in the Rosa Gold picture, he had to find out whether he'd been seen with Jennifer.

Swann picked up his order and went and sat next to the old men at the bus stop. There was no need for him to keep out of sight. He took off the wax paper wrapper and started on the roll, good as always. He'd been eating Culley's rolls all his life. He sat forward so the shredded lettuce and carrot and onion fell at his feet. Two seagulls edged closer. A young dero with wild red hair and haunted eyes came and cadged a cigarette from one of the old men, who passed it over reluctantly, had to be badgered into lighting it. The dero was far gone, feet cracked and yellow, wore a greatcoat despite the heat, shuffled and put his hand out to the hippie buskers, who gave him some coin. Good kids.

Jennifer Henderson came out of the narrow doorway between the barbers and the bookshop, carrying a suit. She stopped and put on her sunglasses, looked around and clocked him but didn't hold his gaze. She set off around the corner towards the council car park while Swann continued to eat his roll. When no-one followed, he binned his wrapper and tossed the hippie kids some more coin, then went back to his car off Market Street. Some Italian boys were

standing near it, dressed in the Freo Rocks uniform of black desert
boots, tight black jeans and muscle shirts. The gang was part of the
reason Fremantle was dangerous at night, but they respected quality
cars and nodded when he took out his keys, went on their way.

Swann drove around the corner onto Parry Street, circled the
markets and turned into Henderson street, where the car park for
the Queensgate Building exited. He took his sunglasses down off
the visor and parked in the bays of the police station. From here he
could see across the street to the exit, and he rolled down the windows and waited. He ignored the front desk of the cop shop beside
him, duty sergeant looking through the mesh screen doors.

Jennifer's Karmann Ghia rolled out of the car park and turned
left. Swann reversed, turned towards the cop shop and curled around
to face the street. Two cars had exited the car park after Jennifer, but
neither the old Morris nor the Kombi looked likely. Swann waited,
then saw what he was looking for: a white VB Commodore sedan,
looked like a fleet vehicle. The driver was a large man with a big
moustache in a tan business shirt. Swann didn't recognise him, but
got a good look as he adjusted his radio coming out of the car park.

The Karmann Ghia was back on High Street and headed for the
lights at Hampton Road. Swann sat two cars off the Commodore
as it turned to follow Jennifer past the old women's asylum, before
crossing the traffic bridge into North Fremantle. Swann knew where
she was headed so he kept his eyes on the Commodore. The driver
looked like a detective but drove like a civilian, keeping under the
speed limit and always indicating to change lanes.

This worried Swann. Considering who Jennifer Henderson
was doing business with, the driver of the Commodore was either
another PI or a hired killer. If there was a contract on Jennifer, they'd
want to make it look like suicide or natural causes. Hogan could be
counted on to manage the investigation, but perhaps they weren't

taking any risks. A hired killer with a police or military background would serve the purpose well. Someone efficient and not likely to boast about it down the track, when drunk or in jail. The kind of killer who worked with legitimate business rather than organised crime, whose thugs were more valued for their ability to inspire fear.

Or perhaps Swann was letting his mind run. Chances were, the driver of the Commodore had been hired to monitor Jennifer Henderson's movements and meets – to keep her fellow directors abreast of likely decisions regarding her stake in the company.

Swann scribbled the rego of the car as he drove, the Indian Ocean flat to the horizon behind Rottnest Island. The Commodore continued to sit a few cars behind the Ghia as they entered Peppermint Grove, but the driver now looked more consciously in his wing and rear-view mirrors. Had Swann revealed himself? He saw the man lean down again and suddenly understood. It wasn't a radio the driver had tuned upon exiting the car park.

Swann turned on his CB handset, but too late. He heard the sirens and watched helplessly as the Commodore cut down a side road into Cottesloe. Two unmarked sedans shot into his rear-view mirror, mobile sirens fixed to their roofs.

'Just comin' up on him now,' said the driver of the first vehicle. The car swung past Swann and cut him off, turned to the kerb. The second vehicle, another white Kingswood, pulled in behind. Swann turned off the CB and tuned it away from the police frequency. He could see Ben Hogan and a couple of familiar faces in the car behind him.

Swann pulled out his wallet and climbed out of the car, his guts a mess of nerves. That Hogan was after him could only mean one thing, and he cursed Percy Dickson under his breath. Swann locked the door behind him, his keys still in the ignition. He had a spare key hidden under the chassis. There was no way he was going to sit in his vehicle and take a bullet, have a throwdown tossed onto his lap, or be loaded with something else.

The traffic, heavy enough for there to be witnesses, slowed to negotiate the three parked cars. If they were going to shoot him, Swann wanted it known that he was unarmed. He put his hands in the air and stood quietly and waited, making eye contact with as many passing drivers as possible.

Had the driver of the Commodore clocked Swann early on and called his mates in the detective branch? Or was this an unhappy coincidence?

Hogan strolled casually around the EK while buttoning his suit jacket, looking down at the seats. He had a black eye and a split lip, stitched where his teeth had broken his mouth. He saw that all the doors to the Holden were locked, and sneered. Swann looked to the hands of the five detectives gathered around him, rather than their eyes. He wanted to know what they were going to load him with. They gathered close and left a space where Hogan slipped through.

Protected from the view of the passing traffic, Hogan stunned Swann with a punch to the solar plexus, then, as he hunched backwards, an uppercut to the face. Swann braced himself against the door panel that largely protected him from the blows of the others, except for Hogan's boot, which was kicking into his torso and head. Swann refused to lie down, to let those arms hold him. A beating was preferable to being fitted up, to what would come later at the lockup. He took the boots to his ribs and face, while the others continued to shield Hogan from the view of the motorists, the strobe effect of the flashing lights, no sign of handcuffs, just the kicks that kept coming.

When he was finished, Hogan leant down and spoke quietly into Swann's ear. 'Been looking forward to this talk, Swanny. Been a long time coming. Your mate Percy Dickson had a bad accident this morning. Surprised you haven't heard. Those bikie dogs you sent are next . . . then *you*.'

Swann let the blood stream from his nose onto the bitumen. His nose was broken again, and he spat blood and saliva. But no real harm done. He had taken worse beatings. Hogan spieled on, his voice a monotone, trying not to get excited and split his lip again. Hogan's mouth was so close to his ear that all Swann had to do was brace his feet and hands, and slam the point of his shoulder into Hogan's face.

He heard him cry out, felt teeth in his collarbone, then stood with his hands in the air once more, looking to the halted traffic, the motorists staring while waiting for a red light. Hogan's mouth was split again, and the blood was flowing down his chin. They stood across from one another, the junior Ds not sure what to do.

Hogan didn't say anything, make any more threats, meaning he didn't trust all of the coppers present. But his eyes said enough. His eyes were bright with hatred, and knowing. He reached for his handcuffs and snapped them out.

19

Gary Quinlivan put on his seatbelt as instructed. Marrone grinned and plugged himself in. Gary wondered why, with all the cars at Marrone's disposal, his used-car lot filled with Triumphs and Mustangs and Porsches and Alfa Romeos, even a red Maserati, Marrone had chosen an old Land Cruiser with dented fenders and red dust in its wheel arches.

The trip to the Perth Mint had been more eventful than Gary liked. He'd helped carry the cash from Marrone's office to the Toyota, a foot-high stack of used notes that had been cycled through Marrone's automatic counter, taped into bundles of five thousand. Two hundred thousand dollars in cash, covered with a hessian bag.

The old banger hadn't even started first time, and one of Marrone's mechanics had to jump it with a portable charger. Worse still for Gary's nerves, Marrone stopped twice on the way to the mint, killing the engine both times. The first time was to buy cigarettes, the second to collect a debt from a mechanic in Subiaco. When Gary asked who the debt was owed to, Marrone just shrugged and replied, 'A friend. You go.'

Marrone parked down the street from the garage and told Gary what to say. 'You did bad work on Mr Jeremy Harper's Mercedes. He's asked you to refund the price of his reconditioned engine nicely, three times, and you haven't called him back. I've been sent to collect the debt you owe him.'

Gary laughed. Marrone was joking, right? Sure, they were testing him, and sure, he'd lost forty-five thousand dollars of Marrone's money at the pool table, but this was something else. Gary no longer believed he'd actually lost Marrone's money. He suspected he'd been set up, that there was some link between the worker in the overalls and Marrone, and that the money handed over to the man had come right back to Marrone. Merely to put pressure on Gary, to see how he ticked.

Well, if it was a test, then he would do it. The opportunity to become part of Adamo's crew was too good to miss. Gary was no hard man, but he'd give it a go.

Predictably, the owner of the garage laughed in Gary's face. A wiry older man with red hair and freckled forearms, he didn't even put down the socket handle, or wipe his hands of grease. Turned and went right back to working.

Gary heard Marrone's footsteps and stood back. The mechanic ratcheted a nut, peered under his armpit, saw Marrone's immaculately polished shoes. Spun around in slow motion, hands in the air.

Marrone didn't need to speak. He was a well-known face who sometimes went by the term businessman, other times mediator.

Now the mechanic wiped his hands of grease, backed away into his chipboard office, emerged with a cheque, proffered it to Marrone, who shook his head. Made the man pass the cheque to Gary. Still no words were spoken.

Marrone waited until they were back in the Land Cruiser, engine jouncing on its axle. 'You want that respect, Gary, you gotta earn it. You gotta make a name.'

Gary didn't reply. It was worse than he'd thought. Adamo hadn't just instructed Marrone to show Gary the ropes. He was going to make him do things. Things Gary doubted he could do.

And there'd been a third detour on the way to the mint, although not one that required turning off the engine. On James Street, Marrone suddenly put his foot down, cranking back a gear to give him extra control, left the road and mounted the footpath. Gary braced his feet into the floor pan and put his hands on the dash, gritted his teeth. Marrone grunted as he yanked the steering wheel and took out the first in a line of card tables where protestors were collecting signatures. The sound of splintering wood and a burst of yellow flyers like a flock of startled birds. The engine screaming as Marrone sighted on a young woman who hadn't budged, standing there defiant or frozen, Gary couldn't tell, the plywood stave of her placard wedged between her legs.

'How many people you count here? Pigs aren't doin' their job. More than three and they're supposed to arrest 'em.'

Marrone shanked the steering wheel so that he struck her with the right fender. The sound of a mallet hitting meat. Instead of coming over the car, she smashed into the fence. Screams from her friends and then Marrone had them back on the road, turning with a squeal onto Roe Street, his hands at two and four on the wheel and his face calm, not even looking back.

At the mint Gary signed for the gold, using what he discovered was Adamo's money as payment, passed to him by Marrone. His nerves were still shaky, especially when he saw a shred of torn denim caught in the front fender, now even more dented than before. At the desk in the foyer he was forced to come up with a name, on the spot, for the registration forms. At least he wasn't asked for ID.

Marrone was scuffing his shoes and whistling a Kiss song whose name Gary didn't remember. The cash disappeared off the counter

and Gary lit up a cigarette, staring at sepia photographs of prospectors dry-blowing in ancient riverbeds, dusty abandoned mine sites
and mutton-chop and cravat-wearing company directors out in the
goldfields; a panorama of the view from the mint over Perth Water
before Adelaide Terrace was built up, all Cape lilacs and colonial
mansions and black swans in the shallows.

It was cool inside the limestone walls, with the metal-stamp hiss
of coin presses at work in the rear of the building. Then the clank of
a door opening and a trolley gliding over the floorboards. Marrone
greeted the security guard by name, shook hands. Once Gary had
signed, the guard wheeled the trolley out into the fierce light and
oven heat to the rear of the Land Cruiser. Gary watched as the gold
was loaded, heard the plate shockies of the Land Cruiser creak as the
glinting one-kilo bars were laid out in three lines.

The foundry was on an alley off the rail sidings at Midland Junction.
A wreckers and towing company on either side, dogs on heavy
chains panting in the heat. The foundry was made of corrugated
iron, high walls and skillion roof, open eaves and windows, heat
shimmering off the rusting metal, a car park of packed sand and
mounds of broken castings.

Marrone pulled open the twin doors of the shed and motioned
for Gary to back the Land Cruiser in. Inside it was dark and hot,
smelt of carbonised bricks and propane, the air ragged with the
sound of burning fuel. Down the far end Marrone spoke with a fat
man in a leather apron and bare feet, otherwise naked except for his
jocks. Streaks of sweat ran over his shaved head and his eyes burned
red. He hoisted open the rear of the Land Cruiser and had a look,
then the three of them carried the gold bars to an iron table.

The man donned long leather gloves and with some tongs took

the lid off a pit built into an earthen mound, flooding the shed with a deep red glow. The sound of the burning propane reminded Gary of a jet engine, and the arid heat burnt his nostrils. Marrone tapped him on the shoulder and they walked to the entrance of the shed. Outside it was close to forty degrees but felt considerably cooler. They watched as the man carried three gold bars in his tongs and dropped them into the fiery pit.

'You stay and watch him. Don't let him out of your sight.'

Marrone returned ten minutes later with two cans of Tab. Gary rubbed the beaded steel over his forehead, put it into his neck, his face.

'How long does it take to melt the bars?' he asked Marrone.

'Too fucken long.'

Gary stared into the fiery hole of the shed, the heat pressing against him, the bald man standing beside the furnace reading the paper in the red light, immune to the searing heat, a creature of hell.

'*Lasciate ogni speranza, voi ch' entrate . . .*'

'*Cosa?* Eh?'

Gary laughed. 'It's Dante. An Italian poet. From the *Inferno*. Abandon hope, all ye —'

'I know what it means. Where was he from?'

'Florence.'

'You speak Italian?'

There was wariness in Marrone's eyes, the things Gary might have heard.

'No.'

'You should learn, but Cosentino, northern Calabrian, or at least Napoletano. Not that Firenze shit.'

'I thought you were from Sicily.'

'I'm from Osborne Park, fuckhead. Adamo speaks Calabrian.'

'All right, I'll give it a go. Should we watch?'

Marrone nodded, and Gary followed him into the shed. The bald man in the leather apron had donned his long gloves and lifted the lid, pulled out a glowing red beaker, carried it quickly to a sheet of scavenged asbestos cladding. Gary couldn't help himself, he gasped like a child when the man began to tip the molten gold into what looked like pieces of terracotta, the beauty of the liquid bullion in the hard red light.

Rosa Gold became real for him at that moment.

He thought of all the glittering metal that waited beneath the ground at the Rosa Gold stake. What it stood for. What it would make him. Felt a shiver of deep longing.

'That's our moulds,' Marrone told him. 'Made of clay and graphite, some loose gravel. When they cool, we crack 'em open. Looks like real alluvial gold.'

'And then?'

'You take 'em into the mint, sell them back under Adamo's real name. The cash you get is now clean cash. Legit.'

The man carried the beaker back into the fire-pit, the sound of hissing diminished. He used the tongs to drop three more kilo bars into the beaker, replaced the lid.

'Where do I say Adamo found the gold? On the Rosa Gold stake?'

'Fuck no. There's thousands of eavesdropping pricks with metal detectors all over the city. We don't want 'em anywhere near our stake. And you can't take the gold in all at once. It's gonna take weeks, bit by bit. What's wrong?'

Gary shrugged the look off his face. He got it now, why he was here. 'There's got to be a better way. Banks, offshore accounts . . .'

Marrone laughed, slapped Gary on the shoulder. 'About time you twigged. Welcome to the team, laundry man. I gotta go, but I'll leave you the Toyota. And watch this prick. Make sure any spillage goes back into the pot. If he tries to nick any, wait till he's not looking, clock him with something made of iron. Put his head in that fucken oven. It burns at 1330 degrees. All that blubber, he'll go up like a fucken candle.'

Gary thought of the woman Marrone had run down in the Land Cruiser. He didn't want to be caught driving the car, especially not with twenty-five kilos of gold ingots in the back. 'What do I do with it all?'

'When the prick's finished, you weigh it, make sure it all adds up. If it does, you take it to Chisholm's safe in Northline. If it doesn't, you torture the prick, kill him if you have to. Fucked if I care either way.'

Gary watched the man reading his paper by the blasting light of the furnace; he must have heard Marrone's threats. Gary had a plane to catch in a few hours, but that wasn't something he could tell Marrone – to do that would mean Gary's head in the furnace.

Quoting Dante Alighieri earlier had been a joke, a way of showing off his schooling, but it had been a mistake. Now the words wouldn't leave Gary's head. *Lasciate ogni speranza . . .*

20

Swann wedged himself into the corner of the cell, his sweating shoulders against the angled walls keeping him upright. He was alone, and it was quiet and still, only the stink of sour sweat and piss. The other cells at East Perth lockup were full of drunks and street people, their grunting wheezing comedowns and shouts of anger and wheedling clamour when the coppers were near.

He sat forward on the concrete bench, put his head in his hands to still the dizziness, then remembered, sat himself upright, made himself look calm, contained, like he still had some dignity left. They would want him to look broken, to make what happened later seem logical, a matter of cause and effect.

When Hogan had shoved and yanked and hoisted him across the Central police station foyer, on the way to the lockup, followed by the jackboot drumbeat of his posse behind, he'd made no effort to conceal Swann's identity, and Swann had wondered why. He'd assumed Hogan would secrete him somewhere in a suburban station perhaps, and then let whatever happened take place in private, away from the scrutiny of others.

Now he understood.

It was the change of shifts at Central and there were dozens of uniformed and detectives behind the desk, coming in and heading out on patrol. Swann was held there by Hogan, his face pressed into a wall, while the paperwork was done.

The ex-head of Perth Central, Superintendent Frank Swann, now under arrest in his own station, bloodied and beaten while resisting arrest, the obvious charge to hold him on.

Word quickly got around Central that Swann had been arrested. Stickybeaks and their whispers, echoing in the halls. A few looks of concern, some of disbelief on familiar faces. Men and women who had saluted him not that long ago, before he was labelled a rat, run out of the force.

Swann didn't know the duty sergeant, so there was no angle there. He had to hope that someone would tell someone, who'd tell someone, who'd call Marion.

It was a long shot.

Hogan made the humiliation real. Wanted everyone to see it. A great man, fallen from grace. Now one of *them*, on the other side of the bars. Wanted the serving coppers to imagine how that might feel. What a proud man might do to himself, to end the shame.

They hadn't taken Swann's belt, or shoelaces, as they were supposed to.

Now he had to wait, for what happened next. For the darkness to fall, for the early hours, when they would come at him, and string him up. Paint it as an act of desperation, and despair.

His nose was still bleeding, but he made no effort to staunch the flow. He felt the blood seep over his chin and run into his collar. His need for a cigarette competed with the nausea. He was still dizzy. Concussion vertigo. He'd had it many times before. The walls rocked left and right when he shifted his head, the floor rose and fell.

An odd sound nearby, a wrong note, his own laugh. Sounded like a bark. The image of him sitting in the swamp, watching the subdivision, bored and restless, complaining to himself. From where he sat now, that was nothing to complain about.

Percy Fucking Dickson.

Swann put it out of his mind. Drew comfort instead from the coolness of the walls, breathed deeply to calm himself. He had to save his strength. He had to remain awake. Refuse all food and drink, as potentially drugged. He needed to be ready to explode. Make as much noise as possible, from his cell at the end of the row. Use deadly force. If he could kill one of them, then suicide was not an explanation. If he could kill one of them, they would kill him too, but questions would be asked. What were they doing in his cell, in the early hours . . .

Two sets of steps approaching. A pair of leather-soled shoes, the other police-issue boots, the heavy clump and squeak on the painted cement floor familiar to him, after all these years. One detective and one uniformed?

Swann pulled himself onto his feet, the dizziness overwhelming him, had to put a hand on the wall.

Two would not be enough, he would make sure of that.

The iron teardrop over the judas hole turned, revealed a blue gaze that stared, unblinking. Around the judas hole someone had drawn a cock, a pair of saggy balls. The unblinking blue eye looked out through the eye of the cock, the old crim's way of mocking a screw's gaze. Swann looked back, waited, heard the keys at the sergeant's belt, the tumblers in the lock. He took the stance, bare hands raised before him, ready to rush the door, get inside the baton blows, go for the eyes, the throat, the neck.

The heavy door swung back. He heard the sergeant's boots creak. A murmur. Cartoonish aftershave amidst the sour smells. Then the sergeant's boots retreating down the row, the rising pitch of the beseechers at him, pleas for cigarettes, blankets, a human voice, to know that they hadn't been forgotten.

Minister of Police Terry Sullivan entered the cell with his hands raised, a wrinkle in his nose at the smell, the sight of Swann's bloodied face, spattered shirt, his balled fists.

'No need for that, Frank. I heard you were here. Not my doing, of course. Take a seat. Cigarette?'

The cell door remained open, and Swann listened for footsteps.

'There'll be nobody joining our party, Frank. It's you and me, for now. Depending on how we get along.'

Swann took the offered cigarette and leaned into the flame, the roll of dizziness making him stagger, saw the look of exhaustion on Sullivan's face.

'Not sleeping well, Sullivan? Polls crook again?'

'No need for that.'

'Come to rub it in? Express your concern? Right a wrong?'

'You don't look too good, Frank, if you don't mind me saying. We've had our differences in the past ...'

Swann grunted, tried not to move his head. Sullivan's face dissolved in kaleidoscope, cigarette smoke, duplicates and triplicates of the smug eyes and grim smile, jug ears fanning out like a cut deck of cards.

'Call my wife. Let her know I'm here.'

'Can't do that, Frank. But I can go one better. I can let you out. Sit down, you're about to chunder.'

Swann sat, and Sullivan stood, looked at his watch.

'Hogan know you're here?'

Sullivan shook his head. The Police Minister had helped run Swann out of the force, had signed off on the paperwork, had spoken against him at the Royal Commission.

'I've got a few concerns with our Detective Inspector Hogan. Let me be frank, Frank. I'm beginning to suspect that Ben isn't a team player. That he's taking things for granted. His promotion, for example. But leaving that aside, I wanted to make you an offer. You see, Ben's gone into the mining game, and I'm hearing things . . .'

Swann could see Sullivan reading him, looking for cues.

'What's that got to do with me?'

'You've offended him, for a start. And I'm in a position to help —'

'I don't know anything about Hogan's business.'

'Perhaps not. Let me fill you in.'

Sullivan steepled his fingers beneath his nose, an odd gesture that implied thoughtfulness, an attitude of prayer. But his eyes were all rat cunning, and resentment.

'It's not only Hogan that I'm concerned about. His mining outfit's called Rosa Gold. Leo Marrone and Tommaso Adamo are involved, Bernie Isaacs too, a couple of others.'

'You're on the outside. They reckon you're gone at the next election, not worth including. You want in.'

Sullivan dropped his hands, examined his palms, scuffed a thumb over fingernails. Looked Swann in the eye.

'The fire yesterday, all Tommaso's property. I've heard that there were witnesses. One in particular, who's come forward. Some lezzo, a self-proclaimed anarchist. Civic-minded enough to call the Premier's office. Said she wouldn't go to the police. Wouldn't leave her name, but claimed she had photographs. I want you to get me those photographs, or something else I can use. I've also heard that Bernie Isaacs is up to his old tricks, fixing races. Take a look at him too. Hard evidence only.'

'Hogan?'

'Leave Hogan to me. But make no mistake. You don't get me

something good on Isaacs or Adamo, and you're back here. You're the only man I can use who won't tip off Hogan. I don't want Adamo to know either. I want it to be a surprise.'

Sullivan stood back and waved Swann to the open door. 'You go first. I'll follow in a few minutes. It's all arranged. You're on bail, judge's orders. Walk out and don't look back. And not a fucking word, to anyone. Your bail can be revoked, just like that.' He snapped his fingers.

Swann climbed to his feet, felt the nausea rise into his throat. He stepped towards the open door, felt his feet land, cushioned, like walking in a dream. Took another step, and then another.

The desk sergeant wouldn't make eye contact with him, busying himself with paperwork. Swann walked out of the main doors of the station, the curved walls of Central looming behind him like a satellite dish tuned to the suburbs. The light and heat nearly brought him to his knees. He gripped the railings, avoiding the eyes of the coppers entering the station, the blood across his shirt, drying on his face. There were bore-water taps on the foreshore at Langley Park. He needed to get cleaned up before he called Marion.

'Swann!'

He glanced up and saw Jennifer Henderson, sunglasses on, looking cool despite the heat. She stood beside her Karmann Ghia, no expression on her face as Swann lurched towards her.

21

Peter Henning drew a cloth across the sweating flank of the horse and spread the fine auburn hair between finger and thumb, inserting the needle into the vein. The mare smelt odd, was sweating something noxious. Isaacs stood behind him, too close as usual, observing the process, silent and smug. Another mid-week meeting, another race with minimal prize money, but Dandy Mandy had come in by three lengths in a 1200 sprint, at twenty to one, backed in from sixty to one.

Between races, Henning had watched as two young men and a young woman, who Henning knew was Isaacs' daughter, moved from bookie to bookie laying bets of five hundred dollars on the nose. Unlike the other stewards and sundry officials, Henning hadn't watched the race from the trackside box. Instead, he had stayed in the concourse and watched the faces of the bookies when Dandy Mandy came in. They didn't look happy. Had sworn and muttered and made eyes to one another, and especially at Ron Bevans, the bookie most closely associated with Isaacs. Bevans merely shook his head, pretending to be as badly done as the rest of them, but Henning had been watching. No bets on Dandy

Mandy had been placed with Bevans.

Since yesterday's incident with Rum Punch, Henning had been gathering intelligence on Isaacs. From one of the stewards, Henning had heard that the payout insurance on Rum Punch was likely to be in the order of fifty thousand dollars. Now he knew why Isaacs had knobbled his own gelding. He'd wanted the insurance, although Henning didn't know why. Rum Punch was down to race in the big winter carnivals on the wet tracks that his father, Sir Keith, was renowned for dominating.

It didn't make sense. Henning had demanded that the stewards question Isaac's helpers, who must have seen what Isaacs had done with the length of four-by-two. But they had claimed ignorance. Allegedly, Rum Punch had slipped while being loaded onto the float. And Isaacs had laughed in their faces. Worse still, the swabs that Henning had taken from Rum Punch had come back from the lab negative.

Which was impossible. The horse had clearly been doped.

Now here was Isaacs again, breathing down his neck. Beer breath and stale sweat, watching as Henning corked the syringe and placed it carefully into a plastic specimen bag, stowed it away in his Gladstone.

Henning wasn't going to engage with Isaacs, not if he could help it. He had ignored the sarcastic comments and intimidation while Isaacs followed him around. A horse's trainer had the right to be present during the after-race examination, so Henning couldn't ask Isaacs to leave. But he would have the last laugh. Henning was certain that Dandy Mandy had also been doped. All the signs were there. Distress. Foaming spittle. That peculiar chemical smell.

Henning had asked permission from no less an authority than Sir Irvine Lee-Hastings, the head of the Western Australian racing federation, to deliver the swabs in person to the laboratory and then to personally oversee the testing process.

Henning glanced at Isaacs and was pleased to see that his silence was having the desired effect. Isaacs was fuming. Hands on hips. Gut drawn in. Drawing himself up to his full height. Black eyes enraged.

Henning smiled politely. 'Take her away. I'm done with her.'

Isaacs waved at one of his minions. Watched Henning fix the steel clasp of his Gladstone bag, clicking shut. Take up the bag and his old trilby and head for the door.

Outside it was clear and warm. Most of the crowds were still on the terraces. The final race was under way. Shouts and cheers came from the nearest stand, the drone of the caller rising in pitch and volume. The macadam of the car park was still wet from the earlier rain, and Henning could smell the algae from the nearby river. The laboratory was in the city, and if he hurried he would make it before closing. He looked at his watch to confirm that he had time, removed his sunglasses from his jacket pocket and stopped in his tracks.

The reserved car bay where he parked his Rover was empty. Dry car shape where it had rained, only half an hour ago. He turned as he heard the footsteps and took the blow of the tyre iron on his face, dropped like a stone. Bitumen gravel, inches from his eyes. Busy ants. One of his teeth, a spray of blood. Darkness.

22

'You've done this before.'

Jennifer Henderson's mouth was by Swann's ear, so close he could smell the gin on her breath, juniper hot. 'I was a nurse in Vietnam, based in Vung Tau. It's where I met Max.' Her voice airy, childlike. Spaced out.

'One of your patients?'

'Max? More than once. I was a shy little thing, but he was injured often. Not always in the line of duty. He was a wild one, after a few drinks.'

Having washed the abrasions made by the soles of Hogan's boots, she applied iodine salve and butterflied plasters to the deeper gashes around Swann's nose and forehead. They were in one of the Hendersons' investment properties, a ground-floor flat on Broome Street, Cottesloe, all linoleum floors and Formica bench tops, the standard Westinghouse oven. Cheap bamboo blinds and beige-painted walls. Idiot box in a steel frame bolted into the wall. The Hendersons owned the block of eight.

Swann sat quietly on the stool. He was still dizzy. His jarred neck sent flares into his head. He heard Jennifer open the lid of the washing machine. She'd taken off his shirt and run it through a short cycle. Now she hung it in the sunshine and he heard the Hill's hoist creak as the shirt caught the wind. In direct sun it would soon dry. The bloodstains wouldn't be totally removed, she told him, but she could lend him one of Max's shirts.

Swann was startled by the touch of her hand on his bare shoulder. She pushed a glass of whisky into his fingers, held one of her own. Obviously the gin was finished. She sat on the stool opposite him and smiled wistfully.

When Swann was tailing the Commodore tailing her, Jennifer had seen the flashing lights and then the unmarked sedans pull him over. She'd circled back and watched his arrest and followed them into town. She hadn't asked him why he'd been bashed, but apologised for not bailing him out, saying she was unsure because Swann said they shouldn't be seen together.

At first, Swann appreciated her distance, working the angles in his head. He was going to have to keep Sullivan buttered up if he wanted to stay out of prison. Sullivan didn't know about Jennifer and her connection to Rosa Gold – if he had, he would have used it as further leverage. Sullivan wanted dirt on the Rosa Gold directors and didn't care how he got it. Hiring Swann was both a clear indication of the man's waning influence and a cynical move. He could burn Swann after he was no longer useful, and nobody would care.

Swann finished his whisky and rolled his neck, felt a wave of nausea break over him. He put his hand over his glass as Jennifer splashed another finger into her tumbler. That pale light in her eyes, coming from a great distance, a place of comfort that no longer existed.

Swann sat forward. 'The man who did this to me was settling an old score. It has nothing to do with Rosa Gold. But you were being followed. He looked like a professional.'

Whatever tender fantasy she'd been enjoying patching him up, reminding her of tending to Max, perhaps – it was gone. She bit her lip to stop it trembling. 'The car you say was following me. Did you get a look at the driver?'

'He's not a local. But I lost him.'

'And he must have lost me, which I'm grateful for. I couldn't have come here otherwise. I feel safe, for the first time since . . .'

She didn't finish the sentence. Her eyes turned inwards, the hard focus of whatever bad memory blocking everything out.

'That look in your eye,' he asked her. 'It happens often.'

He imagined she would describe the trauma of finding her husband dead in the backyard. Or the sight of her home, trashed and violated. Or the memory of being a nurse in a war zone.

She would finally say it and they would talk it out. He would listen. He would tell her that she needed to leave, forget Rosa Gold – the money, the principle of the thing – it wasn't worth dying over.

'You really want to know? It's the first time I've felt safe since . . . I met you.'

She laughed, watched his reaction, amused and self-conscious, a glint of mischief, the perfect triangles of her incisors when she smiled, that gap between her front teeth.

'I don't follow.'

'I'm just saying I trust you, Frank Swann. It's a compliment.'

'Now that I'm laid low.'

'Perhaps. Or now that I've made the first move . . .'

'The first move?'

'. . . away from my home.'

'Start of a new life.'

'You have a bad concussion – I can see it in your eyes. A bath, then sleep.'

She wasn't in her right mind. She was drunk. He'd talk to her when she was sober. Tell her what she needed to hear.

Swann got to his feet, knees wobbling, head spinning. He felt like throwing up. Immediately she was over, a hand supporting his bicep. 'Or perhaps you'd like me to call your wife. Have her pick you up.'

It was a statement, no genuineness in it, knowing that he'd refuse.

There was nothing going on, but it didn't feel like that.

Just like last time.

'Thanks for patching me up. But I need to visit a friend of mine. About another matter.'

She let him go, as if stung.

Swann's injuries weren't out of place amongst the battered and broken in the public wards of Royal Perth Hospital, where he'd finally tracked down Percy Dickson, admitted under an alias. Dickson had been gone over with a ballpein hammer, just like Dennis Gould. The same shattered kneecap and ankle, on the same leg. The other unharmed, for later if need be.

Swann stood at the foot of Dickson's bed. Percy didn't try to speak. He made no mention of Swann's own black eyes and broken nose, the visible bootprint on his forehead, lacquered with iodine salve. Percy was an old soldier and storing it up. He was in bad pain. His entire leg was in a cast. His eyes were small and sunk into his head.

The shock of what had happened to Dickson could kill, let alone the fear that worse was to come, the anger at knowing his attackers would get away with it. Through gritted teeth, Percy described the two men in balaclavas who surprised him at his front door, coerced him with a pistol to his temple, tied him down and worked him over. He'd given them nothing more than they already knew, and so they'd shattered his kneecap, then his ankle. They were already aware that the stolen jewels were back in the hands of their owners. One of the jewellers, out of ignorance and against Dickson's explicit instructions, had mentioned it to members of the Robbers Squad.

Percy claimed that he'd told the thugs nothing, but Swann knew this wasn't true. Otherwise, how had Hogan made the connection with him so quickly? Or learned that it was Swann who'd brought the bikies into it? These were conclusions that Swann kept to himself. There was no point making Percy look at what he'd done, which was to put Swann right in it.

There could be no walking away now. Hogan's intention was to have Swann killed in the lockup, of that he could be sure. If Swann didn't stay one step ahead of him, keep Sullivan happy, that was where he was headed. By now Hogan would know that Swann was free, and that Sullivan had ordered his release. He would put two and two in the hat. Sullivan could delay Hogan's promotion, but only so long as he remained Minister. There was talk of an election within the year, and a landslide win to the younger Labor team. In the meantime, Hogan wouldn't defy Sullivan and kill Swann in the open, although the chances were good that he'd have a warrant out for Swann's arrest, hedging his bets. But Hogan could easily have Swann killed by an Adamo stooge, then control the flawed investigation into his murder. Neither Adamo nor Marrone would hesitate if they knew Swann was snooping around Rosa Gold.

Hogan would be expecting Swann to visit Percy. He couldn't linger. He nodded goodbye but the old soldier wasn't finished yet.

'While yer here,' Percy spat, 'you should speak to my neighbour. The same thing. But Bernie Isaacs, Hogan's old chum. Hogan's Heroes, they could call this fucken ward. Speak to him. I told him about you. Nothin' to do with the jewels, but might be some work in it.'

Swann peeled back the curtains along their silent tracks, and saw that a man the same age as Percy Dickson was in the next bed, no more than a few feet away, listening. His grey hair was neatly combed in a side part, but he had the same haunted look. His jaw was broken, and fixed with steel plates. One of his forearms was in a cast. Defensive injury.

Swann glanced at the chart hung on the rail, just as the man began to speak, stiffly, through plated teeth.

'My name is Peter Henning. I'm the Chief Veterinarian at Ascot, Belmont and Gloucester Park. I want you to help me. I was bashed, in the Ascot car park. I've told the police, and there will be a steward's inquiry, of course, but . . . you see . . .'

Swann listened while the man laid it out, precisely, in great detail. So Bernie Isaacs was working the insurance companies, just like Tommaso Adamo. Just like Hogan, with his facilitating the jewel theft, his ongoing links to the drug trade, managed by Adamo and Marrone. Isaacs, Marrone, Adamo and Hogan – all of them directors of Rosa Gold, all of them prepared to burn everything they owned, take down anyone who threatened them. Whatever was going on with Rosa Gold, it was important enough to have Sullivan sniffing at the closed door, trying to get in. It wasn't like the directors of Rosa Gold to work in the open, to take these kinds of risks. Disorganised crime, nobody wanted it, unless the money was worth it.

23

The scrub on the edge of Mount Eliza smelt of aniseed and baked dirt, the smog rising off the freeway. Swann sat on a park bench and waited for Donovan Andrews. The sun had gone behind the cenotaph and the Esplanade was cast in shadow. At the foot of the Barrack Street Jetty a crowd had gathered, dressed in colonial-era clothes. The men wore britches and the women bonnets. Somewhere amongst them was the Prince of Wales – the future King of Australia – invited to participate in the re-enactment of the first landing at Mounts Bay. Swann had seen photos of him in the morning paper, getting kissed by a beautiful model, down at the beach. Unsurprisingly, Prince Charles didn't look like he minded.

Swann smoked a cigarette while he waited, could hardly taste it, staring at a skiff making its way through the chop towards the break-wall, canvas sail, passengers in their old-fashioned clothes. A cheer went up from the crowd on the foreshore, and then something else, booing, jeering from a megaphone. From the trees by the Supreme Court came a group of Nyungar, a couple of dozen, moving quickly across the open ground. Police met them from the riverbank and soon they were outnumbered, surrounded. One carried a flag, another a scroll. They tried to get to the Prince but were kept back, as the booing and shouting continued. The skiff reached the shore and two men dressed like soldiers carried an older man in a triangle hat through the shallows to the beach. The Union Jack fluttered at the back of the skiff, the Aboriginal flag flew in the midst of the mob, planted in the grassy bank.

The commemoration party were forced to retreat within the police cordon to where Mounts Bay had once lapped at the city, before it was filled with dirt, reclaimed for the freeway. When Swann was a child, Langley Park was an occasional airstrip and the foreshore was lined with jetties and shanty-town allotments, the river still a major source of transport down to the Fremantle port. The East Perth power station had burned a brown coal smear, heavy industries stinking up the Claisebrook Creek, sewerage outlets at Burswood turning the river green with algae. The top end of Hay and Murray streets were filled with run-down tenements, whole families to a single room, East Perth the same.

Swann turned at the sound of Andrews' Gold Flash growling over the lawn towards the bench, where he cut the engine and kicked down the stand, hoisting off his full-visor helmet. Oblivious to the palaver on the foreshore, he slapped Swann on the shoulder, slumped onto the bench and showed his palm, smirking.

'My info done you good, detective.'

Swann placed the bills into Donovan's fingers, immediately secreted in his leathers.

'Goes without saying, Don.'

'Jesus, what happened to your face?'

'What I wanted to speak to you about.'

'Ah, shit. My info didn't do you so good?'

'Nothing to do with that, Don. Something else.'

Andrews looked around, nervous. 'You know Marrone knocked

one of Hogan's fizzes here a couple months ago? Bloke Hogan was feeding stuff to from the drugs locker. Found burned in his car over there, melted like a black crayon.'

'Don't worry, there's nothing to link me, or you.'

There was a tang of sweat on Andrews, unwashed leathers and sockless feet in his boots. Donovan shook his head and wiped his mouth with the back of his hand, burped a little. 'There's a weird vibe about, is all. That fucken fire, took out half of Little Italy. Somethin's goin on. Biggest thing in years, nobody's even talkin' about it. Cops *or* robbers. Happened two days ago, now it's like they already forgot.'

'That's what I wanted to talk about, Don. You hear anything about that fire, I want to know. I also want you to keep your radar on Hogan, and Tommaso Adamo. Leo Marrone. Bevans and Isaacs. Farquarson.'

'Jesus, detective, I'm happy for the reward, but you were in the force . . . last time, you had the uniform behind you.'

'You offering me advice now, Don?'

There was a hardness in Swann's voice that he hadn't intended, the copper trait of putting blokes like Donovan in their place.

Andrews shrugged, let it go. 'For the same reason you used to give me advice, detective. You can pretend we're still fizz and copper, and that's all . . .'

Andrews' concern came from a good place, his voice like a child's.

'I'm just keeping an eye on something,' Swann answered. 'Surveillance. My bread and butter now.'

'I'm just sayin . . .'

'It was different back then, Don. Forget it.'

Andrews nodded, but he didn't look convinced. Swann stared down over the city, where the evening shadows cast by the buildings loomed like grasping arms. The black hole in Little Italy was still smouldering, a city block loaded with burnt timber and drifts of grey ash and cinder, wafting about on the sea breeze. Traffic up the Terrace and off the freeway over the Narrows Bridge, commuters returning to the suburbs, and flocks of seagulls headed the other way, back from the coast and the council tips, thousands gathering on the broad field of grass, settling in for the night.

Exactly what he should be doing.

Swann would like to take his own advice, and forget it. Forget all about it. Seemed to him, watching the colonial skiff setting off from the seawall beneath the bluff, that Donovan Andrews was right, and that the city was good at forgetting.

Gould's apartment smelt no better than on Swann's last visit. Mildew, ash and dirty washing. Gould and Reggie sat on the couch across from Swann, both nursing a neat Jameson, pointedly ignoring the damage to his face. Swann had explained the reason for his beating without telling them about Dickson's crippling – he didn't want to trigger Gould's anxiety.

Swann had just called Marion to tell her he wouldn't be home. He also told her to expect a visit from the coppers, some tossing of their things. He made no mention of his injuries, or when he would return. The last thing he wanted was for Hogan to take him at home, put his family at risk. If Swann's car wasn't parked in the street, Hogan was likely to seek him elsewhere. In the meantime, Swann needed time to work out a plan, find a way into Rosa Gold.

Gould had been working the phone, digging up information on Gary Quinlivan, the unknown quantity on the board. Swann listened to Gould speak, but it wasn't easy to concentrate, or keep his eyes open.

'Gary Quinlivan,' continued Gould, 'was pursued for debts over a real estate development in Yanchep, in 1977. Investments totalling some million and a half dollars. Some of the investors claimed to be family friends. Declared a bankrupt. Settled out of court, in the end.'

Reggie coughed, sat forward. His blue eyes shone even in the diminished light. 'Shouldn't really be a director of Rosa Gold if he's a recent bankrupt.'

'Indeed,' said Gould bitterly. 'But who's watching, right?'

Reggie patted him on the forearm, eyeing his nephew's withered leg. The two of them had met a couple of times, as Swann had hoped.

'The question then becomes,' Reggie said, 'what specific talent does Quinlivan bring to the table? Why is he useful?'

Dennis Gould sipped his whiskey. 'Perhaps his expertise is purely financial?'

'But this is different from a pump and dump, isn't it?' Swann said. 'If what we're hearing is correct, then all of the other directors are scrambling to raise serious money. We know how the others make their cash, but what about Quinlivan? If he's an equal partner, what's he doing to raise the same kind of stake?'

'Family money?' Gould ventured.

Reggie shook his head. 'I know old Judge Quinlivan. He's well-to-do, but not rich, and something of a philanthropist. Besides, I heard that his son is still in disgrace after fleecing family friends. Once bitten, and all that . . . I doubt the Judge would be giving his son a red cent.'

'Is the Judge someone we could go to?' Swann asked. 'If he's as straight as you say, then —'

Reggie shook his head. 'Perhaps, when the time is right. But thus far it's all legit, despite the company young Quinlivan is keeping. If what I'm hearing is correct, then Rosa Gold is looking to shape itself into a genuine mining enterprise.'

'But the fires?' Gould asked. 'The bashings. The jewel thefts . . .'

'The birthing pains of frontier capitalism, Dennis. Still, there's something odd going on.'

After Dennis Gould had phoned his contacts in the broking houses, and heard that there was nothing current on the wire about Rosa Gold, not even rumours, Reggie had called one of his old friends, now the CEO of one of the largest mining companies in the world – Plantagenet Lewis Australia. PLA had been in the gold business since the beginning, the bastard child of young English aristocrats who'd come out in the 1890s to seek their fortune. PLA still ran one of the largest gold concerns in the world, the Super Pit in Kalgoorlie. They owned mines in South Africa, in the United States and Canada, in the Philippines, in Papua New Guinea and Irian Jaya.

The conversation between Reggie and the CEO, Barry Nichols, had been polite and familiar, until Reggie mentioned Rosa Gold. Nichols had gone silent. Then he became suspicious, and angry. Who was Reggie working for? What had he heard about PLA and Rosa Gold? The call had finished with Nichols advising Reggie to keep out of it, or their friendship would suffer.

Swann laid the map of the Rosa Gold stake on the coffee table. The total area was some forty square kilometres, about eighty kilometres west of Big Bell, near Cue, six hundred kilometres north-east of Perth in the heart of the granite mulga country. Reggie wrote down the coordinates of the stake and the claim numbers of the adjoining stakes. Further details would be kept at the Ministry of Mines. It would be worth discovering, given the tone of Barry Nichols' reaction, whether or not some of the adjacent claims had changed hands recently – whether Rosa Gold was buying up the nearby land or whether other, larger predators were on the ground.

Swann had one last question for Dennis Gould. 'You've been involved in raising venture capital for new mining operations, and for turning them into publically listed companies. Assuming that Rosa Gold wants to keep the company in private hands, and bring the mine into operation with their own funds, how much are we talking about?'

Gould's glass was empty but he didn't reach for the bottle. 'That would not only be unusual, but almost impossible, depending on the size of the deposit. If it's a small deposit, then a few million. The drilling alone costs a fortune, then there's the equipment when the mine goes into operation. Transport. Permits. Gifts to public servants, ministers. Staff costs. It's why most companies go public, to try and secure sufficient funds. But if the deposit was large, in terms of estimated ounces in the ground, and this would depend upon the assay results coming in, to get a big mine up and running would cost more money than Rosa Gold could afford, rich as they are. That's another reason most companies go public, to not only raise sufficient funds but to share around the risk, should the mine not pan out as indicated.'

Swann lit a cigarette and took it in. 'So if Rosa Gold hasn't gone public at this point, then they must be absolutely certain that the claim is a bonanza. Which means I need to get my hands on the assay results, to confirm.'

'Good luck,' Gould replied. 'The assay lab is part of the Perth Mint, and equally secure. The big companies use armed security to transport their cores to the lab. And once there, the security is the same. Armed guards. Cameras, you name it. The mining industry runs on discretion, and confidence in discretion.'

'And rumours, and gambling,' Reggie added.

'Yes, those too. Although sensible money likes to keep them to a minimum. And the Rosa Gold directors seem to be doing a capable job of keeping things quiet. But as Max Henderson's wife, shouldn't Jennifer have copies of the assay results?'

Swann shook his head. 'She only knows that her husband thought it was a three million–ounce mine. Rosa Gold was Max Henderson's baby. I get the feeling she was against the whole thing – kept her distance.'

'Good instincts, as it turns out.'

Dennis Gould stared down at his ruined leg, evidence of the truth of his last statement. Reggie patted his forearm again and refilled his glass, didn't offer the bottle to Swann.

Swann wasn't drinking because he still felt dizzy, had a fierce headache. His left eye had swollen shut, and the bridge of his broken nose ached. Several of his ribs were bruised, possibly fractured. He stood up, got the staggers, braced himself on the back of his chair until the dizziness passed. Reggie noticed, but said nothing, passed Swann the folded map and his notebook, and accompanied him to the door. 'My place. My spare bed. Your car to get us there.'

Swann waited while Reggie said his goodbyes to Gould. In the morning, Swann would call Marion from Reggie's place. And then he would call Jennifer Henderson. He needed to find Garth Oats.

24

There was no use trying to sleep any longer. Swann sat up on the couch and put his head in his hands. The old fears had reawoken during the night; the fizz of nerves in his chest, the racing of his mind; the voice in his ear telling him what he already knew. Headed down the path that Gould had gone, of doubt and self-pity. Swann knew where it led. Didn't want to go there again.

The most effective thing was to focus on your enemy.

But how to bring Hogan, Adamo, and the others down?

Swann pulled on his trousers and T-shirt, rolled his shoulders. The first slivers of light pierced the venetian blinds. Reggie's dog, Mutt, followed him into the kitchen where Swann drank water from the tap. Mutt wasn't a mutt but a pedigree British bulldog, who'd won shows before Reggie had rescued her from his dead sister. Mutt's body trembled with age and anticipation. He filled Mutt's steel bowl with water and stood while she drank, the sounds of her tongue sloshing through the largely empty house. Clearly, Reggie had already started the process of divesting himself of property. His once crammed apartment now felt like a hotel room, functional and bare. There were noticeable blank spaces on the walls where paintings had hung. Afghan carpets were missing. Mutt knew something was going on, and trailed Swann back into the living room while he slipped on his socks and shoes.

The phone rang, and it was Marion. Right away he could tell. 'That woman's been calling again,' she said, her voice pinched.

'*Enough*,' Swann said.

So far Hogan had no reason to connect him to Jennifer Henderson, but there was every chance that Swann's phone was now bugged.

But Marion continued to talk over him, her voice rising in pitch, and he realised it was too late. If Hogan had been listening, he would already know. 'Three times already today. The first two, I told her you weren't here, to not talk about her business, to give me her number and I'd call her back, but she just hung up. It was dawn, and she was drunk. Said she wanted to know whether you were okay, the concussion, the beating. It was news to me, I said. She told me that she was worried about you. I told her I didn't want to hear it over the phone. She told me she'd meet me. I told her I didn't want to meet her. That I'd pass on her message. So here I am, at the phone box on the corner of Market Street, in my thongs and happi coat, haven't even brushed my hair . . .'

The image deliberate, to remind him.

'It's not her fault. She doesn't know the rules.'

But by calling, Jennifer had put Marion in danger. Marion had her own contacts in the force, and she would use them if anything happened to Swann. She would put herself in the same position Swann was in now.

'There's a question I wanted to ask you. You mentioned your clients in the burned-down tenements. Can you contact them? It needs to be done discreetly.'

'They'll be living rough, or in nearby boarding houses. I can track them down. Anyone in particular?'

'I've heard about a young woman, a housing-reform activist, an anarchist.'

'Mattie – she's an everything activist. Burn the bra, ban the bomb, give it all back. This is sounding serious.'

'She claims to have seen something on the night of the fire, to have photographs. You need to tell her to shut up. And you need to hide her somewhere. Take her to Brett's, or better still, tell her to piss off over east.'

'I know where to find her, don't worry. She needs her methadone. I'll be careful.'

'I'm going away for a day or two. I'll leave messages with Reggie.'

Marion didn't ask the question he could feel down the line. *With her?*

'You'd better, Frank. I love you. And school the woman.'

That tone in her voice, concern, but also knowing. Something she'd picked up from Jennifer Henderson, or from him? The fear that the payback from bent cops wasn't the only thing happening again.

'I love *you*,' he said, and meant it more than ever.

Hung up, pulled out his notebook. Whatever Max Henderson had discovered out at the Rosa Gold stake had made it necessary to kill himself. Swann had to get out into the desert and take a look for himself.

He dialled Jennifer at the flat but there was no answer. Mutt whined and nudged his leg. Swann ran his fingers through her coarse fur, scratched behind her ears. She scuttled sideways like a crab, towards the door.

'All right. Let's go.' He took the lead off the hatstand by the window. Reggie wasn't up to walking, and the poor thing looked like she needed a break from the apartment.

The sun hadn't risen over the blue scarp to the east. The surface of the Swan River was still as jelly. Fishermen were hand lining for mulloway down the end of the jetty, live baits out in the deepest waters. Swann and Mutt walked along the edge of the tideline where the sand was packed hard. Three pelicans sat on the prow of a yacht moored in the bay. The muddy footprints of water rats on the white walls of the mansions of the rich, feeding on the fruit trees that grew over. Jellyfish swooning in the shallows. The clear imprint of a large flathead in the sand below the tideline. The silver flanks of mullet breaking the surface at the edge of the weed beds.

Mutt sniffed the old rope and polystyrene chunks and blow-fish carcasses that lined the sand. The folds in her face were a mess of drool and samphire shreds, which she'd licked for the salt. She barked at the pelicans on the yacht, the sound ringing clear over the morning, making the three birds lift with loud beating wings as they flew to the remnant bush of Point Resolution.

25

The first tank of petrol lasted four hundred kilometres through the wheat belt to the desert at Paynes Find. The crop between was high and ready for harvest, the roads empty but for the tractors moving out from the small town silos into the endless fields of wheat.

Jennifer Henderson came awake when they reached the truck stop. Until then she'd slept against the passenger door with a hat low over her eyes, her long legs stretched beneath the dash, hands drawn into the sleeves of a cotton check.

He'd picked her up from the Cottesloe flat, where she was already packed and dressed, freshly showered but weary, her face drawn, bruised rings beneath her eyes. Two swags and a milk crate of pots and plates, enamel mugs and teabags and instant coffee in pastel green Tupperware. Twenty-litre bottle of water. Max's kit, from his regular trips to the desert, with her own touches: milk and cigarettes in a small cardboard box, fresh bottles of Seagram's and Jameson, disprin in a glass jar – everything her home contained in the way of sustenance and nutrition.

The easterly off the desert was hard and dry. Jennifer sipped water but she didn't want to speak, kept closing her eyes as she sobered up.

They drove with the windows down as the EK rose and fell between the granite mesas and saltbush plains and the dry washes where winter floods engulfed the road. The cyclone had brought early rain to the desert, and some of the soaks were damp, but the sun-baked road was all red dust and kangaroo roadkill, picked over by cautious crows, defined on either side by the shredded tyres of road trains and the smashed amber glass of beer bottles tossed from passing cars.

Swann drove and smoked, his forearms reddening in the sun, eyes on the long flat road that stretched into a wash of glimmering mirage.

Jennifer had called Gary Quinlivan last night, as instructed. She told Quinlivan that she couldn't sell her share because the conveyance of Max's will wasn't complete. She told him that she would sell once probate was settled – that she had no interest in mining, something that Quinlivan was clearly pleased to hear. Before hanging up, Jennifer had asked, as a courtesy, that Gary Quinlivan invite her to the next Rosa Gold board meeting, where she would tell the other board members exactly what she'd told him. Quinlivan replied that Jennifer should consider herself invited to the first AGM, on the weekend, at the offices of Chisholm Gold, joking that before long they would have their own office tower.

Swann had made his own quick call, to the Minister of Police's office. Unfortunately, Sullivan wasn't out playing golf, or down the racetrack. Once his secretary had put Swann through, Sullivan waded right in. The business card that Swann had taken the number from – it wasn't a get-out-of-jail-free card. It wasn't a licence to piss around and waste time. It wouldn't save him if he was arrested again. Sullivan wanted dirt on the Rosa Gold directors, *yesterday*.

Swann replied that he had a lead on some racetrack fixing done by Isaacs and Bevans, and that he was looking for the activist witness with the big mouth. He'd be in touch. Sullivan laughed. He'd better be. He'd better have evidence in forty-eight hours or he was back in prison, for life.

Meaning, death.

Swann had no intention of giving Sullivan the activist, should he ever find her. He didn't want her blood on his hands, although he had to give the Minister of Police something.

Perhaps he would find it on Tommaso Adamo's vast cattle station to the west of Cue, near the Rosa Gold stake. He'd bought the property after Max Henderson had gifted Rosa Gold the IPO to the site, the mining rights that made further exploration possible. The station wasn't far from the gold mines of Big Bell, the site of an early-20th-century gold rush that had attracted tens of thousands of men and prostitutes to the area. There was no other mine operating on Adamo's station, as far as Swann could make out, even though it was well known that Adamo was cleaning dirty money by claiming gold finds on his land. Swann wondered what else might be on Adamo's property that might have led to Max Henderson's death. Adamo and Marrone were wholesalers of marijuana and heroin, and there was plenty of room on a place that size to run plantations and set up an airstrip.

The road stretched north into the red desert scrub. The gnarled corkwood and sheoak and kurrajong trees that spread evenly over the plain were ancient and black and stunted, their leaves thin and dun coloured, their fruits small and hard and bitter. In a few months the regular winter rains would come and the land would blossom with a carpet of pink and white everlastings, purple flannel bush, grevillea and mulla-mulla, but that seemed a long way off.

The sun was headed towards the horizon and the land became infused with a calm light. A wedge-tailed eagle hovered in the updraft off a red bluff, looking for rabbit. Shadowy granite monoliths started to mark the horizon. Crows cawed in the branches of the quandong and mulga scrub. Swann got the Holden up to 140 and they settled in for the last stretch before their destination. They hadn't seen a single other car for close to two hours. The wind blew so strongly through the open windows that there was little point talking, and they savoured the cooling air on their arms and faces.

As the road rose over a long scarp to the broad horizon, tilting towards the coming darkness, Swann started to think about what the night would bring. There was little chance that they would make the Rosa Gold camp by nightfall. Swann had camped in the desert often when he'd been stationed in Kalgoorlie, and the first night was always the hardest – the eerie stillness after the rattling day on the road. Voices carried in the stillness and were muffled by the endlessness of the land. The feeling of being watched as you clung to the campfire when the darkness fell, the only point of light for hundreds of miles. The cold coming so quick that you scrambled to get dressed. Talking in whispers for no reason but the feeling that there was listening.

And this time he would be alone with Jennifer Henderson, the awkwardness already there between them.

Up ahead the lights of Cue came into focus, bright on the horizon. But the lights were deceptive. Cue was quiet and empty when they arrived. The servo on the edge of town was open, and so was the gold-rush pub on the main street. A few men in singlets stood outside drinking and smoking, workers from the nearby Day Dawn mine.

Swann was suddenly tired. His eyes were sore from the brightness of the day, the lack of sleep. The skin on his face hummed with windburn. His throat hurt from too much smoking. His broken nose ached. They filled up with petrol and headed for the pub.

26

Gary Quinlivan saw that the seatbelt light was out. He reclined his seat to the furthest extent, and lit a cigarette. The plane had levelled above the clouds. It was the rainy season in the Top End, and the clouds were an electric grey, massed like glaciers, the sound of thunder and bursts of sheet lightning making the Boeing rise and fall. The Thursday Qantas flight from Singapore to Darwin had been booked out, but he'd been able to secure a seat on stand-by. His trip had gone better than expected, and his expected stay of two nights in KL had been abbreviated to a single overnight and morning. The majority of passengers were smoking; Asian businessmen and the odd returning tourist. Nervous, perhaps. Although not as nervous as Gary should be.

It was only a short flight and so he had better get cracking. He stood, and pretend yawned, took a look at those around him. Nobody taking an interest. He'd gotten the hard part out of the way, made it across the Malaysian border past Singaporean customs, such as it was. He was dressed in a straw-coloured linen suit, with white tooled leather shoes. A bit showy, perhaps, but he was feeling optimistic. A pity the girl couldn't be with him. She'd have loved KL.

He made his way down the seesawing aisle to the toilets, bolted the door shut. To begin, he stood and looked at himself in the mirror, passed a hand through his hair, wiped the oil off his nose with a tissue. He knelt down and ran his finger along the seam beneath the steel washbasin, found the screws. From his pocket he took out a Phillips head screwdriver and worked out the four screws that fixed the plate over the plumbing. The sound of the engine grew louder as he removed the plate. He stood and unbuttoned his jacket, rolled his shirt up his waist. He found the edge of the white electrician's tape and began to peel, holding the edge and turning on his heels in the confined space, watching himself in the mirror, the image of a dervish, tanned and entranced. He spun away the six metres of tape and pulled off the five packets stuck to his waist. The skin at his belly was red with sweat and chafing.

There was a knock at the door, but he ignored it. There were no cameras in the toilets. He knelt and placed the packets in amongst the faucet piping, tight so that they wouldn't slip with the vibration. He replaced the plate and fixed the screws. He made a little spool of the tape with the fingers of his left hand and wound the tape until it was a solid lump, then pressed it smaller with his hands and put it inside his jacket pocket.

By the time he returned to his seat the service trolley had gone past it. That was too bad. He could do with a drink. There was time for one more cigarette before the seatbelt light came on and they began the descent through tumbling clouds. He sat and watched out the window, the possibility of a lightning strike. The last layers of cloud parted and there was the city below, bathed in grey rain.

He removed the wedge of tape from his jacket and stuffed it deep inside the seat lining. He was clean now. Customs couldn't touch him.

It wasn't more than a twenty-minute taxi ride into downtown Darwin. The taxi driver was a heavily tattooed Thursday Islander. He wanted to talk, and so Gary Quinlivan talked, just enough to not annoy the man. The TI had worked in Western Australia laying track for the iron-ore mines. He had beer on his breath, and smelt of bacon grease, smoked bidis. Gary told him nothing about himself, and let him talk about the rainy season, the coming dry.

He had the man drop him in the central mall, where he entered the post office and picked up his package, mailed to himself c/o Poste Restante. He sat at a quiet booth inside the PO and broke open the package. He binned the wrapping and pocketed the driver's licence and open Qantas ticket.

Outside, lugging his shoulder bag, he took another taxi to the airport, careful to not be seen by his original driver. This driver did not want to talk. He dropped Gary outside the terminal in good time. Inside, he used his open ticket to book a seat on the next Darwin–Perth flight. The ticket did not contain the number of the plane but Quinlivan had done his research. He knew that the same plane he'd arrived on, once cleared in Darwin, was cleaned and refuelled then sent on the domestic route to Perth. A different pilot and cabin crew. Potentially some of the same passengers, but they weren't to know that he was now travelling under a new name.

Gary took his seat at the rear of the plane, as he'd requested. *The safest*, he'd joked with the check-in girl. He'd freshened up in the toilets, and smelt of good cologne. This was a substantially longer flight, and he hoped he could sleep. After lunch, perhaps. At some point he would enter the same toilet and remove his packets. Two kilos of pure. Enough to make a serious dent in Adamo's market, if he played it right.

With his regular earnings from the casinos, brothels, plantations of pot coming into harvest, and his usual smack wholesaling,

Adamo had already secured his portion of the start-up money for Rosa Gold. When his insurance payout for the North Perth fires cleared, he'd also have enough to help bring the mine into operation. The others were doing their bit too. Now, with these two kilos, paid for in cash with the proceeds from his bank robberies, once Hogan had taken his cut, Quinlivan would be able to sit at the table as an equal partner. He had a buyer lined up that he trusted. He would keep a half-kilo to deal to the rich kids he knew, and some for himself.

The plane had taken off without him noticing. He hadn't been at all nervous, both at the buy and later going through customs, but now the fatigue washed over him. How long was it since he'd slept? Since he'd woken up to find the dead girl, whose name he couldn't even remember.

That was one good thing about smack. It certainly kept the conscience clean.

27

The darkness grew out of the shadows in the land. Swann pulled over by a stand of curara amidst a field of caustic bush, sweet samphire laced around the saltpan they'd just crossed. Behind them, the black stitches of the EK's tyres over the crystalline flats that caught the muzzy light of the Milky Way and the brighter stars in the moonless sky.

The air was fresh and cold, the dirt crusty after the hot day and recent rain. Swann drifted into the darkness and drew up fallen boughs of beefwood and acacia he couldn't name. Sandalwood already burning in the small fire Jennifer Henderson had built in the lee of the wagon, her swag laid beneath a low branch, the sweet perfume hanging in a shroud.

They'd eaten a quick meal in the Cue pub; Lancashire hotpot spooned over mashed potato and carrots, several ponies of Emu Bitter. Swann hadn't slept for two days, and his windburned face felt like a crepe-paper mask. Jennifer Henderson had freshened up in the women's bathroom at the pub, combed out her hair then cinched it again, but the hot dusty afternoon was there in her red-rimmed eyes.

She passed him an enamel mug half-filled with whiskey, poured herself some gin. They tapped mugs and smiled. The fire burned high between them and for a moment Jennifer Henderson was clothed in flame, a trick of the light, melting inside a fiery throne like a Hindu widow, but smiling.

Swann stretched his bare feet towards the first coals in the bowl of dirt and cracked his neck, ran a hand through his hair.

She was good company. They'd had some laughs on the muddy dirt road from Cue, sliding around the graded embankments in the darkness, her hand on his forearm when she thought they were going to crash, the night air smelling of melaleuca and cooling pine sap. Her first laughs for a while, perhaps. He hadn't expected that she could be so unburdened. He had a picture of her as an eighteen-year-old nurse, hair in a sixties bob, that cute gap between her milky front teeth and those china blue eyes, fresh from the country, savvy about matters of life and death but wide-eyed in the markets of Saigon, with her friends at the bow of a sampan on the Mekong.

Now her eyes were heavy-lidded in the flickering shadows, strands of twisting black hair over her face while she told him about Max, how they'd met: that place in her memory Swann had guided her to.

Swann's head was pulsing with pain, a spike driven into his neck when he moved his head, the flames disorienting him. He needed to sleep, close his eyes to the dizziness, let himself fall. But he listened, and not only because he'd asked.

Jennifer's story explained the occasional hardness in her eyes, her knowledge of men. Her first husband, Steve, another SAS veteran she'd married in Melbourne, was charming and funny when sober. When it got too much she'd run, but he'd always find her. Each time she ran further, was free longer, but one eye on the rear-vision mirror was no freedom at all. Finally, she drove without sleep across the Nullarbor.

'You knew Max was here.'

A moment of hesitation while she thought about lying.

'Yes, I'd written to him. I knew he was here. And you're right. I put him in a terrible situation, almost immediately.'

'He moved you in.'

'Watched over me while I slept, a day and a night. When I awoke, Steve was there. He knew about Max.'

'Max saw him off—'

'Yes, but it wasn't like that. I don't understand how he did it. There was no talking, or shouting. It had just gone dark and they were in the drive. It was all done in their eyes. Like a shadow dance. Not a word spoken, but somehow Steve knew . . . He got back onto his Triumph, and I never heard from him again.'

'Reminds me of the story Garth Oats told me, his first meeting with Max.'

And he's no longer here, to protect you.

They'd got there quicker than Swann had hoped. He'd intended to be lighthearted about it, take his time, put her at ease. Then he was going to ruin her fragile happiness – and lead her instead towards stories that would make her think twice about continuing with Rosa Gold. Perhaps the race-track veterinarian whose jaw had been broken, or the gelding whose legs had been smashed with a four-by-two, or Percy Dickson's shattered kneecap. Stories of cruelty enjoyed, violence as ritual.

The campfire had burned low, and his scalp ached with the cold, the glow of warmth against his face and chest, the frigid cloak of night over his shoulders.

Her next question took him by surprise. 'Have you ever wanted to . . . tried to kill yourself?' Her mouth a dark gash, her inkblot eyes unreadable.

He didn't answer right away. Shook his head. It was none of her

ZERO AT THE BONE

business. He felt himself blush with anger, then swell with something else – the wanting to tell her. The things he'd only ever told
Marion. But it was all right; Jennifer was just trying to understand
Max. And it was the same story Swann had intended to tell, but
with different characters.

He told her about the murder of Ruby Devine, the Royal Commission that followed, the price he'd paid. How he'd thought his
eldest daughter had been murdered over it, how he'd lost his wife,
after his affair, lost his family. How he'd sat there night after night,
unable to sleep, gun loaded in his hand, hoping they'd finally come
through the door so he'd stop pointing it at himself.

'I'm sorry, it's none of my business. You've gone white as a sheet.'

Concern in her voice, but her eyes searching. She was trying to
trust him, he could see that, but she wasn't telling him everything.

'The policeman who bashed you yesterday. Was he part of the
gang, the ones who promised to kill you after the brothel madam's
murder?'

'Yes.'

And then Swann thought, I'm not thinking straight. And then he
thought, why not? *She should know.* It was why he was there. Beside
her, looking into her unreadable eyes. 'That man is Ben Hogan. He's
also on the board of Rosa Gold. What he did yesterday had nothing
to do with Rosa Gold, but he's not a man to —'

'I know that's why you brought me here. Not because . . .'

She'd nearly said it, but he felt it anyway. Her eyes flashed in
the orange glow, but her anger only made her beautiful. A smudge
of charcoal near her mouth, lips pursed with drunkenness and her
pale hands shaking as she lit a cigarette, filled his mug with whiskey,
glancing into his eyes.

Hours later, Swann woke from a dreamless sleep, unsure of the
time, looked out at the only source of light – the campfire burned

to a mound of coals. Jennifer was still awake, staring into the fierce glow. She sipped gin and swallowed, wiped her mouth with the back of her hand, an unguarded moment. He looked closer, saw that she was crying, letting the tears run, cold slicks on her porcelain face, seeping out of her burning eyes.

28

The dawn chorus of zebra finches and budgerigars in the curare chirruped in waves that lofted and fell. The track cut through a low rise and there was Wulga Rock in the distance, a hulking monolith of crimson granite near a well-treed riverbed. The view was clear to the horizon, the land shrouded in blue cold.

The sun rose quickly and soon the bush glowed with a buttery yellow light. A great perenti stopped them as they passed the first granite bands extruding from the rock. Top of the food chain, the dusty old lizard stared down the middle of the road, tongue flickering. Swann drove around it and continued on his way. The track widened out where it had been recently graded. There were deep corrugations in parts, which meant heavy traffic. It was getting hot and he drove with one hand on the wheel while he smoked.

Off the main track, he let the Holden grind forward over the bumps and ruts and creek beds in first and second, and they started to see big mobs of kangaroos and emus in the bush around them, a couple of foxes with dusty red coats and a large wildcat in some bushes near a termite nest, glaring amidst a cloud of flies.

The sun was almost overhead and the country was baked flat.

The plain of turpentine and poverty bush and occasional stands of sandalwood were evenly spaced and it was like trying to navigate inside an orchard. Because the track skirted the termite mounds and occasional granite extrusion, it was hard to get a measure of which direction they were headed. He couldn't see above the tree line and he couldn't see far ahead. This was cattle country, and he saw herds of wild goats and the occasional fresh cowpat on the track. The road began to rise up a sandy gradient and he saw the tall canopy of rivergum, and that's when Jennifer Henderson clutched his forearm and pointed to the west. 'Nearly there. I recognise the riverbed crossing.'

Swann edged the Holden through a small stand of gimlet gum when he turned to see Garth Oats on the riverbank, aiming a hunting rifle at his head. Oats was slick with sweat, dressed in a pair of baggy shorts and an old army bucket hat. Swann immediately cut the acceleration and put his hands on the steering wheel.

Oats' eyes were dull and empty. His lips were cracked and dry, his skin a deep nutty brown. He disappeared over the lip of the riverbank and they followed. On the other side of the gully, Swann could see a granite bluff pockmarked with caves over a gouged truck turnaround, a couple of blue shipping containers and a small camp beneath tarpaulins.

Garth Oats didn't look happy to see them. He indicated that Swann and Jennifer should sit on upturned milk crates by the camp-fire, which was burned down to cinders. He unloaded the rifle, pocketed the shells and hung the firearm from the branch of a dead sandalwood tree. Swann could smell the sandalwood in the coals of the campfire, sweet and aromatic. Oats scraped away the surface layer of cinders and dropped some grass tinder on the live coals, blew gently until it caught. His arms were striped with cuts and one of his elbows was capped with a ruby red scab. He waved away the flies from the scab but they settled back, until he waved them away again.

'Sorry about the drama, Jen. Had a bloke snooping around a few days back. Went off to shoot an emu and caught him here at camp, trying to get into the containers.'

Swann had noticed the two brass locks on the container doors. 'What's in there?'

Jennifer answered. 'Split cores for the assay. The other half goes to Perth.'

'How does it get there?'

'Drive it myself,' Oats said. 'My van's behind the bluff. But I'm not going any more. In case the bloke comes back.'

'You thought I was him?'

Garth Oats looked at Swann for the first time. Didn't answer.

'Did he have dark hair? Big mo?'

Oats' eyes said yes. He wouldn't look away now, and it was unnerving. 'He was following Jennifer around,' Swann said, 'the day before last.'

Oats surprised Swann by laughing. 'Made good time then, didn't he? His ute's still here somewhere, where I set it on fire. Gave him a water bottle and sent him on his way. He asked to use the CB before he left. An hour later a helicopter flew low over camp, must've picked him up.'

Swann thought about that. 'You don't think he was with Adamo, the others?'

Oats laughed again, but it didn't look easy. His face settled into its hard, still emptiness. 'No, I don't. They've all been here before, when Max was in camp. We showed 'em the whole operation.'

'Who's the guy, any ideas?'

'He was ex-army, I could tell that much. Not real talkative, but cool under a gun.'

'Might be federal police. They'd have access to a chopper. But why would they be interested in your core samples?'

Oats poked the boiling billy with a hooked stick and lifted it onto the red dirt, glanced at Jennifer. He took a pair of pliers from next to the fire and tipped the billy tea into three chipped enamel cups. Swann offered him a cigarette and he accepted, used Swann's zippo and flicked it shut, took a long draw.

'He find out what you've got here?'

Oats shook his head. 'Only thing he didn't have was boltcutters. Tried to use a tyre iron as a jemmy, but they're good locks. He was set to blow them off when I arrived. Plenty of gelignite around the place. Helped himself to some sticks and was set to blow the doors when I came.'

Swann looked closer at the nearest cave, emitting a loud buzzing. Saw a Coolgardie meat safe in the shade. Emu feathers in a pile nearby.

'Where's the drill rig?'

Oats tweaked his head towards the bluff. 'Back over the hill.'

'How many men working it?'

'We're not drilling any more, since Max. Waiting on some money from the others, and a deeper rig.'

Oats pinched off his cigarette and walked over to the corner of the nearest container, where he'd dug a hole, and dropped the butt in.

'Jen said you want to take a look around.'

'That's right. Ask you a few questions.'

Oats spat in the dust at his feet, nodded. He took a sling of two army-issue water bottles, put them around his neck. Took up his rifle and reloaded. 'Wait over there on the rock. Some things I need to speak to Jen about.'

Swann took up his hat and sunglasses and left the thin shade for the blaze of white heat. He stood at the base of the rock and watched them, Oats completely still, Jennifer's head bowed, muttering to him on the hot gusts, hard to make out.

One phrase snatched clearly, from Jennifer. 'Tell him what you want . . .'

Oats nodded, did something that surprised Swann. Put an arm out and brushed away a lock of her hair, rested his hand against the back of her neck, drew her towards him.

The embrace was brief. Comfort given. Jennifer Henderson glanced up at Swann, watching.

Swann followed Oats as he clambered over the granite extrusion pocked with dried namma holes. Wallaby droppings and knots of fur and chewed bones and teeth spread across the baking rock. Oats stopped suddenly and put his palm down to signal that Swann should be quiet. Beneath them on the rock a bunggara was sunning itself, a metre away from its shadowed lair of broken granite slabs. It was a big old lizard about five foot long, with a fat belly and a broad slabby tail. It opened one eye and watched them as they skirted around, then opened the other eye to watch them leave.

'He likes you, Garth, I can tell,' Swann said.

'He should,' Oats replied. 'He's the boss round here. Winter he lives off tadpoles in the namma holes. Summer I bring him goats, and he drags them up the rock and into his cave.'

Smaller lizards skittered across the rock as they approached. The bleached skull of a giant cat, distinguished by its curved forehead and great fangs, lower jaw intact, sat in a dry namma hole amidst a rug of fur and claws. 'You bring him that too?' Swann asked.

'Last year,' Oats answered. 'Shot him down by the river, by the soak I've dug there. He killed my dog. Bit his throat out before I could get a bullet into the thing.'

'Small dog?' Swann asked.

Oats shook his head. 'Big dog.'

They came to the edge of the granite hill and walked onto the hard red dirt. Oats pointed out some snake tracks that followed the tree line around the base of the rock, keeping out of the line of sight of the wedge-tailed eagle that had followed them since they left camp.

'He knows you too,' said Swann, lifting his eyes to the great bird riding the thermals coming off the baking granite.

'She,' Oats corrected. 'Nests over the hill there. I make sure she doesn't miss out either. No shortage of goats. Get a few camel too. I take the back strap, leave the rest for her and the wild dogs.'

Swann could see the drill rig over at the next granite island, rising out of the red desert like the hump of a whale, small flukes of cracked boulder to the rear.

'Whale rock?' Swann asked.

Oats laughed. 'Yep, that's him.'

'That's a small rig. How many crew?'

'Just me and Max. Goes fifty metres down. Good for exploratory drilling. Need a new one now, like I said, once some money comes through. Proper crew.'

But they weren't headed towards the rig, as Swann had expected. Instead they followed a dried creek that ran off the nearest granite hill, which rose in a sheer face above the desert sand. A stand of green myall grew beneath it, and there were caves behind the scrappy grove. Oats led Swann up the first ledge of smooth rock that climbed in staggered layers. Swann didn't know much about geology, but even he knew that these were the oldest rocks on the planet, Gondwana stone worn by billions of years of baking sun and freezing nights. It was odd, but there seemed to be a path of smoother rock in the centre of the route Oats was taking him, turning up the face of the great granite wave that rose over the red desert beneath them.

They came to an area like a balcony in the rock face, and then Swann saw the depth of the cave that was invisible from the ground. Oats went into the cave and Swann followed. There was plenty of light and Swann saw right away the smaller ledge of rock against one wall where a campfire had burned for so many years that the rock had melted into a smooth blackened bowl. On the walls around him were sprays of faded white ochre that framed the perfect handprints of dozens of children. The floor of the cave was a mess of dried sheep and goat droppings, and there were shotgun cartridges and broken glass swept into a corner. Oats passed Swann one of the bottles from around his neck and Swann drank the hot water. They walked back onto the deck of rock and gazed over the land that stretched unbroken as far as the eye could see.

'Beautiful,' Swann remarked. 'This what you wanted to show me?'

'Nope.'

Swann followed Oats along the ledge of rock and down through some boulders until they walked again onto the ocean of flat red sand, marked only by the prints of emu and kangaroo and sheep and goat, the intermittent scrape of lizard tail and the curved patterns of snake. Out of the wind, these tracks would stay for months. Their own tracks spread in a line off the rocks behind them. Oats walked directly through some tangled wait-a-while about a hundred metres into the scrub, zebra finches thrumming as they passed. He stopped Swann with a hand that reached back against his chest. 'Careful.'

At their feet was a mine shaft that sank vertically into the hard dirt, braced with boughs of hand-sawed rivergum. Swann shook his head. Beneath the thin layer of dust, the dirt was like concrete. Backbreaking work. He could see the pick-marks and the square edges of the shovel used to dig the shaft out by hand.

Oats spat into the shaft. 'Max's dad, Clarrie, made this hole back in the late thirties.'

'Hole's a funny choice of word, Garth.'

'Hole's dry. It's just a hole.'

Swann looked to Oats, whose expression was bitter. 'Nothing came of it?'

'Ruined what was left of his health. See those bands of greenstone down there?'

Swann looked deep into the shaft.

'He was following banded greenstone, a vein of quartz in it. This little area . . .' Oats waved his hand in a tight circle around them. 'Max's dad saw it was a diatreme. Had a conical mound here, a cap of greenstone, granite and quartz. Diatreme's just a vent of molten rock pushed up from below. Extruding's a good sign . . . What they call brecciated rock over this area.'

'So he dug down to follow the diatreme?'

'With a pick and shovel. Then had to crack the rock with a sledgehammer, break off fist-sized pieces. Crush each of them by hand, in an old whaler's try-pot. Into a slurry, mixed with cyanide. Then added mercury, to draw out the gold from the cyanide paste. Then superheated it, to burn off the mercury.'

'Dirty job.'

'The oxidised mercury did for his lungs. The digging did for his back. And the hole was dry. Bit of silver in there, just enough to cover his costs.'

Swann stared into the shaft and imagined what it must have been like, in the heat of summer, the digging, the crushing, the burning of lethal substances.

'What made him stop?'

Oats nodded, as though he'd been waiting for the question. 'Clarrie's wife, Max's mum. Did for herself with the cyanide one day. That cairn up there . . .'

Oats pointed to a group of rocks on top of the granite wave. 'Max was four. She's buried in Cue, in the cemetery there. Clarrie and Max made the cairn. It was the Depression years . . .'

Swann was familiar with stories of hardship and tragedy, part of the mining game, the common history of the hundreds of thousands of men and women who'd flocked to the state to strike it lucky, but had foundered. Stories forgotten in the triumphal noise coming out of the big corporations, the government. What a man and his wife and his son had started, and so many others like them, long gone. But this was something different. Because now, all these years later, not more than a few hundred metres away, Max Henderson had struck the big one.

'Jennifer told me Max's dad had a stake at Day Dawn, just outside Cue. What made him come out here? That land's still producing.'

'She told you that, eh? But she didn't tell you why?'

The tone in Oats' voice was odd, almost a challenge. Swann stared at him, waiting for him to continue. But Oats wouldn't meet his eye, until something passed over his face that resembled anger. He spat again into the pit. 'He had a stake, all right. But he was one man. They ran him off. Easy done in those days. Plenty of broke bastards willing to heavy for cash. Made him sign it over for peanuts. Threatened to cut off one of his hands. Depression years, a man with a wife and kid out here, with one good arm, is a dead man.'

'Did the claim run?'

'Oh, it ran. Still running, like you say. It's all part of the same mob now, consolidated, all those small claims. Blokes like Max's dad, who did the hard yards, got edged out.'

Swann smoked his cigarette until it was burned down. Oats stood beside him and said nothing, in the way that a mourner might stand beside a grave.

'So that's why Max Henderson had an IPO on this land, then wanted a piece of Rosa Gold. Because it's here. Where his old man went under. Where his mother died.'

'Guess so.'

'Why are you telling me this, Garth?'

'Because I want you to understand. Max, Jennifer, me.'

'I get it. But Jennifer's out of her depth. Max left her alone. You're way out here, no help to her.'

Oats made no reply, or any sign that he'd heard.

'Tell me about Max,' Swann said. 'You were here with him the months before he killed himself.'

Oats shook his head, his smile not quite right, eyes working hard.

'Did Max see something he wasn't supposed to? Did you?'

Oats weighed his answer, frowning. 'Sure. They're smuggling. There's a runway not twenty clicks from here. Once a month a plane lands from the north. Beech Baron, with long-range tanks. Meets a small Cessna that comes up from the south, heads back that way. We watched them plenty of times.'

'Does Adamo have anyone stationed here?'

'No. There's a plantation or two, but they use windmills to power the bore, drip feed the plants. Never any visitors, though there will be soon. Plants aren't far off harvest.'

'You told me that story about Max when he was a chopper pilot. A hero. He try and do anything heroic out here?'

Oats set his jaw. There was pain in his eyes. Like so many who show nothing, the man felt deeply. Swann had to remind himself that Max Henderson had abandoned his best friend too. Hadn't left him a note either.

'Did he say anything to you about his state of mind, the last time you saw him?'

'No, he didn't. We better get back.'

The sun had fallen behind the rock and thrown the land into glowing relief, each rock, bush and tree foregrounded in the pure light. The only sound the flies and cawing crows, zebra finches in a mistletoe nearby. That feeling of being watched again, as the bush quieted and settled.

29

Swann woke on the floor in the grey Perth dawn, a wattlebird calling in the callistemon outside. The air was cool and the blanket was tangled around his legs, his swag peppered with the red dust of the north. He could hear Jennifer grinding her teeth in the next room, the sound that had woken him. His hip and right leg still ached from the accelerator, and the muscles in his lower back were in spasm.

The drive from Cue had taken twelve hours. Jennifer sat beside him in the dark, drinking quietly, singing to the radio as she became drunker, talking to him about her childhood, asking him about his own. They'd arrived in the early hours of Saturday morning. All he'd wanted was to go home, to sleep beside Marion, but that was impossible. He walked down the driveway of the block of flats and into the back garden, stripped off and washed under the hose, the smell of the sandalwood smoke in his hair, his closed eyes filled with the vision of the road running beneath him.

He helped Jennifer inside, guiding her to the bedroom, carried in her belongings. It was then that he discovered the cardboard packet of gelignite, in the milk crate full of dirty enamel cups and plates. Garth Oats had said there were plenty of explosives lying about the

Rosa Gold site, but Swann hadn't seen any, and he didn't remember seeing the packet when he'd loaded the car. He picked it up, weighed it in his hands, the same weight and size as a packet of candles. The only indication of its contents the red hazard sticker emblazoned across its front. Swann took the explosives outside and put them in his Holden, hid them under the front seat.

Now he let himself out of the flat, closing the door quietly behind him. In the car he headed north to Girrawheen, to the house of Marion's cousin Brett. Marion was an only child, and her father had worked detective's hours. She spent a lot of time with her cousins, sometimes weeks when he was on a big case, or coming down after a bad one, needed to drink for a few days to clear his head of the pictures. What he used to call a Homicide Holiday.

Brett was the same vintage as Marion, and her closest remaining kin. He'd been an outlaw bikie for a while, and had done a stint for his part in a stolen car racket. His own father had run horse stables in South Fremantle, one of the local hard men. Marion's family was like that. Some worked for the law, some against. Nobody cared. Family came first.

Swann had always liked Brett. He was reckless, too independent to remain a patched bikie, but you could tell he cared for Marion like a sister. He'd gone his own way, the same way Swann might have gone if he hadn't met Marion's father.

He pulled up outside Brett's house, parched verge and rusted letterbox, wild oats knee-deep across the front yard. It was a squat clinker-brick cube on a sandy quarter-acre block, like all of the others on the street.

Brett answered the door and cracked a smile, fewer teeth than when Swann had last seen him. His eyes were bloodshot and his face was burned, his mullet of thick black hair splayed across pale shoulders. Black jeans and bare feet. Heavy silver bracelets on his wrists.

Bowl of soggy cornflakes in his hand. Milk on his whiskers.

Swann followed him through the stale smells of the house, out onto the rear patio. Heat radiated off the unpainted cement, mica and quartz catching the light. A few withered pot plants amongst the wild oats and nasturtiums. A string of green pigface in the grey sand. The emerald buds of Brett's home-grown peering behind some fibro slats.

Marion and a young woman sat drinking tea at a plastic table. Marion rose and Swann kissed her, realised that he'd rushed to kiss her, to get inside that worried look. The press of her cheek on his broken nose, the smell of citrus in her hair.

She didn't let go of his arm as she sat beside him at the table, moved her hand to his lower back, both of them facing the young woman opposite, who seemed embarrassed by their affection.

'This is Mattie. Mattie, Frank.'

Mattie had a round face that contained a bowlful of resentment, and with good reason. The Premier had recently declared that people like Mattie were public enemies, communists and deviants, a major threat to state security, saboteurs of progress.

Section 54B had been designed for people like Mattie and the trade unionists who supported them, and Swann guessed that Mattie's paranoid eyes had probably seen a thing or two. She didn't look like the kind who tolerated fools, and Swann didn't bother with the chitchat.

'Marion told me you might be able to help. I've been made aware that after the fire, someone anonymously contacted the Premier's office. Was that you?'

The wariness in her eyes, a glance at Marion, who nodded. 'Yeah, it was me. I told 'em I was taking it to the press.'

'Did you?'

She looked at him like he was stupid.

'Tell me what you saw.'

Her shoulders and her jaw were set, but there was a tremble in her hands as she rolled a cigarette.

'I'm a photographer. I've been documenting inner-city life. The real life of the city. The bands. The people. The streets. Was going to collaborate on a book with a poet I know.'

'What did you see?'

'Some of my mates, well, a few weeks ago we stopped paying our rent. Changed the locks, started our own squatting commune. That didn't last long.'

'You changed the locks knowing who the landlord was?'

'Yes. And his plans for the area. We did it as a protest. The National Trust didn't reckon our buildings were significant. Or our way of life. They're all toffs.'

'Go on.'

'The poet I live with. She was bashed, after they kicked the doors in. They threatened her with rape. Held her down. Then joked she was too ugly.'

'Were you there?'

'No. But I know who it was. We all know. His name's Leo. We call him Cleo, because of the way he dresses, the pride he takes in his appearance. He'd been around a few times before.'

'Was it Leo you saw the night of the fire?'

'I started following the bastard when he was around. Photographing him about his business in James Street. Making his standover collections from all the shops, his trips to his boss Adamo. I started photocopying my photographs, made flyers out of 'em, clagged 'em up on walls and poles.'

'Jesus. He know you?'

'He used to be my dealer, when I was on the gear. But I was care- ful. The project I've been working on, I'm used to taking candid snaps, being discreet.'

'The night of the fire . . .'

'Well, he'd been coming around. He wanted us to get out, him and his goon squad. But we still had months on our lease, and refused to vacate. We knew what they were up to, right from the beginning. Even the reason they'd leased the homes to our collective, rather than other tenants. They expected us to trash the place, but instead we looked after it. Even more so after we heard about the plans at council, for the office tower and all that. They wanted to kick us out, so they could let the place run down, or trash it themselves. Give the council no option but to allow them to demolish it. We got suspicious when they stopped making threats. We set guards at night, in shifts, to keep an eye on the street. And that's when it happened, on my watch.'

'What did you see?'

'Cleo and his meat axes rocked up in an old Land Cruiser, started dousing all the front porches with petrol.'

'You get photographs of that?'

'Yes, until Cleo saw me. Then they lit it up. We had an early-warning system rigged, one of those boaty horns in each house, the kind they use to start yacht races. So I started blowing on the horn, and people started blowing on theirs and getting the hell out, over the back fences, all up the street. Most of us had bags already packed, we were that suspicious. If we hadn't been well prepared, a whole lot of us would've died.'

Swann lit a cigarette and looked at Mattie through the smoke. She was a smart kid, but right off the edge. How far had she gone? 'Why did you call the Premier's office? Tell me what you really said to them.'

She looked away. 'I told them I was going to start pasting up pictures of the men doing it. I wanted the Premier to know.'

'Where are the photographs?'

'I haven't developed them yet. My darkroom and everything got burned down.'

'They're in your camera?'

'Obviously, I can't take 'em to a chemist, or a commercial developer.'

'Frank . . .'

Swann looked at Marion, and shook his head. He developed his own surveillance photographs in their bathroom at home, but he didn't want these pictures anywhere near his family.

'Will you trust me with the roll of film?'

'Why? What do you want it for?'

He looked her in the eye, but didn't answer. He wasn't going to lie to her. By giving the film to Sullivan he would put her in even more danger, unless he got her right out of the picture. Finally, she broke eye contact, looked at Marion. 'If you can get me the chemicals, and the paper, I can develop them here.'

Swann shrugged, put out his cigarette, stood to leave. He didn't need to tell her how much danger she was in. Once the photographs were developed, he'd put some of Percy Dickson's money to good use, get Mattie on a bus with a one-way ticket to Sydney. In the meantime, she was safe with Brett.

Swann kissed his wife again, held her embrace. Her look told him she would keep Mattie safe.

He shook Brett's hand at the door. 'Brett, a question. Does your brother Darryl still work at the track?'

'Ascot or Belmont?'

'Ascot.'

'Yeah, he's there, getting by on Dad's good name. Still a demon for the punt. But yeah, he's a strapper for one of the trainers. You want to speak to him? Saturday, he'll be there today. I'll tee it up.'

Swann thanked him and walked across the yard to his Holden, felt the weeds and wild oats stippling against his shins, smelt the hot dust in the air. The sun was like barbed wire on his bruised face, the cuts around his eyes. But the dizziness was getting better. One foot in front of the other.

30

Gary Quinlivan's ancestors had entered a horse in the very first race in the colony, on South Beach in 1833, although there was no point Gary mentioning it. No point either in mentioning that one of his ancestors had helped create Ascot, on a loamy floodplain sprawled across a serpentine kink of the Swan River, as a place for the gentry to indulge their love of the thoroughbred, some of the same horses that Gary's ancestors shipped to the British Army in India, to the cavalry officers in the Boer War, even the Great War.

Tommaso Adamo had no real interest in the horses – that much was obvious. And so Gary watched Adamo watching Marrone, prying into that same weakness Gary had sensed over the pool table, the sparkle of rashness in his normally dull eyes.

Gary had done what was requested of him, and no more. He had taken twenty thousand dollars of Tommaso's cash and bet it all, had returned with fourteen thousand dollars of clean money, the torn winner's chits as evidence for the taxman. Ron Bevans had facilitated the bets, spread across the concourse full of bookies, their tote bags and chalk boards and tilted fedoras and wary eyes on one another. Losing bets went with Bevans, the winning plunges with the others, on Bevans' advice.

But Leo had kept going, with his own coin, had dropped tens of thousands of dollars for little return. He didn't seem to care, kept returning to Tommaso for more, the indulgence wearing thin. Even after Gary told Leo that the inclined straight finish was designed to wear the weaker horses down, which meant that smart money went on the best stayers with the best handicaps, Marrone kept betting on long-odds horses who carried little weight. He would smile and cheer when they shot out of the gate, leading easily for the first stretch, some leading into the final turn, but his face would drop when they were inevitably mown down in the final furlong by the better stayers.

It felt good to sit next to Tommaso Adamo, and watch as he watched, the Victorian-era grandstand filling as the races grew in importance, the prize money increasing in line with the betting, the cheers from the stand and the golden light softening over the emerald green track, the bright silks of the horses and their jockeys.

Gary had never met anyone quite like Tommaso Adamo, whose gravitas needed nothing in the way of reinforcement, or justification. He spoke softly, and his movements were decisive for an old man. His honesty could be unnerving, however. Adamo was not Machiavelli, Gary had decided, but the Prince. His cool observations and the orders he gave made Gary feel like a pretender in comparison. And yet there was also a lightness of touch about Tommaso Adamo. Those in his company appeared happier than when they were not, Gary included.

In a word, *charisma*, and Gary wanted it for himself. Would need it where he was headed.

Gary waited until Marrone wandered away to squander some more cash. He leant forward, put his hands on his thighs, but Adamo spoke first. 'You don't like to bet?'

'I don't see the point.'

'Something for nothing, Gary, is the point. People who want something for nothing, they our bread and butter.'

Gary looked around the crowded concourse, listened to the shrill laughter, the colourful hats and champagne flutes and huddles of men, going over the form. There was more to it than Adamo suggested, there was the pleasure of the occasion, but Adamo had the essence of it, as always.

'You don't want something for nothing, Gary?'

'I'm my father's son. He has money, but grew up in the Depression. Old habits . . .'

'Your father is a smart man. My father, he had the weakness. Something for nothing. For my family name, I had to . . . how you say . . . replace him.'

'Yes, replace . . . supplant him.'

'Is that how you feel about your father, Gary? You go against him?'

Gary understood that the question was a diversion, from where Adamo was leading him. 'That's what we're counting on, isn't it? With all our . . . business. The something for nothing people. The earlier share floats.'

'But not Rosa Gold.'

'No, not Rosa Gold. That's for us.'

Gary felt Adamo stiffen, not a physical movement, but a change in the atmosphere between them. He looked down at the stairs to the grandstand and saw the Minister for Police waving his hat in Adamo's direction, making his way through the crowd towards them.

Adamo muttered something in Italian that sounded practised. '*Lichate u spittu.* For this one, the free ride is over.'

Sullivan's sweating face looked Gary up and down, expecting him to move away, but Gary didn't budge.

31

Swann sat across from Darryl in the cement-floored stables, both of them perched on steel buckets, the smell of hay and horse shit. It was Darryl's smoko between races, before he had to saddle up the next horse, unsaddle the last.

'What you're asking, Mr Swann, I'm asking myself: is it worth it?'

Swann was ready for the question, passed over a fifty-dollar bill. Darryl's eyes sparked, then settled back into their cool hard stare. Overcompensating, for his stature perhaps, or more likely his weakness for the punt. Swann could remember when Darryl was a shy boy who spent most of his time with horses, leading them down to the beach to swim.

'Thanks. I'm down to my last two bucks. Got here in a horse float, with a nervous fucken gelding.'

You would never know Darryl was Brett's elder brother. He was a scratch over five foot, whereas Brett was taller than Swann. The stablehand's features were crowded around a grim mouth, his face tobacco-coloured and his eyes bloodshot and malicious, grown into his father's son.

'Yeah, I've heard about the vet. Who hasn't? The bloke took on

Isaacs. Point needed to be made.'

Darryl didn't sound too sympathetic, and might even have been involved. The vet had broken the rules. 'The juice. What is it?'

'Dunno what it's called. Elephant juice? Horse goey? To be used sparingly, is all I know. Works on the dogs, too.'

'Everyone on it?'

'My bloke doesn't, much. Special occasions an' that.'

No angle there, either. Swann remembered Bevans, assumed that Darryl needed to keep in good with the other bookies.

'What the vet told me. Isaacs and Bevans have been playing the field. A big plunge recently.'

Darryl rubbed a surprisingly large hand over his small chin, pulled at a stray whisker. 'I heard about that. Cleaned half of 'em out, is what I heard. Isaacs and Bevans behind that, you say? Any proof?'

'That's what the vet was going to squeal about, before he was bashed. More than just the juicing. He watched Isaac's kids lay the bets, with everyone but Bevans.'

Darryl's eyes took on a cheery malice. He had debts with most of the bookies. And with what Swann had given him . . .

'I'll pass that on. They'll watch the fuckers more closely now. Fuck it, I'll offer to watch 'em myself. And if it happens again, and they find out it's real . . . Wouldn't want to be them two.'

Swann looked at his watch. Outside the stables, the announcer called the places and odds of the last race to a roar of appreciation, the sound of excited clapping. Another big hit for the bookies. Darryl shot to his feet, dropped his cigarette in the hay, swivelled a booted toe on the butt. With Swann sitting down, they were about the same height. Darryl thrust out his hand, his eyes daring Swann to mock him.

Swann sat beside Minister Sullivan in the aisle seat of the highest row of the grandstand, in the place cleared by a departing minder. Five rows down he could see the perfectly combed hair of Tommaso Adamo, in a crisp white shirt with his sleeves rolled to his elbows. He was seated next to a young Anglo man Swann didn't recognise.

So this was why Sullivan had organised to meet at the races. Swann had come in the side entrance, and had only seen Adamo after he'd sat down. Swann realised then that he'd been positioned. It was only a matter of time before Adamo turned and noticed them together. Tommaso Adamo knew Swann well, in the same way that he knew every serving detective; their appetites, their vulnerabilities, their moral code. It was his business to know.

'Bit of a stupid place for a meet.'

Sullivan grunted, sipped on his can of Emu Bitter, not in the best of moods.

'I presume you paid your respects to Tommaso.'

'Was the fucking fire deliberate or not?'

'It was deliberate.'

'The ding prick. The smart-arse little prick.'

'There were eyewitnesses, who saw Leo Marrone and his boys.'

'And the proof? You got photos?'

Swann had thought about it on the drive over. 'No, there weren't any photos. That was bullshit.'

'Where's the witness? I need an address.'

Swann shook his head, saw the white knuckles gripping the can, Sullivan's anger noticed by those around. Swann leant forward, pretended to look down at his paper.

'Think about what you're saying, Sullivan. You give Tommaso the witness, she's dead. You really want into Rosa Gold that bad? Can't you use something else? Planning permits?'

The hot glance from Sullivan said it all. That was the Premier's department, not his to touch, not yet.

'The fucking address.'

'No *fixed* address. Courtesy of Leo Marrone and his mates, the fire. Last I heard she was sleeping rough in Kings Park. She wouldn't tell me where. She was headed east too . . . May have already gone.'

'Then a name.'

'They aren't going to enthrone you at the head of the Rosa Gold boardroom table on a name.'

'Then you're fucked, Swann. Bail revoked. Back to lockup. Lonely way to die.'

Whatever Tommaso Adamo had said to Sullivan had hurt him bad. The Minister's voice was rising, not caring who heard.

'It's you or her, Swann. You got that?'

'I'll get you the name. But I need time.'

'A name, and an address. Or you're history.'

As Swann rose to leave, he saw Leo Marrone walking up the rows. Leo would also recognise him, something the Minister clearly wanted. It was an indication of how expendable Swann was to Sullivan, and a bad sign of things to come.

The next race had started. People around him rose to their feet, binoculars at their eyes, form guides in the air, shouting. But Swann couldn't hear a thing. He slipped amongst them, along the next row. Leo Marrone's eyes had taken in the glowering Minister, which made him smirk.

The race over, Swann joined the line of punters headed down the rows, the sounds of laughter and conversation echoing like a swarm of bees around the arched ceiling, a few doves up there fast asleep.

32

Gary Quinlivan reached across Ben Hogan and took a Sao biscuit, a slice of gherkin and a cube of cheese. There was a pot of coffee and a couple of bottles of riesling that Quinlivan had brought. Old Chisholm had a bar fridge full of king browns and he'd knocked the top off a couple, which sat foaming in the middle of the table. Gary had asked him to make room in the fridge for the riesling but the old man had ignored him. Now he was standing by the door and keeping an eye on the stairs as they prepared to start the meeting.

Chisholm was an ex-copper and trusted by Hogan and Farquarson. He had his offices debugged on a regular basis and the place was a good front. He bought and sold gold, much of it stolen or found on other men's claims, and kept it in a walk-in safe at the back of the office by the toilets. Gary would love to get a look behind those solid steel doors. He knew Adamo's gold ingots were in there, but the rumour was that old Chisholm's safe also contained half the stolen jewels in the city, and that Adamo rented it when he needed a place to board his smack. No raid by local coppers would ever take place on Chisholm's property without the courtesy of a phone call first.

Hogan and Farquarson helped themselves to the beer, pouring

into identical Löwenbräu mugs. Farquarson was a senior sergeant in the Robbers Squad but he didn't seem too bright, and he barely acknowledged Gary when he was around. Hogan, the younger of the two but senior in rank, could have passed for any Dalkeith lawyer. He was well dressed in a tailored grey suit, a well-chosen tie. His hair was recently cut, pale edges around his barbered neck, combed in a side part that sprang loose at the front, giving him a boyish look. Unlike Farquarson, whose ravaged face looked ready to explode at any moment, Hogan looked well in control, despite the stitches in his lip and the bruised eye.

But Gary knew that Hogan could turn in a moment. The man was becoming more demanding, despite the generous cut he was taking off the bank robberies. Hogan had what Gary's mother would have called slick eyes, intelligent and watchful and charming, even though his face was often grim.

Today Hogan's face was particularly grim. Gary had no idea what had happened to Hogan over the past week, but the man's attitude made Gary nervous, just as he was newly nervous of Marrone and Adamo, who sat at the head of the table. Marrone had cast Gary a couple of smiles but the effect was not friendly, despite their afternoon at the races yesterday. Marrone had taken Gary into his confidence, on Adamo's orders, but he still gave Gary the creeps. Even as he smiled, Marrone's eyes were hunting for weakness.

After the races, Gary had wholesaled the greater part of his smack to the only dealer not in the Italian syndicate – Robby Barns. Marrone's territory was the city north to Balcatta and Wanneroo, supplied by Adamo. Fremantle was sewn up by some of Adamo's cousins, fishermen who took their vessels out to the international waters for prearranged meetings with passing ships. Robby Barns, on the other hand, controlled most of Belmont and the south-east. His brother was a senior copper and that was his insurance. Gary had wholesaled to Barns at a cheaper rate on the condition that he protect his anonymity.

Gary had every right to sit at the table as an equal. He had raised the two hundred thousand he needed, as agreed, to guarantee his share in Rosa Gold. But here was another smile from Leo Marrone, sipping his coffee, and it made Gary's heart quicken. That morning, Gary had bought his regular amount off Marrone to sell to his dealers in the western suburbs. To cancel his order would raise suspicions. Gary wondered whether Marrone had heard about the overnight overdoses, one in Nedlands and another in Claremont. As far as Gary was aware, the two deaths had been kept out of the papers by the influential families concerned, but perhaps Marrone had heard by way of Hogan? Two overdoses in a single day didn't look good, not in one area – Gary's area. The smack Gary bought from Marrone was 30 per cent pure – he always had it tested. He in turn usually cut it down to 20 per cent, before passing it on to his dealers, who cut it down to 10 per cent.

But this time, with his own supply, Gary had passed it onto his dealers at 40 per cent pure, on the strict instructions that they only cut it down by half. He wanted a name for quality product, to differentiate himself from the regular shit. The risk was Marrone getting hold of some and testing it – he would know from the purity that it couldn't have come from him. Marrone would kill him for that, no doubt. He had done it to others. The two ODs, if Marrone got wind of them, would be enough to arouse his suspicions.

'Here's Isaacs.'

Old Chisholm waited until Bernie Isaacs was seated before he closed the door onto the stairs, waited outside. Isaacs nodded a greeting and shook out a Winfield Red, sat forward with his elbows on the table. The man was physically repugnant, but there was nothing Gary could do about that. They were all, together, the directors of Rosa Gold, for better or worse, and he was going to make them very rich.

Gary cleared his throat and tapped his coffee mug on the table. The conversation dropped off. He was the youngest in the room by a factor of a decade, amongst some of the most powerful men in the state, but he had their full attention.

'Robert's Rules, gents, as we agreed. As this is our first official meeting, no business from previous. I'll concoct the minutes later, to go with the second set of books. Pressing items are the commitment of funds to bring the mine into operation, the potential floating of Rosa Gold stock, at a price determined by us, the attention we're getting from the Minister of Police, and the suicide of Max Henderson.'

Gary had to force himself not to look at Tommaso Adamo when he said this. He still suspected the old man was responsible in some way for the geo's death, as a way of removing a one part share in their impending wealth, although this could hardly be said to have worked – the geo's share had now gone to his wife.

'I'll start by inviting comments on the threats we received from the Minister of Police, at the racetrack. Basically, he told Tommaso he could stymie the redevelopment of properties lost in the fire. The Minister believes he has proof that they were deliberately lit . . .'

Ben Hogan sat forward. 'All very interesting, but what does the fucker want?'

Gary looked to Adamo, who nodded his assent. 'He wants a share in Rosa Gold. He's using the fire as leverage. We think that —'

'With all due respect to Tommaso,' Isaacs interrupted, 'that's for him to sort out. Sullivan's a liability. He's out at the next election. He's just looking to set himself up, for retirement. We'd be better off giving money to the other mob, a political donation.'

There were mutters down the table. Gary didn't look. He kept his attention on Isaacs, who was staring at him, waiting for him to respond. 'I just wanted to raise the issue. A point of concern. He might put some pressure on others —'

'Moving right along, Quinlivan.'

Isaacs still reading him for weakness, Gary the only man there he didn't know, didn't yet trust.

Gary shrugged. 'Moving right along, then. I'll start by reading out the numbers. Money in, money out. And bearing in mind our agreement that all money submitted to the Rosa Gold account must be clean money, in anticipation of our accounts being scrutinised in the future. This statement is from the Rosa Gold account with Town & Country, city branch.'

Gary met Ben Hogan's eyes, before looking away. The city branch of the Town & Country was the one building society that Quinlivan hadn't hit, as per their agreement. For the price of getting the green light, Quinlivan had agreed to pay Hogan 70 per cent of whatever he stole. The number was high, but having been bankrupted, Quinlivan had little choice if he wanted to take his seat at the table. Gary had even gone along with Hogan's little joke, wearing the leathers and riding the Harley of some bikie goon. Gary didn't care, as long as he got paid.

He read out the deposits made by each of the directors the previous day. He read out the total, and the result of his simple division. He, Isaacs, Bevans, Adamo and Marrone, had paid their share. Max Henderson had already paid his share. Farquarson and Hogan were short, particularly Hogan.

He put the sheet down on the table and let the silence settle over them. He had read the numbers out, as was his job, but he wasn't game to draw the obvious conclusions. He left that to Adamo and Marrone, or Isaacs.

Hogan topped up his beer, but Farquarson didn't move. He stared at Gary as though the insult was deliberate. He appeared about to speak, when Hogan put a hand on his arm. 'I had something lucrative on, fellas, that fell through. I'll admit to being distracted. I didn't plan on it, but it looks like I'm going to have to sell my properties. I just need a little more time.'

'I'll buy your share. The lot,' said Isaacs, looking around the table. 'That's what we agreed. If you don't have it today, you lose your share.'

'The fuck you will,' said Farquarson, shovel-edged hands pressed on the table, face reddening.

'Fucken coppers,' muttered Bevans. 'Used to gettin' a free ride in everythin'. Youse been creamin' off us for years. We took risks to raise our stake. We all did. Tommaso burned half of North Perth. I risked my licence to shank a dozen races. Bernie here sacrificed his best gelding, the health of his other horses. Leo's been busy too. I been hearin' about ODs all over the place.'

'That's not on me,' said Leo Marrone, roused into action. He looked sharply at Gary down the length of the table. So he did know.

Bevans looked to Gary too, though for a different reason. 'I don't know where young Gary's raised his stake, and it don't matter. Point is – he's got it.'

'Easy for him,' shouted Farquarson. 'He's workin' for us. But me . . .'

Hogan put his hand on Farquarson's arm again, and this time he didn't take it off. 'Gary's been doing the banks. Leave him out of it.'

The whole table looked at Gary now.

'That's you, eh?' asked Isaacs, a new respect in his voice.

Gary shrugged, didn't want to be involved in the argument. Didn't feel like there was anything to be gained by making an enemy.

'I'll lend you the difference,' Adamo told Hogan. His voice was quiet, but firm. 'No interest, but if you haven't got it in a week, I'll take your properties as collateral.'

Nobody spoke against him. Gary nodded and picked up the piece of paper again, when Hogan finally spoke.

'What about the geo?'

'What about him?' Gary's voice was as polite as he could make it. The temperature had gone up in the room, and it made him uncomfortable. All the other men were used to conflict, some of them clearly enjoyed it, but he was different.

'His money was in there first, right? Take what we owe off the geo's share.'

Gary looked to Adamo for help. He held the old man's eyes until everyone else looked to Adamo, who simply shook his head. 'We talk about the geo last, right, Gary? Robert's Rules. He's last item on the agenda. You get the money from me, or you lose your share.'

The others muttered in agreement. Farquarson looked like he was about to say something rash, but thought better of it when he saw the looks on the faces of the others, even Hogan. An angry detective is a bad enemy, but these men, Gary knew, would rub out a copper and not think twice.

'Money out,' he continued. 'We've spent twenty thousand on the drilling. Eighty thousand buying up most of the claims around, in a circumference of about forty k's. Which gets me to my next point. When I was buying the claims, I noticed that PLA has also bought a large number in nearby areas. A suspiciously large number. They own a fair chunk of the Day Dawn mine at Cue, but in seventy years have never bought near where Rosa Gold is. I think they've heard something on the bush telegraph. Though we've been pretty discreet.'

'That fucken stockbroker who was goin' to do the float,' suggested Isaacs.

Marrone shook his head. 'No, he's fixed.'

Adamo put both hands on the table, shifted forward in his seat. 'Perhaps, the geologist's wife.'

The threat in Adamo's voice was implicit, but sufficient. Again, he was making his point. Max and Jennifer Henderson were outsiders, mug civilians, not to be trusted.

'Fuck the Robert's Rules. Tommaso's right. What're we goin' to do about her?'

Bevans' look around the table was met with silence. Bad news for Jennifer Henderson.

It was Gary who'd first allowed the geo to the table. Gary who'd negotiated with his wife. He leaned forward and spoke into the silence. 'She's no threat. The geo mortgaged everything to get his stake. She's inherited his stake, and his debts. I spoke to her, as I told you I would. She wants out, but she can't sell their share until the settlement of his will. Could be a matter of days, or weeks, or even months.'

'We don't *buy* it back. We take it. Fuck her.'

Farquarson's face hadn't lost its flush of anger. He was a hothead, not thinking straight. Nobody else met his eye, and that gave Gary the courage to correct him.

'We don't want an aggrieved widow making noises. With the Hendersons' wealth, she's probably well connected. We've got to stay under the radar, for the near future.'

Gary made sure to stay calm, as Adamo had stayed calm. 'We humour her. We act like she's the geo's legitimate proxy, until the time is right. We've got two hundred and thirty thou in contracted equipment: crushers, trucks, graders, drills and diggers. We've got to keep quiet until the mine's in operation, and producing. Until we decide whether to float the company or not.'

'Fuck the float,' snarled Isaacs. 'I thought we agreed on that. We keep the company in our hands. We keep all the profit.'

'That's right,' Gary humoured. 'That's what we agreed. But it's going to be expensive to do that. Our first million is already spent, before a spade has been sunk. But down the track, if we get tight for money there are others who'll be hungry for our action.'

'What are you talking about?' Farquarson demanded. 'We can fix any bastards who try that. We've put the money in —'

'Come again?' Isaacs snorted. '*Your* hand's short. Tommaso had to put in for you.'

'Ben told you, you ugly mutt, something fell through . . .'

Gary shook his head. The man needed more humouring. 'It's a bull market. There's millions of dollars in capital floating around, looking for a home. If word gets out that we've struck the big one but are having cash-flow problems, it won't be easy to keep it in-house, or make good terms. We can always go to the banks to finance us . . .'

Isaacs snarled. 'Fucken banks are fucken thieves. They're not comin' anywhere near us.'

'And the big players, the PLAs of the world, they won't be put off by a few broken legs.'

Gary hadn't meant to say it, but it was too late. What Marrone's thugs had done to the stockbroker, and some of the miners around the Rosa Gold stake who'd averred in selling up their claims . . . it was one thing to know it, another to say it out loud.

Marrone's eyes were dark bitten. He sat back in his chair and wiped his hands on a serviette, smiling cruelly at Gary down the table. Beside him, old Tommaso Adamo stood and looked down over them all, indicating that the meeting was adjourned until after lunch, when the widow would arrive. Adamo's silence said everything about the bickering and the suspicion. He looked directly at Gary Quinlivan, and bowed his head slightly. A nod of respect, or of parting? Gary couldn't tell.

33

Swann glanced through the *Sunday Times* while Jennifer Henderson dressed, the front page still given over to the North Perth fires, photos of bulldozers clearing the charred land and interviews with the newly homeless. Tommaso Adamo was saying he was devastated to have lost so many buildings, particularly in this year of celebration for the city. The block was significant to the heritage of the area.

Jennifer emerged from her bedroom dressed entirely in black. She wasn't wearing any make-up.

Before Swann could compliment her, she asked, 'Is this okay? I don't want to look like the Black Widow.'

'It's perfect,' he assured her, and he wasn't lying. Jennifer Henderson looked newly vulnerable, fragile, perfectly in keeping with the role they'd agreed she should play.

'You don't have to do this,' Swann tried one last time. 'You can just keep away from them.'

He saw that it triggered something, as he'd hoped. But the anxiety in her eyes didn't make it to her voice. She shook her head, laughed. 'How did you sleep last night? I'm getting used to this place. My tenants in the other flats still don't know I'm the landlady. They fight and drink and rev their engines in the morning, but they're nice people really. I don't know that I can ever move back home.'

They drove into Perth in separate cars.

Swann sat with Reggie Mansell at the front bar of the Great Western, across the road from the entrance to Chisholm Gold. They faced the street and sipped from middies. The evidence of the fire was still in the air, the smell of damp ash and the stench of scorched rubber. Cinders had settled on eaves and in gutters. The pavements were covered with black footprints, the windows streaked with grey smuts.

They heard the strumming of the Ghia long before they saw it outside the pub. Jennifer knew they were watching, and didn't put any coins in the parking meter, as discussed. Many of the coin-filled heads of the parking meters on the street had been cut off and stolen by junkies, so no ticket could be issued if she parked in one of those bays. But Jennifer had chosen her park wisely. This was one occasion when a parking fine would be useful, as proof of her visit.

Jennifer Henderson was about to enter a room full of violent men. She lit a cigarette and removed her sunglasses. She looked every bit the grieving widow; pale, wasted, upset.

They had agreed that if she wasn't back in an hour, then he was going in.

Swann tapped the .38 in his shoulder holster beneath his jacket, as he'd done several times already.

34

Gary Quinlivan had gone to some effort, but it appeared to have been wasted on the woman. During the break, he had gone to the trouble of buying a plate of antipasto from the Italian deli around the corner, and a tray of fresh cannoli. He made sure that the riesling was chilled and Chisholm's glasses were clean, but Jennifer Henderson had politely refused both food and wine.

Of course, her husband was dead, and her appetite had presumably gone with him. Instead, she chain-smoked Capstans and stared at the empty pad on the table before her. Gary had tried to be polite, but it didn't work, due in part to the malevolent stares of Farquarson and Isaacs. He'd told her that no notes were to be taken. That he transcribed the contents of every meeting upon completion, and that he would mail her a copy of the minutes, by courier if necessary.

Gary was keeping two sets of books, of course, something known to the others but not to the woman. They all looked bored as he went over the false figures, designed to make her investment of two hundred grand seem an equal share. He outlined how her husband's initial investment of forty thousand dollars had been spent, and described how it would be necessary for her to invest additional funds to help bring the mine into operation.

She seemed very interested in Inspector Hogan. When Gary had finished speaking, apropos of nothing, the woman had said, 'I used to be a nurse. That cut on your mouth looks infected. You should get it seen to.'

Hogan grunted in reply, looked around the room and raised his hands, a gesture that translated as, 'Do I really have to put up with this shit?'

It was then that she dropped the bombshell. Her demeanour didn't change; she remained diffident and avoided eye contact, although her words were delivered with an uncompromising firmness.

'All of my money has gone into this venture,' she said, tapping into the ashtray. 'Our house, investments, all mortgaged to give you cash. Which you claim you've spent already. A pity. I would have been willing to sell my share to one of you, as soon as the conveyance of my husband's will was settled.'

'Meaning?'

Ben Hogan asked the question, although it was in all their eyes.

She was calm. 'I've been approached by the CEO of PLA Mining. A Mr Nichols. Word has got out, I'm afraid, despite your attempts at secrecy. I have been offered a very large sum of money, something in the order of double my investment, to sell my share to PLA.'

'You fucken bitch!'

Isaacs was off his seat, leaning over her, his fist clenched in her face. 'You were right, Adamo, this snake-in-the-grass bitch has sold us out.'

Adamo didn't say anything. He shared a glance with Leo Marrone, a quiet glance that said nothing to Gary but was meaningful enough for Marrone to shake his head.

'Please hear me out,' the widow continued. 'I have cut no deals, made no guarantees, I can assure you. And neither did I invite their attention, I promise you that.'

Her voice was surprisingly loud. Her face was flushed, her hands trembled, but her eyes were clear. She stubbed out her cigarette and looked at them, one by one. Gary Quinlivan was beginning to admire this elegant and rather remarkable older woman.

Adamo had his hand up. 'Let her speak.'

'They have offered to buy my husband's . . . my share of Rosa Gold. But more than that, they asked me to put to you the following proposition. For a minor interest in the company, based on our sharing with them the assay results of the cores drilled so far, they are willing to foot the entire bill for not only bringing the mine into operation, but running the mine into the future.'

'Tell them to get fucked.' Farquarson this time. 'Better still, let me know who to speak to, and I'll tell them myself.'

She shrugged, looked around the table again, watched them closely, caught Gary's eye, and held it. If she was looking for an ally, she had judged well. What PLA had offered was common enough in the mining world, and it suited Gary just fine. PLA would spend most of the money, and Rosa Gold would reap the greater reward. The perfect business model. Minimal risk, maximum return. And it would give him the time and freedom to convert that money into more money, by allowing him to invest his energies elsewhere.

PLA would know that the directors of Rosa Gold were amateurs, novices at the mining game. They would have done their research, due diligence. Drug dealers, bent bookies and bad cops, a bankrupt. What PLA offered instead was experience, a proven capacity to make the most of their little hole in the ground. All for a minor, non-controlling stake in the company.

But the idea didn't take with the others. Gary Quinlivan had missed something while holding the woman's eye. Adamo finished whispering in Marrone's ear. Hogan and Farquarson smoked silently, grimly watching Isaacs and Bevans, who stared back, none of them looking at the woman. Not for the first time, despite the ground that he'd made with Adamo and Marrone lately, Gary was reminded of his lowly status among the directors of Rosa Gold. The men hated one another, certainly, but there was recognition there too. They were never more dangerous than at moments like this, silent and comfortable, an implicit understanding having been reached.

Clearly, they all thought he was working with the woman; they were too stupid to see the worth in her offer. The more he tried to convince them otherwise, the more they would suspect him. He kept silent, waiting like the others for the woman to leave. A three million–ounce gold mine, at least. And they wanted it all, every piece of it.

Jennifer Henderson looked around the table a final time, but none would meet her eye, not even Gary. She got the message. She stood, picked up her handbag and shifted her chair. Leo Marrone, ever the gentleman, guided her to the door. As he did so, he whispered something in her ear. Whatever he said made her freeze. Her face a mask of terror. Then he smiled, pushed her amiably in the lower back, and she was gone.

35

Swann had to wait. It was too dangerous to approach in case Jennifer was being observed. He'd sent Reggie home in a taxi, where a GP was due to visit him. Reggie had told him his pain was no longer eased by alcohol. He was about to go on the morphine.

But Reggie had given him something to work with. Swann had been wondering why Rosa Gold meetings took place at Chisholm Gold. Reggie had mentioned that Rosa Gold would certainly be keeping two sets of books; one for the Taxation Department auditors and another that properly reflected their outlays and inputs.

It was then that Swann understood. The black money would be kept in cash. Lots of cash. The drug and casino and bookie games were all cash economies. On the second floor of Chisholm Gold was reputed to be the best private safe in Western Australia; a solid-steel walk-in that was concrete clad and double-locked and alarmed. Perhaps Adamo and Marrone kept their heroin there too. Old Chisholm stored gold there himself, but not enough to justify a walk-in safe with better security than most banks. Why wouldn't he rent it out to those with plenty to hide from rival crims and honest cops?

The safe might be a good thing to hit, if it came to that, reminded of the explosives in Jennifer's belongings. Swann had decided they were a present from Oats, having being made aware of the danger Jennifer was in. He hadn't mentioned them to Jennifer and she hadn't said anything either.

Swann watched them leave, one by one. Adamo first, spritely and dapper, grey fedora and sunglasses, followed by Marrone, oiled hair catching the sun. Hogan and Farquarson next, buttoning suit jackets and shooting cuffs, faces grim. Bevans and Isaacs soon after, slobs in work pants and T-shirts and thongs, the only odd note the briefcases they carried. Finally, the young man from the races, who must be Gary Quinlivan, looking furtive and hot, slinging his jacket over his shoulder with a fake casual air.

Quinlivan lit a cigarette and ran a hand through his hair, shielding his eyes from the sun. He was a rich kid in bad company, and he looked soft. If Swann had to get heavy, Gary Quinlivan was the one.

The Karmann Ghia wasn't in the drive of the flats, nor was it at Jennifer's Swanbourne home. This was a concern, although she'd have her reasons. Perhaps the white Commodore had been following her again. Perhaps she'd been threatened, and didn't want to return home. The best scenario was that she'd gone somewhere to think, having understood that Max's dalliance with Rosa Gold was foolish. Either way, she would call him, and then they would meet.

He left a note and decided to case Gary Quinlivan's riverside apartment down on the Peppermint Grove foreshore, the address used on all the Rosa Gold paperwork.

The sun had already fallen behind the limestone cliff above Devil's Elbow, and Swann parked by the shallows that stretched clear beneath the hulls of the yachts in the bay. Families picnicked on the buffalo grass down by the white sandy beach, and children swam and tossed jellyfish at one another and climbed the peppermint trees that gathered around the shore. The yacht club was loud with the sounds of a party, and a speedboat ran laps of the sand spit over at Point Walter, dragging a fat man on an inflated tyre. Further out on the water the bass thuds of a charter boat sounded between the drunken cheers of men gathered around the deck; a buck's party with a stripper in the hold.

Swann cracked his windows and peered up at the peach stucco building where Gary Quinlivan lived. He was supposed to be a bankrupt, but the rent on the apartment suggested otherwise. Peppermint Grove was Perth's premier riverside suburb, native bush until last century when the gold rush hit. A consortium led by the Premier's brother had quickly subdivided the area into large blocks that ran down to the waterline, bought up by those who'd struck it rich. There was some remnant native cypress and sheoak in the corner of the bay, but the rest was gold-rush colonial mansions and new apartment blocks like Gary's.

Donovan Andrews had tipped Swann to Quinlivan's sideline in dealing smack, exclusively to the rich kids of the local area, and to some overdoses of late. That would mean pressure on the Drug Squad coppers to find the dealer. Perhaps Swann could help on that one.

Swann was about to climb out, take a seat in the park, when he saw Quinlivan exit the Deco arches of the apartment block. Dressed in jeans and a short leather jacket, he stood smoking under a jacaranda tree staring over the river. Swann hunkered down to wait. The only set of wheels in the car park that looked like Quinlivan's style was a flash new Mazda RX-7. But Quinlivan stayed smoking under the purple canopy and scuffed the toes of his cowboy boots on the broad roots of the old tree and continued to stare at the river.

A few minutes passed and Swann heard the smooth whirr of a gear-box changing down, bursts of deceleration and then a Statesman cruised into view.

Even from a distance Swann could see that the driver was Ben Hogan, pilot sunglasses and black sideburns. The Statesman's electric windows slid down and Hogan said something to Quinlivan. The young man shook his head but did what he was told; walked around the car and climbed in. He looked even unhappier when he was sitting alongside Hogan, who'd raised his bulk off the driver's seat and was speaking rapidly. The windows rose and the Holden took off with a squeal, headed along the riverside road that climbed over the bluff until the view of the river was blocked with the walled mansions of the rich.

The Statesman wasn't Hogan's regular ride, and Swann had to assume it came from the pool of confiscated vehicles used by the Drug Squad for undercover operations, something that made Swann even more curious. The Holden turned onto Stirling High-way then crossed the bridge over the river and swung east along Canning Highway. Hogan drove at speed and wove between slower vehicles, then turned off into a quiet suburban street and parked. Swann turned down the next street and waited at the corner, hoping his guess was correct – that Hogan was doing routine counter-surveillance.

Hogan's Statesman passed the intersection and returned to the highway by way of a bottle-shop car park, tyres squealing as it manoeuvred around car bays and came out the way it had entered. This little number almost exposed Swann, but because the EK was so much slower he was able to park before the Statesman returned the opposite way. Swann U-turned when it was out of sight, and followed Marmion and then Carrington, past the Fremantle Cemetery, where the Statesman turned into the

O'Connor light industrial area.

The sun-bashed verges were wide, with few trees, and there was little weekend traffic. Swann dropped back and saw the Statesman disappear down a small laneway that he knew well; crowded on both sides with unpowered lock-up garages, too small to use as work-shops, too run-down for anything but storage. Swann pulled the EK into a side entrance of the cemetery and drove until the Holden was invisible from the road. He parked next to some Orthodox headstones with patriarchal crucifixes, slanted crosspieces and slabs littered with plastic flowers. He got out of the car and put on his peaked cap and sunglasses, crossed the road to get behind the alley, where he crouched amidst a stand of hakea scrub near a car wreckers and had a good view of the road that flanked the lane.

He didn't have long to wait. Within a minute, the Statesman pulled out and turned east towards the hills. The car's only occupant was Hogan. By the time Swann reached the first sheds of corrugated iron held upright with star pickets and salvage timber, it was too late. He heard the low chugging of the Harley rattle the bones of the laneway shacks – it was hard to credit, but there he was, the Judge's son, the weedy white-collar rip-off merchant, astride the Harley Knucklehead, helmet visor down, giving it the throttle as he fol-lowed Hogan east into the brush-lined southern streets, the sound of the hog a metal bubbling and then a low spitting as it disappeared onto the main road.

Swann hurried out of his cover, intending to follow and photo-graph the bikie-suited Quinlivan and Hogan together, maybe even catch the next robbery, take it to the media. He was halfway across the street when he heard the single gunshot from the cemetery, close enough to echo-slam against the shacks behind him. He ducked and skirted the low cyclone fence along the bank of bleached grass and zamia palm, jumped the fence when he had sufficient cover and drew his own revolver, edged through the graves towards his car.

From behind a headstone he saw that the right rear tyre of the EK had been blown open. He left his cover and stood crouched on the track, just in time to see the red brake lights of the white Commodore as it squealed onto Carrington Street.

Swann changed the tyre, drove out of the cemetery and down into Fremantle. He called Marion from a public phone in the National, and she told him what had happened to Louise's friend Penny. He could tell by Marion's voice that she had company, but the fact that she was talking meant her company could be trusted. This was confirmed when he saw Detective Constable Terry Accardi's silver Pacer parked in the drive, behind Marion's Datsun. Terry wouldn't let himself be seen at Swann's house unless it was important.

Swann drove around the block and pulled into the car park of the Seaview Hotel. The Seaview backed onto the rear of his yard, hidden by the shed. He climbed over the fence and worked his way past the rusted chimney of a Metters stove, a pile of spare louvres and an overturned wheelbarrow, the spools of old wire from their chicken coop.

Marion was sitting on the rear verandah with her arm around Louise, who was crying. Terry Accardi stood across the table from them. He had his notebook out and a pencil behind his ear. There didn't appear to be any other police presence. The sight of Louise crying made Swann's chest tighten. Louise's friend Penny had gone, and he needed to be with her.

'Daddy!'

Swann put his arms around her, squeezed her tight. Louise hadn't called him Daddy for many, many years. He felt her sobbing against his ribs, the dampness on his shirt. He stroked her hair and looked to Accardi, who with a nod indicated the driveway. Swann kissed Louise on the forehead and wiped away her tears. She looked at him, her eyes full of pain. Penny was a junkie, and Louise understood that an overdose was always likely, but it didn't make it any easier.

He led Accardi around the corner, where the detective's disguise collapsed. Swann had mentored Terry Accardi for many years, but that wasn't something his colleagues could know.

'You knew Penny?' said Swann.

'My little sister's friend, Beacy Primary together. My dad played soccer with her father for Tricolore.'

Accardi lit cigarettes and passed one to Swann. The man was shaken. It can't have been pretty.

'What's been left out?'

Accardi started speaking automatically. 'Twelfth floor of Johnson Court, single room. At least a few days. Neighbours reported a bad smell. Summer heat. She was completely black. Unrecognisable. Been years since I've seen her. I've had three showers. Changed clothes three times, and I still can't shake the smell.'

Swann let Accardi go into the details, for the detective's benefit, not his own. He didn't need to know. He'd seen it before. Smelt it before. But Accardi needed to tell someone. It wasn't the sort of thing you could tell your father, your mother, your lover. Not without spreading the ugliness.

When Accardi had talked himself out, he appeared relieved. His eyes had started to shine. His voice had changed, a little tremolo.

'Why a homicide matter? Anything unusual? Signs of other people?'

The question forced Accardi to focus. 'There were no fits in the place. And no gear.'

'Nice of her mates to call it in.'

'The neighbour, an old lady, reported seeing a young male coming out of there on Tuesday morning, well dressed, cowboy boots, pastel T-shirt, newish jeans. Said his hair was nicely combed. Said that made him stand out, enough to remember. Good-looking, thin, pale.'

'She see a vehicle arrive or depart?'

'Not from the twelfth floor. But Louise described the same young male fingered by the neighbour. He'd been waiting for Penny in the car park after their Monday-night gig. The bloke hadn't come over to Justin's van. Louise thought that was suspicious, but assumed the man was a druggie friend. Assumed right. You didn't see him that night, did you?'

Swann shook his head. He'd headed into town as soon as Louise's set was over, in search of Hogan and Cassidy.

'Have a think about it,' continued Accardi. 'The suspect won't be charged with anything except leaving the scene, not rendering assistance, but it'd help to find him. As a junior detective, they're giving me all the ODs. This is my third today. That's three sets of parents I've had to break the news to. The others were in Claremont.'

Swann considered telling Accardi about Gary Quinlivan, but he wanted to speak to Quinlivan first, try to turn him. 'You'd better beat it, Terry – if anyone else turns up and word gets back to Hogan, your career's over.'

Accardi's face softened, became apologetic. He was a good kid. Most young coppers were good kids, until they met the likes of Hogan and Farquarson.

'You haven't heard, have you? Christ.'

Swann shook his head. 'Shoot.'

'It's not just Hogan's Ds you have to watch for. As of an hour ago, every uniformed in Perth is after you. It came over the CB. No mention of a charge, but arrest on sight. Potentially dangerous suspect.

Don't apprehend alone. Call in the tactical response group.'

'My car?'

'Rego given out. You need to lose it, or at least swap plates.'

'Why haven't they raided here yet?'

'No idea. But you'd better go.'

Accardi left by the driveway, but first Swann had to make a call.

He entered the kitchen with Marion close behind, just as three of Louise's friends came in the front door. Swann took up the phone and walked the long extension through to the lounge room. He dialled Sullivan, waited while the secretary put him through. Swann's phone was probably bugged, but he didn't care if his conversation with the Minister was overheard.

'You prick. I told you I'd find her . . .'

'Not enough, Frank. You didn't do enough. Not yet. I said I wanted evidence. I know there's something else. I was told there were photographs taken. I want them.'

'Then call off the uniformed. If I'm arrested I'm no use —'

'Think of it as an incentive, Frank. We all have to work within certain constraints. Yours now include avoiding a thousand armed officers, a hundred Ds. Get me the photographs, and I'll call off the uniformed. Not much I can do about the detectives.'

As soon as Swann hung up, the phone rang. He expected Penny's father, who would want to know more than he'd been told. Picked it up out of instinct.

But it was Hogan.

'Sullivan can't protect you, Swann. He's on the way out, desperate, just like you.'

'I was just leaving.'

Hogan laughed. 'Why did I think you were going to say that? You don't understand. You're not taking me seriously. I want what's mine. And then I want what's yours. And you'll *pay*.'

Swann peered behind the calico curtains into the dusk and saw the white Commodore cruise past, wattles and banksias shivering in the breeze. Then he saw what shouldn't be there, his EK Holden, parked where he hadn't parked it, right outside his home.

'You've got twenty-four hours to get me money. Fifty thousand should cover it. If not . . . you're dead.'

The explosion made the car jump within a ball of fire. The shock blew out the front window and covered Swann in broken glass. A nearby power pole flamed and then the lights went out. Darkness in the house; outside, white heat and orange licks and black smoke that he could feel on his face, his hair.

Swann looked down and next to his bare feet was a growing pool of blood. The shard of glass in his thigh and the blood that flowed down his inner leg glowed in the crimson light. The phone was still at his ear. Hogan was listening, cursed under his breath and hung up.

36

Swann woke up groggy and sore. The fluorescent lights hurt his eyes. Marion squeezed his hand; kissed his forehead. Across the ward, a nurse was taking a child's temperature, the thermometer like a glass cigarette in the boy's mouth. Next to him was a sleeping toddler with her right foot in plaster, a Miss Piggy doll gripped in her fist. Beside her, a teenage boy slept with his face wrapped in bandages. A teenage girl with her arm in a sling was arguing with the desk nurse. She wanted her cigarettes. Fremantle children's ward on a quiet night.

'Anybody else hurt?' he asked.

Marion shook her head. 'Kids got a scare. But we were lucky. *You* were lucky. Cuts all over, but none of them serious. The piece in your thigh nicked a vein. They've put some kind of stent in it.'

'I'm sorry,' he said. 'I shouldn't have come home.'

'I asked you to.' Marion squeezed his hand, a familiar gesture. Their years together, the children, the promise of a future.

'Hogan won't touch you,' Swann said. 'He's thinking of his career. But you can't stay there. They'll be raiding, night and day. The kids. The unregistered guns . . .'

'It's done. We've moved in with Brett. I took the rifle and shotgun with us.'

He looked into her clear green eyes. Acute, shrewd, her father's eyes. The man who'd taught them both. Marion knew what came next.

'I admitted you under my maiden name. They were waiting for you, during surgery. But I got you trolleyed down here to the kid's ward. You'll need to rest up, before you move. Give that stent time to take. If it doesn't, massive internal bleeding. Not the kind of thing I can fix.'

'I'm going to need those photographs,' Swann replied. 'The ones of Marrone, at the fire. I'll keep Mattie out of it.'

'No need. I put her on a bus, gave her some cash. Here. Two copies of the prints, and a set of negatives. The real negatives are safe.'

She picked up a blue airmail envelope. Searching his eyes, looking for something.

'That Henderson woman. She was there, in emergency, while you were under the knife. She gave me this, for you. She said to tell you that *you were right*. That she'd be leaving.'

Marion opened the envelope and fanned the cash, more than he was owed. Paid off. Contract over.

Two things hit Swann; confusion that Jennifer Henderson had known he was there, in hospital, then relief that she'd walked away from Rosa Gold, no longer needed him.

'She say anything else?'

'Just that. Returned your laundered shirt, freshly ironed.'

No relief in Marion's face, cat's eyes in the fluoro light.

Swann pushed Jennifer Henderson out of his mind, tested the idea that with her cash and Percy Dickson's reward, he could withdraw to a safe distance – pay Hogan off.

But that wasn't going to happen. Hogan wasn't interested in the money. He'd made that clear by trying to kill him.

'What time is it?'

Marion looked at her watch. 'Seven. You slept the whole night and day.'

Swann needed to get moving.

Marion kissed him hard on the lips, then softer, then softer again, pushing his hair back in her fingers, parted between her warm thumbs, gently on his cold forehead.

As soon as she was gone, Swann pulled off the blankets, stood on shaky legs and drew the dividing curtain that separated his bed from the others. In the cupboard beside his bed were his clothes, his wallet and something Marion had added – the .38 long-nose revolver he'd taken off Dennis Gould. He knew from the weight that it was loaded.

Marion understood that he would leave the hospital immediately. That whatever weapon he carried, it couldn't be his own. His wallet was stuffed with the remainder of the cash he'd received as a reward from Dickson. And in his jacket pocket was his toothbrush, a packet of disprin and the keys to Marion's car. He finished tying his shoelaces, his right leg stiff with the bandage around his thigh, and combed his hair with his hands. The nurse at the ward station was making the most of a quiet moment by reading a magazine, a picture of Olivia Newton-John on the cover, and didn't look up as he left.

Marion's Datsun was parked across the road. The night was cool and the sea breeze worked to clear his head. He had cuts over his arms and shoulders, and some of them had opened as he dressed. He patted away blood on his forehead, more on the back of his wrist. On the dashboard was a packet of Craven A; on the floor pan, a fresh bottle of Grant's and the cardboard box containing his new bugging device – the receiver, recorder and bug in its original polystyrene frame. On the back seat was a sleeping bag. Marion had even adjusted the driver's seat to suit his height, the length of his legs. The Datsun was a small car, and he felt like a giant sitting in a bucket. He turned the ignition and headed north of the river.

Swann rang the bell outside the tall metal gates of the clubhouse. The door chime was odd amongst the high-tech security cameras that angled over him as he smoked, waited for an answer. When no answer came, he picked up empty beer bottles from the trench by the nearest gate and lobbed them over the razor-edged walls. He threw them in different directions, hoping to take out a window or hit a bike.

The Nongs had built their Morley clubhouse to withstand the potential rocket-grenade attacks and ram raids of their enemies, but the sound of bottles smashing on concrete over the high walls had the desired effect. Within seconds, Swann heard booted feet and then the loading of a shell into a pump-action shottie. He stood back and stubbed out his cigarette with his heel. Zipped up his parka.

A bearded face that smelt of old cigar and green ginger wine. Bloodshot eyes. Hair tied in a greasy bandana. Swann didn't know him, just another of Gus Riley's foot soldiers.

The cold eye of the single-barrelled shottie followed him through the stares of bikie women gathered around fires burning in sawn-off drums. Sounds of Rose Tattoo coming out of speakers on milk crates. A fully stocked bar with a topless barmaid, pinball machines and titty posters on the walls.

Swann was nudged down the length of the bar into a chipboard-partitioned room, where all thirty patched-up members of the Nongs sat in silence around a pool table with a plank surface, clasping tinnies in beefy paws. They stared at him without expression, then looked to Gus Riley, their sergeant-at-arms, who tapped a wooden hammer on a leather gavel, a tiny ceremonial hammer with a nickel plate.

Gus Riley looked around at the others, ignoring Swann for the moment. 'Move to postpone the motion until . . .' he looked at his watch, '. . . 9.15 pm. In agreement?'

There were nods and grunts from around the table, and then the Nong elite stood and scratched and looked Swann up and down, sculling their cans and tossing them in the bin by the door. Soon only Riley and the bloke with the shottie remained. The air smelt of Dr Pat tobacco, leather dew and petrol. And then party pies, carried in by the topless barmaid.

'Not now, Sharon. Later. And you can go too, Bruce.'

When they were alone, Swann allowed himself to smile. 'Bruce?'

'Every mob has a retard, Swann, you know that. Bruce is ours.'

'Didn't even pat me down.'

Swann pulled out the .38 from the back of his trousers, pointed it at Riley, who didn't blink.

'Bruce is cannon fodder, Swanny. His sweetest dream is to take a bullet for the Nongs, die happy. Grab a seat.'

'If I have the chair's permission, sure.'

'Go on, abuse my good nature. It's no small thing to break up a Nong meeting. You can guess what was on the agenda.'

Swann sat on the plastic seat and watched Gus Riley through the remnant smoke, the .38 aimed beneath the table. 'Business is business, right?'

Riley laughed, but his eyes were bitter. 'I know what your EK means to you, same as my Knucklehead means to me, but I did you the favour of detonating it early. You were supposed to be in it. Dead. Kaboom.'

'Hogan won't be happy about that.'

'Human error. It happens. And it's not like it was a paying job. Because of that fucken jewel gig, the bastard's promised to work me over, all of us, until he says it's done. Otherwise it's raids, random traffic infringements, putting the squeeze on our business, legit or otherwise.'

'I suppose I should apologise for Percy Dickson. Putting you in the picture.'

'I ever see that weak prick around, I'll smash his other leg. Then his arms.'

'Your meeting. You come to a decision I should know about?'

'The vote won't make you happy, when it goes down. They'll be wondering why I haven't killed you already. Coming here, you saved us the trouble of looking for you.'

'I've got some business for you. That, and something else.'

'You know where my Knucklehead is, you tell me. Or should I call Bruce back in, some of the others. Torture it out of you, before we sink you in the cesspit?'

Swann nodded at the tiny hammer. 'You're not going to hit me with that are you, Gus? You'll get your Knucklehead. But first I want to tell you a little story. About a mutual acquaintance of ours.'

'This friend have something to do with my bike?'

Swann sat forward, put out his cigarette, lifted the .38 onto the table. He looked Riley in the eyes and started to talk. When he'd finished, Riley looked at his watch, at the hammer and gavel. 'I'll cancel the meeting for tonight. We're going to need a war chest. You've got until tomorrow night, when we meet again, then it's out of my hands. Like I said, the vote's not gonna make you happy . . .'

37

Sullivan's city apartment smelt like a rainforest. He had the top floor of the Mount Eliza, a fifteen-storey block of flats with white fins that had been nicknamed the Thermos Flask. The building was circular, and the view over the city curved around from Kings Park down the Terrace to the line of the Darling Scarp, a great granite wave rising over the plain. The humid air trapped in the apartment during the day brought out the smells of the lush green plants that followed the sweeping glass wall. Sullivan favoured the kind of tropical plants with fleshy white flowers and spiny stems and meaty odours that looked like they wanted to eat their neighbours. The apartment remained in semi-darkness except for the lamps set amongst the broad waxy leaves and dripping green trunks.

Swann stood in the open kitchen and watched Sullivan go about his watering with an attention to detail he wouldn't have expected, carrying his red watering can back and forth from tap to windows. The minister's famous Gladstone bag, something of a joke because of his long tenure as party bagman, was on the floor near Swann. He hadn't planned it, but the opportunity was there, so while Sullivan was busy with a banana tree, Swann reached into the bag and pressed the fingernail-sized ERA2012 bug as deep as he could into one of the corners.

Sullivan turned, put his watering can away and sat at the glass kitchen table, pulled his cotton dressing gown over his crotch and belly. Didn't speak, just put out his hand.

Swann passed an envelope containing photos of Leo Marrone and his goons setting the fire. One in particular was chilling – Marrone looking directly at the photographer, squirty bottle of petrol in his hands, like a child caught in the act, but for his red eyes.

'These the only copies?'

'Yes. The negatives are in there.'

'And the woman?'

'Gone.'

Sullivan slipped the photos back into the envelope and scratched his belly. 'This is good. I can use this.'

'Then we're square.'

Sullivan nodded. 'I'll make the call in the morning. All charges dropped. See yourself out . . . I'm stuffed.'

In the public phone booth in the foyer, Swann pulled out the directory stowed in a silver tray. It was a long shot, but potentially useful insurance. The Leader of the Opposition, a man of the people, lived in a working-class suburb and listed his name in the phone book. His wife answered when Swann dialled, and put the Leader on, who spoke warmly, used to taking calls from constituents whatever the hour.

His voice changed when Swann introduced himself; he became businesslike, and then wary. It didn't matter to Swann if the Member for Armadale's phone was bugged. He described the photographs, and the Minister he'd given them to. He had a second copy. Did the Member for Armadale want the second copy? The answer was yes, but he didn't want to be called again at home. Leave them with his staff in Parliament House. Swann hung up and slid the phone book back into its slot, replaced the Bakelite receiver.

The Datsun was parked at the bottom of Jacob's Ladder, in some shadows beneath a Cape lilac. He fumbled beneath the back seat and withdrew the receiver of the bugging device, checked that the batteries were fresh. No red light came on the receiver. Either Sullivan was already asleep or the thing wasn't working.

38

The mouth of the Swan River was burning with sulphur lights and the clanking of derricks and hawsers, gantry cranes working around the clock. The docks were lined with container ships, their broad flanks forming a sliding wall along the northern edge of the city.

Swann parked outside the prison gates and walked towards the shadowed limestone entrance of the South Fremantle football club, the yeasty smells of Moreton Bay figs squashed beneath his feet. He jumped the turnstiles and kept to the shadows until he reached the dark glass walls of the members bar. It was shut, as he'd hoped, but a small light revealed Danny Yates turned to the till, counting out mounds of coins, sliding them into a cloth bag. There were no kids training on the oval tonight, and even in the darkness the grass in the midfield looked parched and bare, yellow builders sand around the goalmouths. Freo Prison loomed on the hill, the silhouette of a lone sentry with a .22 rifle pacing the rat run, peaked cap over his eyes.

Swann rapped on the locked glass door. Danny paused, reached beneath the till and drew up a baseball bat, approached the glass and peered out. He saw that it was Swann and relaxed, clicked the lock and ushered him inside.

In the light by the bar, Danny gave Swann a shock that he didn't try to hide. The scalp over Danny's right ear had been shaved – a bruised zip of black stitches curled from his temple to his neckline.

'Look at you, eh?' Danny got in first. 'I heard what happened. The car. Didn't know you were near it.'

'Who passed that on?'

'Local coppers. They came here looking for you. Curtis and some of the other mugs. Hogan's Heroes.'

'Second time I've heard that lately. What happened to you?'

Danny ignored the question. 'I told 'em I hadn't seen you, didn't know where you were. They told me they were looking to take you into custody, to protect you. Someone wanted you killed. I laughed in their faces.'

'They did this to you? The local coppers?'

'Nah, a few hours later I was robbed. One guy, but handy with his mini Samurai. Little shit opened me right up, one slice. Scalp slid down on my ears like a Bulldog's scarf. Red and white. And then just red. Shoulda seen the blood, Frank. You'd think a bullock had been decapitated.'

'Shouldn't be at work, Danny.'

'The thing that gets me, the kid didn't need to do it. I'd already given him the money. I wasn't lookin' at him. Playin' along.'

The Bulldogs' members bar was a mere hundred-metre walk to the Freo cop shop. Unheard of, to be done over.

'Bastard knew exactly where the safe was. Out back.'

'Opening time?'

'Yep. A skinny little bloke. Fucken short man's syndrome, to a T. Had to go the big bloke, when I wasn't looking.'

'Much in the safe?'

'Lots. Didn't seem to surprise him.'

Swann rubbed a hand over his jaw. 'Didn't drive a Harley, by any chance?'

Danny poured him a pony of bitter. 'Scarpered on foot, out the gate. After that, no idea. I was distracted, to be fair, scalp hangin' over my ears. I closed up and walked over to Emergency. I know your next question. Been wondering why nobody else's asked. Who knew where the safe was and the best day to hit it?'

'Go ahead, answer your own question. Though I get the feeling we both know.'

'Not many. The boss, a few club people. Some of the local coppers. Farquarson, he's seen me open it. I went out drinking with him a few years ago. He helped me lock up. Apart from that, nobody.'

'I'll ask my fizzes who's doing stick-ups with a sword.'

'Thanks for not sayin', "I'll keep an ear out." Not in a laughin' mood.'

Swann hadn't noticed Danny's partially sewn-on ear. His little ducktail stood off the back of his neck, but in profile his face looked like a zipped-on mask.

Danny looked over Swann's own injuries, the cuts to his face and hands. He seemed about to say something, thought better of it, then tried again. 'I don't know if I should give them to you.'

'You should.'

'Why don't you just . . . Seriously, but. Lay low at my place.'

'Thanks, I might. But I still want them.'

The barman shrugged, went into the office, came back with the cardboard packet Swann had left with him. Danny had peeled off the red danger stickers. Six sticks of gelignite from the Rosa Gold stake.

Without being asked, Danny Yates brought the phone. Swann looked at the clock above the till and saw that it wasn't time to call Riley. Instead, he dialled Donovan Andrews and got some oil from the street. Prossies were complaining of Hogan and Farquarson hitting them hard, he said, above and beyond their usual tithes. Same with the gaming houses, more raids than usual, each time the punters leaving their cash on the table, as was the arrangement. There had been nightly raids in some cases, except on the European Club, which hadn't been raided at all. There were rumours of junkies being goaded into doing stick-ups, in return for drugs; some word of a fallout between the detective branches, heat from above due to the rising crime rate and the fact that the 'Bikie Bandit' hadn't been busted.

Swann thanked Andrews and hung up. Tapped his glass and lit a cigarette, watched Danny pour him a new one. He thought of telling Yates about the probability that he'd been done over by a junkie acting on information supplied by Farquarson, but what was the point? There was no angle in going to the media, either. Same reason. None of the prostitutes complaining of paying bigger bribes could talk on the record, none of the gamblers fleeced or junkies robbing for drugs. Hogan and Farquarson were clearly getting desperate, but Swann didn't know why.

The clock above the till ticked over midnight and Swann dialled Gus Riley. Riley wasted no time, listing the places belonging to Isaacs and Bevans that his men had 'hit hard', acting on Swann's advice. The details would be important to Swann later, because not many of them would make the papers. There had been no incidents to report, no injuries or eyewitnesses.

Then Riley surprised Swann by thanking him. 'It was a good earn, will keep the boys happy. You've got twenty hours left before we come after you. Now, where's my fucking bike?'

'After what you did to my Holden, you prick?'

'I'll get you another one, same colour from our wrecking yard, plenty of parts. My fucking bike, Swann.'

'First I want to know what you did to get Hogan offside.'

Riley cleared his throat. 'That's between me and him. And you don't really want to —'

Swann promised Riley he'd have his bike tomorrow, and hung up over the sounds of Riley cursing.

39

The crowbar was too heavy for Gary. He wielded it and struck it into the palm of his hand but without any real power. He returned it to the boot of the Land Cruiser and took up a small bat instead. It was made of aluminium and dented along its length. Gary didn't want to know. He fell into line behind Marrone and his two thugs. Marrone carried a ballpein hammer and his two Italians a tyre iron and crowbar. They were dressed like housepainters in KingGee overalls and work boots. Gary had been warned to wear something disposable, and had chosen a pair of corduroy jeans and some old Volleys.

The four men made no effort to conceal their faces. The suburban Wesleyan church lay in darkness, the Gothic spire with its Donnybrook stone cross silhouetted by a crescent moon. Marrone led the way along a concrete path down the side of the church, didn't hesitate as he mounted some steps and pushed through into a darkened hall. Gary waited at the rear of the group until Marrone found the lights. Flicker of fluoro then a static hum. Marrone stepped away and allowed Gary inside. He grinned and pointed to a line of cots along the far wall, each containing a sleeper bedded down in an army surplus bag.

Gary nodded and strode over. He chose a young man who was roused by the light, the sound of Gary's squeaking tennis shoes on the shellacked floor. They were looking for a young woman with a crew cut and strong arms, according to Marrone. Anybody who didn't fit that description was fair game. Gary lifted his bat but one of the Italians beat him to it, little grunt of glee as he brought a crowbar down onto the man's legs. The sound was muffled by the layer of blankets but the man's scream was surprisingly loud. The next blow landed on his shoulder and Gary heard the bone break, saw the terror register in the man's eyes.

Gary froze. His mind was clear but his limbs weren't working. Marrone didn't need him here, it was another initiation. People were scrambling out of their sleeping bags now as blows rained upon them. Gary came awake and landed a limp blow on the back of a man crawling beneath him. The tinny sound of aluminium on bone barely echoed, but the man squealed, grabbed hold of Gary's legs. Gary looked up and saw Marrone watching, paused with a foot on the throat of a young woman who was squirming and wailing, snotty tears running down her face. Gary tried to step away from the grovelling man but he hung on, nearly made him trip. Now the man was crawling up him, burying his face in Gary's crotch, begging, pulling at his belt. Gary kicked but his kick was weak. He lifted the bat and brought it down on the crown of the man's head, the sound like the dull ring of a distant bell. Another blow, another to his head and then the man was on the ground, the look on his face dissolving as he went out.

Leo Marrone nodded and went back to work. Gary stepped back and noticed the blue flashing lights, heard the boots on the gravel and looked at the bat in his hands. He slung it over the beds into a stack of boxes and fold-up tables, just as the coppers entered. It was

Hogan and his squad, wielding heavy torches, moving sleekly in a wedge towards them. Marrone kept kicking at an unconscious man, the others winding down, that adrenalised look on their faces, their overalls spattered with blood.

Hogan took out his badge and shoved it into the face of the only man still conscious, a fat Aborigine who was bleeding from his nose. 'You're all under arrest. Illegal public gathering.'

Ben Hogan looked at Leo Marrone and laughed. 'Don't worry, Leo. One of them will give her up.'

40

The sun had risen but Reggie was too weak to get out of bed. He lay on blue pillows beneath a mauve sheet and wheezed through his mouth. Mutt lay next to his legs, staring at Swann and Gould, who sipped coffee in bone china cups so thin Swann could see the shadows of his fingers. The coffee was Greek, sweet and black and muddy, made by Dennis Gould according to Reggie's specifications. The smell of it filled the bedroom.

Reggie had indicated he had big news, that Swann should come right away, that he'd been waiting for him to call. But Reggie didn't look too good. His skin was the colour of dishwater and he had a lemony stain in his eyes. A bowl of cut kiwi fruit on the dresser beside him hadn't been touched.

He closed his eyes, and the breathing stopped.

'Reggie?' Swann said, a little too loud, afraid. But the breathing continued, shallow and grainy, like sand through a straw.

'He's just asleep,' said Gould. 'Still not used to the morphine. Comes in and out. Been like this since last night.'

Swann watched Reggie's chest rise and fall, drank his coffee, felt the strong urge for a cigarette, but waited. 'His friends been around?

Dropping in?'

'Not that I'm aware of. Not since I've been here.'

'He talks a lot about his friends.'

Gould made an apologetic shrug. 'The old days, I suspect.'

'It's good that you're here.'

Gould looked down into his coffee, swirled it around and drank the lot. 'Feel like a vulture. I know what the rest of the family are going to say. You know . . .'

'You're here. They aren't.'

Reggie coughed sarcastically. 'I'm not dead yet, boys. Just needed to rest my eyes. Tell him, Dennis. Tell Frank what you've learned.'

'Well,' Gould said, 'I've still got one or two allies at Capitol. I'm not sure I trust them, but if it costs them nothing they'll help me. They told me Rosa Gold is planning to float tomorrow, AM.'

'But why would they do that? I thought they wanted to keep it in-house.'

'The sharks must be circling.'

Reggie nodded. He still had his eyes closed, but Swann knew he was thinking. Gould jotted figures on a pad. When he was finished, he tapped Reggie on the knee. Reggie glanced at the pad and nodded again.

'My guess would be PLA. You'll remember I spoke to their CEO, my old friend Barry Nichols, about Rosa Gold. His evasiveness makes sense now. Dennis?'

Gould took over. 'What we think happened is this,' his voice rising in pitch. 'PLA have probably made an offer, to let them bring the mine into operation and let them run it, sell the gold – for royalties or a share – their usual practice when a small company strikes it lucky. It's how Lang Hancock made his millions with the iron ore. Never sunk a shovel himself. But it goes without saying that the assay results must be terrific.'

'I thought the assay results were strictly confidential. Aren't they gambling on a rumour?'

Gould shook his head. 'PLA don't gamble. They're big enough to have the inside oil on whatever Rosa Gold's core samples are showing. They'll have people in the lab, in the security detail, in the drilling team probably – all on the payroll. It's their business to know everything mining-related. Rosa Gold have been pretty discreet, but you can't keep something like this from PLA.'

Swann hadn't seen Gould so animated. Gone was the sullenness, the distance in his eyes. His skin had colour, and he no longer smelt bad. Clearly, under Reggie's influence, the boy was putting himself in the bath, eating and sleeping, becoming human.

'Rosa Gold are so scared of PLA they're going public,' Gould continued. 'That way they don't have to worry about keeping the mine a secret. They can use the rumours and the assay results to their advantage. They'll buy themselves a controlling interest of cheap shares, the rest of which they'll sell on the market, try and divide up the minority ownership between the local players and Joe Public. But with the money they raise from a float, assuming PLA or the others don't get a huge chunk and demand a place on the board, they can choose whoever they like to bring the mine into operation, they can tender out different parts of the overall business of running the mine.'

Swann finished his coffee, immediately felt like more. 'But the end result's the same. They give up part of their wealth, even with a controlling interest.'

Reggie laughed, a low throaty chuckle. He slapped Swann on the shoulder. 'Vanity, dear boy. As powerful as greed. Will trump common sense every time. The PLA offer, if it exists, is the rational choice, but —'

'They don't want it to be known as a PLA mine. They don't want to stay in the background.'

'Precisely. A chance to flaunt their genitalia. The only money that matters in this town is mining money. And if it's gold money, even better. A mine this size – they'll be the envy of the city. Impossibly rich. All their misdeeds forgiven. Blood washed from their hands. They'll be courted by politicians, feted like rock stars.'

Swann picked up the pad with the scrawled figures. 'And this?'

Gould pointed to the first line of numbers. 'Not knowing the true scope of the mine, these are estimations, based on Max Henderson's belief that we're looking at a three million–ounce stake. That's the money they'll need to raise. The money they'll initially want to invest of their own, to get the ball rolling. The probable starting price, beside the probable number of shares they'll need to release.'

'If you were handling the float.'

'Yes, if I were handling the float.'

'Is there any way you can find out for sure?'

Gould touched his nose and winked. There was a dark light in his eyes. He too had a stake in bringing down Rosa Gold.

'This is information that might be freely offered from some quarters; from others, it might need to be acquired. But we already have things to barter. Henderson's figures, for example; the range and depth of their drilling. Some of my old colleagues will be very keen to back this, for their own and their clients' benefit.'

'One thing you mentioned. They'll issue themselves shares, in large numbers. Will they have to use their own money for this?'

'The value of the company must be related to real worth, and so they'll put the tenement lease onto the market, as equivalent collateral, based on the assay results. Then they'll issue themselves a controlling number of shares based on the company's worth, which they'll keep off the table, but in cases like this there's a good chance they'll play the open market too, and buy extra shares early while they're cheap, to sell high later, and keep the substantial profit. They'll use every cent they own, presumably. I know I would.'

Swann stared at the figures. Incredible amounts of money. In the hands of men like Leo Marrone and Hogan, Bernie Isaacs. Did such wealth tame the beast, or release its appetites upon a larger stage? He didn't know. He didn't know anybody that powerful.

'You're telling me that by tomorrow night, Hogan and the others are going to be millionaires, many times over?'

'Headed towards billionaires, actually. By the end of the week is the expectation, if well managed. Capitol's management have told its brokers to clear the decks. They expect the shares to rise rapidly and for the phones to run hot, day and night. They've got blokes to take calls from Europe and the States, even after our exchange has closed. No doubt our dodgy directors at Rosa Gold will let their insider mates know to get in early, so some shares will be soaked up there. But expect players like PLA and the other chest-thumpers to land on this hard, buy up as much as they can, boost the share price as high as necessary to get what they want, which is a significant minority ownership. My friend's advice is that a first day ending price of twenty, even thirty dollars a share is not impossible, indeed likely. This company, this float, these shares, are going to be discussed in boardrooms and exchanges the world around.'

Swann pushed the pad across to Gould. 'This money they'll need for their start-up shares, prior to the float. How does that work? Where's it held? How's it transferred?'

Gould looked at Swann with a new excitement. He was at home in the world of numbers, knew the ways and means of liquidity and capital. He smiled, and the smile was cruel.

'Does this have to do with that good news you mentioned?' Swann said.

'You're asking me how much I want to screw with the bastards who've crippled me for life? Let me show you. I was never officially let go from Capitol, and I've still got access to their accounts —'

A crashing began on the front door. Mutt barked. Gould froze. Reggie was jolted out of his light sleep.

Swann peered around the edge of the curtain. Four detectives, one of them Curtis, all of them young. Taking turns slamming into the door.

'There's a back way,' croaked Reggie. 'From the laundry.'

Swann passed Gould the loaded .38 revolver. An ex-serviceman, Gould was at least trained to use a sidearm, and he no longer appeared a danger to himself.

'If I'm arrested, I don't want this on me, no licence. Hide it somewhere it won't be found. And don't answer the door.'

The coppers wouldn't get in the front. During the Royal Commission, when the word on the streets was that Swann was a dead man walking, and Reggie too was in danger, he'd had the doors and frames reinforced with plate steel. But that didn't mean the coppers wouldn't lay in wait for him, and Swann had things to do.

Quinlivan's RX-7 wasn't in the car park beneath his apartment, and he wasn't answering his door. Swann's plan was to take Gary to his father, make him confess his part in the bank robberies, working on Hogan's green light. A confession before the Judge would be enough to get Hogan charged and delay the float of Rosa Gold, give him something to take to the media.

With the float on tomorrow, there was every chance the directors would meet at Chisholm's offices today, to talk it through. If not, Swann was going to blow the Chisholm Gold safe, to bring them running. But he'd do it at night when the streets were empty.

Swann wanted to get there fast, just in case they were meeting early. The river beside him was the colour of tea, shimmering against the seawall along Riverside Drive, beneath the high limestone bluff of Mount Eliza. He turned into the city and crossed the tracks into Northline. He parked on William Street in front of the mosque and walked down to the Great Western, where he took a stool against the bar and tapped out a Craven A, waited to be served. He didn't know how he was going to get at the safe, nor how much explosive to use. He couldn't just walk up the stairs and lob in the gelignite, and the place was heavily secured at night. The sticks were in a Dunlop sports bag at his feet, along with his bugging device and camera. Not even Gus Riley would consider raiding Chisholm Gold, not for ten Harley Knuckleheads. And Swann was unarmed.

The usual barman wasn't there, replaced by a young woman with cherry lipstick and a T-shirt two sizes too small. She chewed gum as she came over and took Swann's order of a pony of bitter, soon frothing on a bar mat.

'Had an argument with a lawnmower, eh?'

Swann wasn't in the mood for chatting, didn't want her to remember him, should something go down, but it was too late for that. It was going to be a long day watching the offices, waiting for his chance.

'Tom not on today?' he asked.

'He's working in the function room until lunch. Private party. Some Japs, business types. The manager puts Tom in there because he knows about wine, and because he's big. He's what they reckon an Australian bloke should look like. How do you know him? He's my boyfriend.'

'He was . . . good to a friend of mine.'

'Well, he's trying to keep out of trouble. He promised. And you look like trouble.'

Swann laughed, ignored the wire in her voice. 'He good at

keeping promises?'

'Good at making them.'

'Easily led, eh?'

'Yeah. What's your name?'

'Frank.'

'Frank, you ever seen a pack of wild dogs hunting?'

Swann shrugged. 'No.'

'Not dingoes. Feral dogs. There's always a big one leading the pack, then others nose to tail, and at the back, small little yappy dogs, the kind that shiver when they get excited.'

'Big Tom's a lapdog?'

'Not when he looks in the mirror. Sees a lone wolf. My name's Melanie, by the way. But that's the kinda trouble Tom gets himself into. Big dog goes for the kill and the middle dogs follow, and the little yappers hang around the edges, barking till they wet themselves. Later they puff out their chests actin' like they're the big dogs, but they're not.'

'Safer on a leash, eh?'

'S'pose you're right.'

Swann watched her go down the bar, begin to wipe and empty. When her hair fell in her eyes, she blew it out in little gusts. He couldn't help smiling. She reminded him of Marion when she was that age.

Swann turned back to face James Street. The owner of the porn shop next door to Chisholm Gold was out smoking in the charcoal-dusted street. He had mirror shades and leathery skin and a many times broken nose. Swann sipped on his beer, which tasted faintly of ammonia. Unlike at Danny's, the pipes here weren't cleaned very often. He put the glass down and lit a cigarette and saw a thin young man with a lairy red shirt exit the Chisholm Gold doorway. Swann recognised him from Mattie's photos; he was one of Adamo's men.

He stood by the doorway and glared at the porn shop owner, who got the message and went inside the folding pink doors.

The goon looked younger in real life. Lean and of average height, black hair cinched in a ponytail. Slav or Italian. At ease, he still looked coiled with energy, ready to act. No obvious weapons. Shirt untucked, gun would be at his back. A knife in a sheath strapped to his ankle. The man's eyes flickered over the passers-by – one of whom was Sullivan. He ignored the bodyguard and went straight up the stairs.

Sullivan, carrying his Gladstone bag.

Swann hoisted up the sports bag and splayed it open, checked that the receiver was on. That the tape was rewound. He popped a single earphone in his right ear, saw the red light of the receiver trip, the tape begin to creak on its spindles. He closed the bag and sat it in his lap. To an outsider, he was just another bloke listening to the races.

Static, scraping of a chair. A distant voice, garbled.

Swann adjusted the earphone, and the voice moved closer. Sullivan's. The photographs of Marrone and his men had obviously done the trick. Got him leverage over Adamo. A seat at the Rosa Gold table, to make his case, perhaps take a slice of the pie.

It was hard to know who Sullivan was talking to. His voice was flat, none of the charming bass notes of the pollie on the make. He was talking firmly, slowly, making his point.

'You have a problem, gentlemen. The investigator I set to observe you is a threat. You all know him. Frank Swann. A threat we need to remove. I'll arrange a meeting with him, and one of you, I don't want to know who, or how . . .'

Swann felt his arms go weak, just as he lifted his gaze to the goon across the street. The man was staring at the Great Western, then moving as the thought occurred to him, crossing the footpath and heading for the door.

Swann tipped the earphone into his sports bag, closed the zip and swung around to look into his beer, did the barfly hunch; crumpled and bent, staring into the glass canoe.

The man was good at his job. Standing quietly, watching, letting his presence register. The pub was an obvious place to survey the Chisholm Gold offices. In the mirror above the bar, Swann saw that there was a second man across the road, a beefy man with a shaven head, watching the street. The bloke in the pub was a forward scout. Meaning they were definitely on to him, but perhaps without a precise description. That would come very soon.

Then Melanie looked over at the pony-tailed goon, clocked that something was wrong. She fronted the wood. 'Oi. Spiv. This is the public bar. The place you're looking for is across the road.' She indicated the porn shop behind the pink doors.

In reply, the man whipped a .32 Beretta out of his back waistband and in a second had it at her head.

'Why you say that, eh? You been watchin', what?'

Thick Italian accent. Melanie's eyes were more angry than afraid, telling the man what she thought of him.

'Come on, son, put it away,' Swann said.

The gun turned on him, recognition dawning in the man's eyes. The wrong tree. Barking up it. He put the pistol in his waistband and straightened his cuffs, fixed his collar. Carbon black eyes. He gobbed spit onto the bar, glanced at the street, rushed out the door.

On the street, coming out of Chisholm Gold, Adamo flanked by his bodyguards, and Leo Marrone, Hogan, Farquarson and Quinlivan. Isaacs and Bevans stalking the other way, faces hard, fists clenched. Sullivan, looking relieved, raising a hand for his staff car.

'What the fuck just happened?'

Swann glanced at Melanie, the adrenalin rushing out of her now, hands shaking, just as Jennifer Henderson emerged from the doorway of Chisholm Gold, looked straight across the road at him, lit a cigarette, turned down the footpath, tilted her hat into the sun.

41

Gary Quinlivan played with his key ring, because it seemed to annoy Hogan. They stood in the afternoon sun beside Gary's red RX-7 and thrashed it out, one last time. Perhaps Hogan could see it in Gary's eyes, the resentment Hogan used to enjoy becoming something else: a confidence that soon Gary would be free of Hogan's demands.

Everything was going Gary's way. He'd been able to persuade the directors of the merits of a float, a way of seeing off PLA and bringing in needed currency. Hogan and Farquarson were still short on their initial investment, and had signed all their property over to Adamo. They were less than a day from the float, and after the stocks rose none of this would matter. Before then, there was only the job Gary had to do, to prove himself to Adamo.

When Sullivan had mentioned Frank Swann's name and the threat he posed, Adamo looked directly at Gary and nodded. It was understood. If Gary wanted to be trusted, he was the one who had to do it. And soon. Marrone would be there to make sure it was done right, but the coup de grâce would be Gary's, and he needed to get his head straight. He needed to concentrate, to build himself up to it. But first he needed to get rid of Hogan. Gary was sick of doing

Hogan's bidding. He'd done his bit and still the copper had come up short. Still he wanted more.

Ben Hogan's forehead and cheeks were flushed, his blue-metal eyes dark. He poked Gary in the chest with hard jabs of his fingers. The jabs would bruise, but that didn't matter.

'I'm not getting through to you, am I?'

Gary tried his best not to laugh. Under stress, Hogan spoke in the tough-guy patois of *Homicide* and *Division 4*, the crime series Gary had grown up with. The language was so familiar, Gary had to remind himself Hogan wasn't an actor, but a real cop.

Hogan's robbing of Bevans and Isaacs had been a big mistake, bloody-minded and stupid. It put everything at risk, making Adamo and Marrone furious. And all because the racetrack pair had insulted Hogan at the previous meeting, goaded him about his cash shortfall. Bevans' house had been raided by two masked gunmen, who forced him to empty his personal safe in front of his family. Bernie Isaacs' offices were robbed and his stables torched, millions of dollars of horseflesh put at risk, and for what? A measly ten thousand dollars, the kind of money Isaacs lost in one night on the tables at the European Club.

Hogan had denied it, of course, but at this afternoon's meeting Isaacs and Farquarson had come to blows over the table. Having signed away all his wealth, Hogan was wild, and threatened Leo Marrone with a gun to keep out of it. Had even pointed the weapon at old Adamo and his bodyguards, who until then had never been present at a meeting. Adamo was always one step ahead. He'd sat there quietly smoking his cigar, a cold fisheye on Hogan.

Gary had serious dirt on Hogan now. Something so good that to speak of it would mean the copper's death. Marrone and Isaacs, even Farquarson, would stomp him.

Gary couldn't believe that Hogan could be so stupid. To assume that Gary wouldn't notice the missing money, or that he'd be too afraid to call him on it. Wrong, on both counts. But Gary would wait. He had the documentary evidence, and the time would come.

Gary Quinlivan had learned a lot over the past few weeks. He understood now that the only reason Hogan had lasted this long was because of his badge. He was a puffed-up standover man who would milk the tit dry. Then ask for more. Gary wished he'd known how these things worked from the beginning. How crims made straights pay and pay. Beyond what was reasonable. Put the fear into them, again and again, just to remind them of their place.

Disrespect, pure and simple.

What was Gary going to do, go to the police?

But Gary was no longer a straight. He'd enjoyed the bank robs, walked taller now. He hadn't enjoyed the bashing last night, but he could rationalise it, understand why it was necessary. Violence was part of their business, a short cut to getting what you want.

'What if I was to tell Leo or Tommaso that you're dealing your own smack?' Hogan growled. 'I know you went up to Malaysia. And why. Eh, smart cunt? Behind their backs, on their own patch?'

Even this didn't touch Gary, as it would have yesterday. He knew the answer of course – they would kill him. On principle.

But not today. And not tomorrow.

Tomorrow, everything would change. Gary's position in Rosa Gold, in particular. He was the only one with business smarts. He'd go from menial to indispensible, in a single day.

As of tomorrow, it was Gary who'd be steering the ship.

'The money you transferred out of the shared account,' he now shot back, 'into your own. Did you think I wouldn't notice? What do you think Tommaso and Leo will do if they learn you've been stealing from them too?'

The look on Hogan's face was priceless.

42

Swann hit the footpath running, made it to his car and headed off in the direction Jennifer had gone. He looked for the Karmann Ghia on the rise up to Francis Street, past the burnt-out block, took a hunch and headed north, doubled back to William Street and saw her get into a white Fairmont.

So she was still in the picture. She'd paid him off, gone off the radar, but hadn't pulled out of Rosa Gold as she'd promised.

Swann needed to speak to her. If everything went well, he'd soon have the Rosa Gold directors at each other's throats. If things went badly, he didn't want her in the firing line.

Swann sat the Datsun three cars back as the Fairmont cruised onto Scarborough Beach Road, through the light industrial area, headed towards the coast. Jennifer Henderson was being chauffeured, but he couldn't make out the driver. Whoever it was deployed the usual counter-surveillance; slowed then sped up, turned off side streets and U-turned at roundabouts. Swann hung back, parking when necessary, resuming from a safe distance.

The Fairmont made another turn down a side street and kept to the suburban road until it broached the hill that overlooked the coast. An area of crummy motels and pizza parlours, kids playing Space Invaders on the footpath, surfers and panel vans, pygmy rooters and kombis in car parks. They headed north above the limestone cliffs and emerald reef pools to Trigg, turned inland and circled the fringes of the city, east to Balga and Balcatta. The petrol gauge in the Datsun was flicking on empty.

Still the Fairmont continued on, trolling through an industrial area of panelbeaters and wreckers and car yards, turning down a track behind a cement factory spewing creamy froth into a holding pond, bumping over ruts and cutaways, accelerating past a side track and raising a wall of limestone dust. Swann accelerated too, then into the cloud from the side-track a white Commodore speared across his path and turned into the cyclone fence, barring his way. Swann slammed on the anchors and skidded up to the Commodore's nose.

The dust settled. The Datsun's engine ticked. The driver of the Commodore remained in his seat. Dark sunglasses. Big moustache. No expression on his face.

The ambush was perfect. Swann was unarmed, having given the revolver back to Gould. It would take him a full minute to reverse down the track. There was no sign of the Fairmont. Jennifer Henderson was gone.

Swann put the Datsun into neutral, left the motor idling. The Commodore showed no signs of backing up, now that its job was done. Swann kicked open the door and stood. The driver waited, face impassive, hands beneath the dash.

Swann rolled his neck, clenched then unclenched his fingers. Dropped his sunglasses onto the seat. The man could not know he was unarmed. He touched the back of his belt in bluff.

The .45 calibre pistol rose from the man's crotch and took aim through the open window at Swann's chest. It would kill him from three metres or one metre, didn't matter. He walked up to the Commodore.

'I want to know where Jennifer Henderson is,' Swann said.

The man didn't answer. Just held the pistol on him. His job was to stall, to let Jennifer escape. Military trained, no doubt about it. Robotic. Not in his orders to engage with the enemy.

He spoke like a robot too, out of the side of his mouth. 'Put these cuffs on. My boss says to keep you company for the next twenty-four.'

'Or what?'

The look said it all. Perfect place for an execution. A shovel and tarp on the back seat.

But not a robot. Not perfect. Swann saw the raised rear door lock and leaped to the handle, threw himself behind the driver's seat, caught the gun hand as it turned over the man's shoulder. The .45 discharged into the ceiling, blowing a coin-sized hole and deafening Swann. Cordite in his nostrils, he turned the man's wrist hard, twisting it over the headrest, putting all his weight on it, pulling it down, shanking it south, until the forearm broke at the wrist. The gun dropped from the limp hand and Swann snatched it up, put it at the man's head, behind the ear, clutching his hair and getting his breath back, waiting for his hearing to return.

The man was good. Breathed through his pain, teeth gritted. Eyes never closing. Swann saw his face in the rear-vision mirror.

That robot voice was unchanged. 'I want you to know, I didn't have anything to do with that bomb. A few seconds earlier, could have done for me.'

'You were tailing me for Jennifer Henderson. Take me to her. You drive.'

The man didn't move. Swann tilted the gun down and fired a shot just shy of the driver's groin. Gunpowder on the man's cheek.

Swann made him get out of the car, kneel with his face to the wall while he locked the Datsun. He returned to the Commodore, searched it, came up with another .45 in a holster taped under the front seat, a knife sheathed beside it, binoculars, Pentax SLR, all the tools.

But no ID, no hint of who he worked for. Swann would leave that question for Jennifer Henderson.

The man drove one-handed, broken wrist in his lap, the automatic purring through the gear changes. They reached the coast and turned with the sun on their right, the ocean rising to the horizon, the cool breeze reviving the driver, skin grey around his lips, hand trembling as he bore his pain. The Commodore slowed and turned past the SAS Barracks. Now Swann knew where they were headed. Jennifer Henderson had moved home to her Swanbourne residence, gutted and empty.

Swann made the PI drive the Commodore across the lawn and right up to the front door. Then had him ring the bell, the pistol in his lower back.

Jennifer Henderson answered. Jeans and corduroy jacket, calf-skin boots. She smiled at Swann strangely, nodded and stood away.

He went in behind the PI, whose shoulders visibly relaxed. He turned to Swann and there it was, a little smile of triumph.

Swann sensed the blow before it landed, but not in time. Sharp pain in his lower neck, sparks in his eyes, cartoon colours in the dark.

Stillness, then the fall.

43

Swann awoke to a sharp intake of breath, then another. Smell of solvents. He shook his head and took a deep inhalation. Then another, powering up. He could feel his heart beating slowly, too slowly. Panic when he understood that he was blind. Hands and feet bound. Something tight across his chest. Panting now, light at the edges. Not a blindfold. Not a bag over his head. A shroud of cloth. He bit it and shook; it fell.

Garth Oats. The smell of him across the room. Wood smoke and bush cigarettes. Stale sweat. Watching Swann struggle in Max Henderson's recliner, tilted back.

The handle cracked at his side and the seat shifted and he was sitting upright, staring into the eyes of Jennifer Henderson, looking at him with concern, lifting a lock of his hair, gentle touch.

The PI was bound to one of the iron chairs from the garden set. Pushed against the wall, his smug look gone. Didn't look like he'd slept, as Swann must have slept – through the night. Sunlight around the edges of the drawn blinds.

Jennifer raised a glass of water to Swann's lips and he gulped it down, already working the angles. 'Jennifer?'

She shook her head and took the glass away, into the next room, leaving water to run down his chin. The pain in his head was strong and sharp, illuminating. He remembered the blow, clean and precise, the tempered edge of Garth Oats' hand delivered to the base of his neck, just enough to knock him out.

But why had they subdued the PI? His broken wrist was bound in calico and masking tape, in a sling made from a T-shirt. A glass bottle of ether was on the floor beside him, stoppered with a cork, away from his bound feet.

So he had not gone quietly.

Their eyes met, Swann looking for an answer. There was nothing in his face. Resignation in his posture. Seeing it out. Part of his military training. The belief that triumph came not because of intelligence or teamwork, but the capacity to endure, to suffer. Cold. Hunger. Pain. Exhaustion. Terror.

The soldier's lot.

But Swann struggled in his constraints. Muscles aching. Chafing at his wrists, his feet. The hot clear pain in his head.

Garth Oats checked the window at the front door. His rifle leant against the wall. He hadn't looked at Swann. He lit another cigarette, and crouched with his back to the door.

'Garth. One of those.'

Without looking at him, Oats rolled Swann a bush cigarette. Lit it and crossed the room to put it between Swann's lips, held it until it took. Swann exhaled through his nose, felt better, much better.

'What's this about?'

Oats didn't answer; disappeared behind him, soundless. Just the man's campfire smell, bad sweat, burning mulch.

Jennifer Henderson returned with the telephone on a long lead. Oats followed her with another outdoor chair, placed it square to Swann, and she sat, like a queen. She nodded towards the PI and

Oats approached him, knelt and took up the ether, uncorked it.

Now the man showed something. Began to squirm and shimmy. Rock on his chair, voice muffled behind the rag in his mouth, face reddening with the effort.

Oats took no notice. From a pocket, he took out a glass dropper and drew up some ether, placed the bottle on the floor, recorked it. Took the man by the hair and thrust back his head. Dropped the liquid into the mouth rag, looked into his enraged eyes, waited for them to roll, dropped the lolling head.

Swann wasn't gagged yet, but the look in Oats' eyes was a warning. He placed the dropper in his pocket, took his position by the front door.

Jennifer Henderson looked at her watch.

Swann could smell her, too. Amber, citrus, honey. 'Jennifer. Whatever's going on, I don't —'

She put a hand up to silence him, dialled a number, waited. Flicked a switch that put the phone on speaker, a novelty he'd seen in executive boardrooms. Lit a cigarette while she waited, her eyes never leaving his. Disappointment there, or was it regret?

'Jeremy Hardman.'

The voice harried, clatter in the background, hard surfaces, more voices, just like Hardman's.

'Jeremy. This is Jennifer. Talk me through it.'

'Oh, Mrs Henderson. You called at the right time.'

Voice different now, unctuous, deferential. All the time in the world.

'As we anticipated, it's . . . mayhem . . . since sliced bread.'

Excited shouting, like boys who've cornered a rat.

'Fifteen minutes and we've seen significant trades. From Carman, who trade for PLA, in particular. Some small parcels from individuals who got in early, but it's mainly big buyers with deep pockets. Started at two cents, already ten dollars. Higher bids coming all the time. The market will pay twenty, perhaps thirty by day's end. Have you considered —'

'Not yet. Call me if it hits twenty.'

'Carman know I'm acting for you. I can make them an offer directly.'

She hung up, exhaled smoke into the air, closed her eyes, bowed her head. Opened her eyes and checked her watch. Stood and left the room.

Garth Oats hadn't moved from his position by the front door. The PI was still unconscious, head slumped on his chest.

What game was Jennifer playing? Like the other Rosa Gold directors, she had a half-million shares in her name. What was it she wanted him to hear?

The phone rang, and the back door opened. Jennifer returned to her iron chair, hoisted the phone onto her lap, lifted the receiver. Looked at Swann, flicked on the speaker.

'Twenty-three dollars forty cents a share! It's something of a record, Mrs Henderson. Not since Poseidon. Carman are on another line, open. They're not going away. They'll buy, Mrs Henderson, but my advice is not to sell . . . the value of your stock . . . tomorrow we can expect . . .'

Twenty-three dollars a share, and rising. Just as Gould had predicted. PLA and the other big players were paying any price. Hogan and the rest, rich beyond greed. Swann felt sick to his stomach. The power they'd wield. Untouchable.

If he got out of this, Swann would have to leave, his home and his family. But he wouldn't be safe anywhere. He'd have to keep moving, until they caught him.

The PI began gurgling, no mean feat while gagged. Oats crossed the room and lifted him by his hair, looked at his face with all the curiosity of a cat examining a dead bird. He wrenched off the gag then let the head slump down.

Went back to his position by the door.

Jennifer Henderson was looking at her watch, the tension radiating from her trembling hands. She lit yet another cigarette, her fifth in the last quarter-hour, and dialled. Flicked the speaker again.

'I'd like to speak to Barry Nichols. Tell him it's Jennifer Henderson.'

She was quickly put through to the CEO of PLA. His voice measured, clearly expecting her call. 'Mrs Henderson, my brokers tell me —'

She cut him off, violence in her voice. 'I'll sell my entire parcel of shares, for thirty dollars a share. That's fifteen million dollars. I expect it in my bank account by the time I hang up, and I'll dial them to confirm. You have my details. The shares are yours.'

'It's above the market price, but done . . . done, Mrs Henderson. On another matter, have you seen my man, Singleton? He hasn't checked in. Is he still with you?'

She hung up without answering him. Swann felt the anger rise through him, surge into his fists. He tried to shift within his restraints, but couldn't move.

Jennifer Henderson dialled her stockbroker, then her bank. She didn't put the phone on speaker, or look up at him, her face hidden behind a veil of black hair.

'It's there?' she asked. 'Then, as we discussed. Transfer the entire amount. Yes, offshore . . .'

She looked at him now. 'Yes, that's right. Mr Frank Swann, a postal cheque, and post it. Ten thousand dollars. Yes. Then close the account.'

She hung up, exhausted but exhilarated, triumph in her eyes. She came over and stood beside him, put a hand on his shoulder and ran her fingers through his hair, looking down at his face.

For a moment he thought she was going to kiss him.

'Don't be angry,' she said. 'It had to be this way. Your conflict with Inspector Hogan threatened everything. When I learned of it, I had to act. I had to disappear. But we knew you'd find us.'

'We? You and Garth? Did he help trash your house? Make me think you were in danger?'

'I took no pleasure in deceiving you. This is about —'

'Greed. I thought you didn't need the money?'

She bowed her head. Tears swelled over the rims of her eyes.

'Now what?'

She knelt and unbuckled the belts at his shins, not meeting his eyes.

'Listen.'

Garth Oats was on the telephone.

'*There is no gold.* How do I know? I salted it myself. Injected the half-cores with alluvial. You're the assay lab. Look at the popcorn shape of the macroscopic grains. Mercury refined. You can confirm by checking the other half of the split cores, out at the stake. But you won't find any gold there. Never was . . .'

Jennifer unbuckled the last bind on his wrist.

'You beautiful man,' she whispered. 'It's done.'

44

Something in Ben Hogan's voice burst, the sound of air escaping.

The others didn't notice, too caught up in getting drunk. Farquarson was toting a cigar the size of a small dog, whisky in his other hand. Neat single malt in a coffee mug. Isaacs, Bevans and old Chisholm were playing cards, Texas hold 'em, for ridiculous stakes. Sheep stations.

Adamo and Marrone and their men were chatting in Italian, taking no pleasure in being around the drunks. Adamo looked like he'd rather be weeding his garden. Marrone polished his croc-skin boots with a silk handkerchief. He'd smirked disdainfully a few minutes earlier when Isaacs had called for some strippers, said he felt like getting his dick sucked.

But now Hogan couldn't be ignored. He was tottering on his heels, had to put a hand against the wall.

'There's no gold,' he said quietly.

Marrone had his gun out straight away, followed by the body-guards, eyes flashing, covering the door. Adamo nodded to him, and Marrone took up the second phone that lay on the table, an open line to the brokers.

Every time the stock price had risen, Marrone had called it out, raising cheers and toasts from the others, and exclamations of disbelief. Millionaires, the lot of them.

And now this.

'The price – it's falling,' Marrone confirmed. 'Dropping through the floor. Five dollars! Four dollars!'

'There's no gold,' Hogan repeated weakly, his voice ironed out. 'That was the assay lab. We've been *had*. It's all over the radio. FUCK!'

He grabbed the phone and flung it to the floor. 'My fucking life savings. You CUNTS! What did you do?' A Winchester .45 appeared in his hand, murder in his eyes.

Gary Quinlivan took the cigarette out of his mouth, arm too heavy to bear its weight.

Bevans stood and drew his own revolver, for no reason at all.

Hogan put a bullet in the man's guts, stepped forward, put another between the eyes.

45

Jennifer helped Swann to his feet. He stood beside her on trembling legs, braced against her.

'We have to leave, *now*,' said Oats. He went out of the room, taking the rifle with him.

The dizziness was clearing. Swann felt strong enough to walk. 'What about him?' He indicated the PI, who slept on, head at a bad angle.

'Garth will drop him somewhere.'

'What didn't you want him to know?'

'About you. If PLA suspect your involvement, there'll never be an end.'

'It's not PLA I'm worried about. It's Hogan, Adamo and Marrone. When they hear —'

'They don't know about you and me. But they were always going to kill me. Just like they were going to kill Max, until . . .'

Suddenly it all made sense. That look in Jennifer's eyes, beyond her worry that the sting would sour, that PLA would smell a rat. She'd already known what Swann had been trying to tell her; the danger she was in, the company she was keeping. Max Henderson had known too; had found out the hard way.

'You're telling me that Max killed himself —'

'To put them off . . . long enough to get the shares floated. They were going to kill him. The older one, Max knew it. Killing himself gave me time to finish what we planned.'

That was where it stopped making sense. Why hadn't the Hendersons fled? Withdrawn from Rosa Gold? Knowing how it would end.

'You don't understand,' she continued, not meeting his eye, or trying to convince him. 'Max was going to die anyway. Leukaemia. All the doctors . . . *nothing* worked. I knew, we all knew, that he was going to do it his way.'

Swann turned away from her, couldn't look, the pain in her voice bad enough.

'He wanted to free me, even though I didn't want to be free. He wasn't supposed to . . . I didn't know *when*. I thought that if we got away with this, together, it would help him, bring him some peace. He believed it was his anger that caused the sickness. I thought that he could laugh . . . at them. You can see why I needed you. You know their world. How they do things. I needed you to watch them, keep them away, until . . .'

Garth Oats returned carrying two duffle bags, rifle slung over his shoulder. 'We have to go,' he said. 'I'll check the street. Swann, try and wake him up.' He indicated the PI. 'He's too heavy to carry.'

But Jennifer didn't let go of Swann's hands. 'Garth has been watching one of Marrone's men. He's out there somewhere, waiting for their call. Garth saw him last night, watching the house. Wanted to get rid of him, but I told him to wait, until after . . .'

'They know you're here? Then Garth's right. We need to leave now.'

'I want you to understand. It was never about the money. It was about PLA, and Max's father, mother. I never planned to deceive you. You're —'

The bullet ripped her chest from the side, wrenching her away. Swann dived out of instinct, brought her with him. He saw her ripped from him again, in slow motion, even as he dragged her behind the easy chair, no protection at all. The image of her dark blue eyes reaching into him, then the disbelief, a moment of accusation, shock, not understanding. He looked around, saw the PI's Webley .455 by the front door.

But she held him, gripped his shirt, blood vessels breaking in her eyes. 'The money,' she whispered. The bullet had torn her lungs, her breathing came in whimpers.

'Don't worry about the money,' he replied. And then he saw Oats brace the side fence, vault over with his rifle. Swann stroked her hair, her face. Wiped the tears from her eyes, the foam of blood on her lips. She pulled at him, and he leant closer. 'Because of Max, I've been *so* . . .'

And then she started keening, the sound of pity and terror, and the darkness came into her eyes.

He smelt Oats before he arrived, scalded earth, wood smoke, the sob breaking deep in him, not making it to his lips, a shy groan. He fell beside Swann and his hands were shaking, pressed to his knees. Swann wanted to say, *look what you've done*, you and Max, but Oats was already feeling it. His only people, gone.

Swann climbed to his feet, blood on his hands, sprayed across his chest, his neck and face. The PI was awake, had seen the whole thing, eyes wide, face red.

Swann knelt and unwound the gaffer tape that bound him, did the same to the cloth binds on his wrist. The man had wet himself, smelt of wheaty piss and old socks, his forearm swollen. The PI tried to stand but fell to the floor, his knees gone, muscles cramped.

Swann helped him back onto the seat, dizziness in his grabby move-ments, throaty sounds, rapid blinking.

The PI had no inkling about what had happened, or why. Better it stay that way.

Swann went over to Oats, knelt beside him. 'Take her to Cue. Beside Max's mother and father.'

'She was going home, to Tasmania,' was all Oats said.

Swann had just retrieved the Webley when he heard car doors slamming in the drive. He switched off the safety, slid in a round. The ether had dulled his head. Of course they would come, to make sure of the assassin's job. Swann watched Adamo's goons stroll towards the front door, the shorter man in the red silk shirt wielding a large ballpein which he swung at the lock, splintering wood but not breaking through. Swann lost sight of the beefier man, who'd presumably headed down the side. First he'd have to climb the high fence that Oats had vaulted, designed to keep Max's dogs in. Swann locked eyes with the PI, who was walking the wall with his one good hand, trying to get his legs to work. For the first time there was fear in his eyes.

Oats had disappeared. Swann took the PI by the arm and shuf-fled him to the back door. Cracked it, and peered around the side. Nothing yet. Only a single brass cartridge, ejected from the silenced rifle beside a duffle bag. The dead assassin dragged into the bed of poppies, cause of death unknown.

Swann helped the PI down the wooden steps and over towards the shed, pushing him inside. Heard the side gate give way. Rushed to the red-brick barbecue across the narrow yard, ducked behind it.

Swann looked to the back fence. Twenty metres and a good leap, he'd be on the other side. It was sturdy jarrah, wouldn't make a sound.

But the PI would never make it. Swann saw the beefy bodyguard, cradling a .22 sawn-off rifle, good for hunting in suburbia – he didn't even pause at the sight of his dead colleague. He entered the back door but came out immediately – the other man must already be inside. Swann cursed and saw the first bodyguard in the upstairs bedroom. The man had clocked him, had raised his hammer behind the glass. Boots were approaching over the paving. There wasn't time to think.

Swann shot the man behind the left knee, an image of Dennis Gould and Percy Dickson guiding the bullet home. The sound of the gunshot slammed into the iron shed, rang in Swann's ears. The bodyguard shrieked, kneecap blown out the front, leg gone beneath him. Firing up into the trees as he fell.

Swann crouched and ran and kicked the man in the face, stamped on his arm, wrenched away the .22 and tossed it inside the shed, saw the PI scrabble for it on the concrete floor, take it up one-handed, draw a bead on the goon's head.

Swann was exposed, and ran to the nearest casuarina, the same one where Max Henderson had taken his life. He covered the windows and back door with the Webley, waiting for a glimpse of the red-shirted bodyguard, knew that he was armed with a small-calibre Berretta.

Swann waited, and still nothing.

Finally the back door swung inwards. Swann aimed and held his breath, pistol steadied on a low branch, partially concealing him.

The red shirt launched himself through the door, hit the pavers and slid beneath the iron table setting. Swann lifted but didn't fire. The man wasn't moving, and there was no gun in his hand.

Garth Oats stood in the doorway, no expression on his face. He ignored Swann as he moved over to the bodyguard by the shed door, face florid with pain. He said something to the PI, who passed him the .22.

'What are you doing?' Swann shouted. 'Garth —'

But it was too late. The nutshell crack of the .22 reverberated around the yard, then dropped away. The bodyguard was dead, a bullet in his left eye, right hand spasming in the dirt, then still.

'Better you get lost,' said Oats. 'Give me the Webley. I'll get rid of that.'

Down the mineshaft, in Cue.

46

Swann found a park between a gold Toyota Crown and a purple Sandman on Beaufort Street. The length of William Street was blocked by huge plaster floats of anchors and mermaids and quokkas on flatbed trucks and performers in costume, the footpath crowded with schoolchildren and kids from the suburbs. Locals slipped out of the cafes and bars for a look at the Mardi Gras, waiting for the signal to begin the procession over the tracks into the city. At the front of the queue was a gigantic plaster black swan, strapped down with wire leaders, rocking in the breeze, the police marching band tuning up in formation beside. Swann slipped through the crowd and turned into the greater throng of rubbernecks at the corner of James and William.

Reggie was perched at the front bar of the Great Western. Tom was behind the wood, as was his girlfriend Melanie, doting on Reggie. The front bar was packed, a good vantage point to watch the action across the road.

Melanie fixed Swann a whisky to match Reggie's gin and tonic, dewy on the coaster.

Swann had heard it on the radio. Double homicide at the offices of Chisholm Gold. There had been a siege, now resolved. One of the dead men was a serving member of the CIB, no further details.

'You smell badly of turps, dear boy.'

'Ether.'

'One of *those* nights, eh?'

Swann tried to smile. He'd washed his face and hands at a tap on a suburban oval, changed out of his bloodied shirt. He put a hand on Reggie's shoulder, gently squeezed the bird bones. Reggie didn't need to know the details of what had happened, even if he wasn't looking too bad. Perhaps it was the air of celebration and drama, the juniper and quinine, cigarillo in his hand.

'Still on the durries, eh?'

Reggie nodded, puffed a cloud of smoke. 'Bum-sucking, as the kids say. Can't inhale. But no point quitting, is there?'

'Suppose not.'

Out in the quicksilver light, beating off the windshields of the paddy wagons and unmarkeds in the street, Terry Accardi scouted the footpaths and gutters, notebook in hand. A plastic tarp was draped over a body, feet out from the doorway, one stockinged foot, brown brogue on the other.

'Were you here?'

'Yes, my boy, I had to see for myself. Dennis received a call from an ex-colleague at Capitol. Half the big end of town have lost their shirts. The Rosa Gold directors have lost everything. Your lady friend, bless her. For her sake, I hope she's gone.'

Swann nodded, his face numb, his throat dry.

'Good for her. A story for another day, perhaps. So, as I was saying, I caught a taxi down here to see what I could see, expecting to find you. Then all hell broke loose. Gunshots. Sirens.'

'Who copped it?'

'That I don't know. I think it's Farquarson over there, under the sheet.'

It was impossible to tell. The feet in the doorway belonged to a large man. Terry Accardi was still scoping the crime scene, jotting in his notebook. It was odd that he'd been given such a high-profile investigation. A police homicide. Unless the higher-ups were confident that giving the case to a rookie would guarantee their control, and fail to be thoroughly investigated.

A big mistake, if so. They didn't know Terry Accardi like Swann did. Swann could feed Terry the good oil on Rosa Gold, suggest he start with a warrant to search Chisholm's safe.

But later.

Two uniformed sergeants appeared from the doorway, hats in their hands. They stood briefly over the corpse, returned their caps to their closely cropped heads. Ben Hogan followed them into the sunshine, his mouth a slash of grey, blood soaked into his shirt. The rubbernecks on the footpath outside the crime tape leaned closer. Hogan put on his sunglasses. Ran a steel comb through his dyed black hair. Lit a cigarette, looked around at the gathered faces.

Looking for Swann?

Hogan would already have a story to explain his presence at the scene. The Commissioner and the Minister of Police would want to believe his story, would *need* to believe it. Whatever other witnesses said.

The other Rosa Gold directors were not the kind to talk.

Either way, Swann was safe for now. Ben Hogan had bigger things to worry about. The brass would be watching him closely. No more stuff-ups. No more embarrassment. There were plenty of others who wanted the top job.

Gary Quinlivan was led out of the darkened doorway, followed by Bernie Isaacs in cuffs, shouting abuse at Hogan, red-faced, spittle flying.

Terry Accardi was listening to Isaacs, catching every word. He'd know that Bernie wasn't the dogging kind. But there he was, still shouting abuse at Hogan, who looked uncomfortable, turned his back on Isaacs and caught the full bank of television cameras and snapping newspapermen. He seemed stunned, bent his head and went to walk back inside Chisholm Gold, but was stopped by Accardi.

Good kid. Smart move.

Accardi didn't want Ben Hogan up there unsupervised, messing with things, as he and Don Casey were rumoured to have done at the Ruby Devine crime scene, those four years ago.

Hogan looked perplexed, put on his professional face, extended his hand. Accardi shook it, but without enthusiasm. Bernie Isaacs was shouting to the cameras now, to the zoom lenses, the fluffy mics thrust on poles. Gary Quinlivan stood beside him trying to look small, doing a good job, face pale and pinched, hair over his eyes like a sullen teenager.

Isaacs and Quinlivan were led towards a paddy wagon, Isaacs kicking against the uniformed sergeants, wrestled into the dark cave, door slammed and locked.

The crowd hadn't dispersed. The show wouldn't be over until the bodies were removed. Then the pub would get busier.

Reggie cackled at something Melanie said. She had her hand protectively on his arm. He looked tired but content. Swann's enemies were Reggie's enemies, and today was a win. His blue eyes watered in their bruised pouches. Reggie's escape route was becoming clear. The booze-fuelled short cut. Exit on a bender, most likely. With a bang and a whimper. And Swann would be there, if that's what Reggie wanted.

'I'll call you.' Swann finished his drink and picked up his cigarettes, squeezed Reggie's shoulder.

'Go home and heal, Frank. A quick healer you always were. And quit the durries, for me, *promise*. No future in 'em, for a man with your responsibilities.'

'Sure,' Swann agreed.

'Good, Frank. And don't forget, dinner at mine, soon. Asparagus soup, in season. Young Dennis is on the job. Claims he can cook soup. Secret's in the stock, apparently.'

'Teaching his grandmother to suck eggs there.'

'Like that as a child, too. My brother's fault. Talked to him like an adult. Not my domain. I'm rambling, you better go home.'

Out on the street, Swann met eyes with Hogan, but only for a moment. Hogan was trying to look important, but he was trying too hard. His posture stiff and unnatural, ciggie near to burning his fingers. He'd lost everything. The product of decades of careful graft, gone. Gust of wind could blow him over.

Swann turned away from the spectacle, just as the Mardi Gras burst into life, steel drums and bagpipes blaring, tin whistles and trumpets, the first crack of fireworks across the city on the foreshore. The black swan float that led the procession wobbled and teetered as the truck beneath it swerved to avoid a pothole, a leader snapped and was grabbed by nearby men, the wind lifting them off their feet.

Swann turned the corner and walked towards the Datsun, dun coloured in the late-afternoon glare. The rear door of the Sandman was open, four sets of bare feet in there, stereo pumping AC/DC, fluffy walls and ceiling, TV and bar fridge, faux fur on the dash.

The Datsun slumped as he sat and dropped the visor, vinyl seat burning through his shirt. He turned the ignition and looked at his reflection in the rear-view mirror. The swelling around his black eye was nearly gone. The cuts on his cheeks were ruby red, lost in his stubble. True, it was the same battered face he'd worn often as a teenager. But that was then. Things would have to change. He twisted the rear-vision away and swung into the traffic.

47

In the back of the paddy wagon, Gary Quinlivan sat with his head in his hands. They were still parked at Central, but Gary was alone. He hadn't been processed yet, and that worried him. Isaacs had been carted away an hour ago, and the two uniformed drivers had never returned. It was starting to get dark.

Gary's hands were shaking; his wrists ached in the cuffs, and he was sweating. He had never seen anything like it. Overdoses were ugly. Collapsed lungs, cardiac arrest, the awful gurgling. But he was always numb. He was no longer numb. The gunfire had jarred him out of something, the dried blood on his clothes, in his hair. The smell of it, like rusting iron. He felt naked. Couldn't get comfortable on the hard metal seat. Every time a firework exploded, his mind snapped, sent a shock down his spine. He felt anxious when he knelt, nervous when he sat. Squirming inside. Shame and fear. The look in Hogan's eyes as Gary had been bundled into the paddy wagon, along with Isaacs.

Gary Quinlivan knew too much.

Isaacs was mad. The things he was saying. Hogan would have no choice. Tommaso Adamo would have no choice. Perhaps when he calmed down, Isaacs would think about what he knew, and what others knew, enough to pull back.

But Hogan had looked at Gary like he was meat on a hook.

He and Isaacs were the only witnesses to the double murder of Bevans and Farquarson. Adamo and Marrone had known to run as soon as the bullets started flying, along with their bodyguards and old man Chisholm.

Isaacs wrestling with Hogan on the floor, like animals. Gary had just sat there, blood on his face, in shock. Ears ringing. Cigarette burning his left hand.

Then the sirens, boots on the stairs. Hogan with his pistol at Isaac's head.

Gary couldn't sit and he couldn't bear to move; either way, the nerves in his chest clawed at him, made him think he was losing his mind. He couldn't control his thoughts. Images of hanging in a cell. Of Hogan's mates coming for him in the night.

He heard boots crunching on gravel, the jangling of keys. But it wasn't the rear door that opened. The Holden sank as the driver sat. Gary crawled on his knees over the tray, handcuffs biting his wrists, peered through the mesh of iron and glass that separated the cabin from the lockup.

Hogan. And he was alone. Jacket off, clean shirt on, looking freshly shaved and washed.

But his eyes. What was in his eyes?

Ben Hogan adjusted the rear-vison mirror so that Gary looked straight at him. Hogan smiled, fluttered his fingers, a wave goodbye. Lit a cigarette, exhaled lazily. Took out the road map from the glove box, opened it at the page for the Gnangara pine forest, placed it on the seat next to him, next to his pistol. Turned off the CB, turned on the radio.

Gary tried to batter his hands against the mesh, but his knees buckled. He wanted to lie on the floor and curl up. He wanted to grovel, whimper. To get rid of the feeling in his chest, behind his eyes.

But Hogan had already turned the mirror away, disgusted.

48

Marion danced with Sarah, and a couple of the prostitutes she visited on her rounds. Swann knew one of them by name, Rose, who lived in the battered women's sanctuary on Pakenham Street. Behind them, on stage, Louise and Justin were plugging through a looping ska number, stringing it out for the dancers. Every now and then, they turned to look at the empty stool behind them, the silent drum kit with folded sticks where Penny once banged away. There were tears in Justin's eyes, singing 'Pressure Drop', his long pale arm around Louise's shoulder, thrumming on the bass.

'Who's that?'

Cameron, sitting at the bar, was as drunk as Swann had hoped, unaware he was sitting Marion's father's test for a new beau. *Get them drunk as possible, and see what happens.* See if any meanness comes out. Any bitterness. Sadness. Anything that might ruin a marriage, or harm your daughter.

Swann searched for hostility in Cameron's unfocused eyes, looking over at the audience of pale drunken sailors, hard-faced stevedores, the odd hippie and surfer, off-duty prostitutes and wide-eyed students. The boy was on his tenth double vodka and orange.

Swann was drinking straight orange juice, although Cameron didn't know that. The barmaid was in on it, and Swann only had to tip his finger at his empty glass.

The song ended and Cameron leapt from his seat, applauding. Marion and Sarah joined them, and Marion winked, came under Swann's arm, sweaty from the dance floor. She sipped from his juice, grimaced, ordered herself a whisky and dry, edged back under his arm.

'Not smoking?' she asked.

'Just quit.'

He got the reaction he expected, and fair enough. 'Oh yeah? Give you two months. What about Cameron, you taking him elsewhere, after?'

Swann shook his head. 'No, I've seen enough. He'll do.'

A hard punch to his upper arm. Sarah, eyes wide but smiling. 'I heard that! He'll *do*. Jesus, Dad.'

She rubbed his arm where she'd punched him, took her mother's hand.

Swann had planned to take Cameron to all the Freo dives, see how he coped amongst the crims and drunks and freaks, but he didn't have it in him. Besides, he'd seen enough now to be sure. Sarah would easily hold her own.

After returning from the city, Swann had slept for a night and a day, while Marion watched over him. He'd felt like staying in their darkened room sleeping forever. He wasn't ready to tell her what had happened, but she'd seen the bloodied shirt, had read the papers. She lay beside him, beneath the fan, held his hand.

Swann roused himself only when he heard about the farewell gig for Penny. He showered and dressed, ate in the backyard, watched a wagtail tormenting a crow, thought it a good omen. Then the sounds of his daughters, their music and shouting and laughter, dragging him out of himself.

He called Gus Riley and told him where to retrieve his Knuckle-head. Then he called Darren Plant at the mortuary, told him about Max Henderson's blood disease, asked him to check the records. Plant shuffled his papers and replied that there was nothing in Henderson's blood to indicate leukaemia, and that if Henderson had the disease it would certainly have shown in the blood.

Swann promised Marion and his daughters that he'd see them later, then headed into the city, to Parliament House on the hill, cut off from the city's inhabitants by the freeway, coursing with traffic. He guessed that neither Hogan nor Sullivan had the stomach now to arrest him, but just in case, he called into the office of the Leader of the Opposition, as promised.

Lush carpet and jarrah floors, Anglepoise lamp, brass fittings. The Leader's large suntanned hands on the walnut desk, the secretary ushered out. Swann told him what he wanted, for Hogan to back off, for Adamo to leave him alone. Swann had no reason to trust the politician, but the man assured him he would do what was asked. That he was sick of the likes of Adamo, that he intended to clean up Northline, that his plan was to create a legal casino that would put the others out of business.

Swann didn't care about any of that. He handed over the photographs and the recording of Sullivan at the Rosa Gold meeting and went out of the wood-panelled foyer into the furnace heat.

It was at Company House that he'd confirmed it all. It took longer than he anticipated but he found what he was looking for.

Garth Oats had told Swann that Max Henderson's father was run off his claim, a stake that became part of the Day Dawn mine outside Cue. Swann requested the PLA files, all seventeen of them, and got down to work. He found it in the file second from the bottom, early PLA operations in the Big Bell and Day Dawn areas.

In 1934, PLA had 'consolidated by acquisition' the northern greenstone bands described as originating in a vast granite breccia on their initial claim, close to the Cue town site, the first miners to introduce 'industrial mining and crushing technology' to the area. Consolidated by acquisition. Or, according to Max Henderson, his father had been forced to give it up, on pain of having his hand removed with a cold chisel and hammer.

For anybody but a geologist, perhaps, fifty years was a long time to hold a grudge. But Max Henderson was used to thinking in terms of billions of years. The human lifespan insignificant, the son completing the father's work.

PLA had always been Henderson's target, right from the moment Max convinced the directors of Rosa Gold that he was a believer, that he possessed the same *disease of the heart.*

But Max Henderson's disease was not the same as the other directors'. Swann had sensed something in Jennifer's eyes when she told him about Max's cancer, the fact that he was dying anyway. Had he lied to his wife about an illness he never had, to justify his suicide? Or was his illness more enduring, the result of damage to his parents first, then to his heart, his mind? Swann had seen shame in Jennifer's eyes. Not shame that her husband had suicided, perhaps, but shame that Max hadn't told her when, or how.

He had abandoned her, trusting that she would pick up the pieces, continue his plan of revenge. After all, she had little choice. He had put all their money into it.

PLA was a large multinational company newly fleeced of fifteen million dollars, and then some. Perhaps Max Henderson had seen in the directors of Rosa Gold the same capacity for ruthlessness that had once transformed PLA from a collection of small-time miners into a powerful mining giant. The same personalities. Same methods. Same weaknesses.

By not going directly to PLA, Max Henderson had controlled the Rosa Gold drilling and logged the salted cores, lured the bigger fish that way. He and Jennifer had turned the tables, used the greed of Rosa Gold and PLA against them. The disease of the heart that drew them deeper into the scam.

Max Henderson had had his revenge.

But at what cost?

Jennifer Henderson had gone into the ether, too, with her millions. But it was never about the money. Jennifer had loved a man who did not love her back. Was never capable of loving her back. Max Henderson flew his chopper in Vietnam in a way that distinguished him from others, won him medals for bravery, because he didn't care, wasn't able to care.

Swann knew what that felt like. To welcome the end; to long for it.

But it wasn't like that now. He looked at Marion and Sarah, back on the dance floor, expertly ignoring a couple of drunk bogs in black jeans and desert boots, rat-coloured mullets, one of them noticing Sarah's pregnancy and backing off, Marion and Sarah laughing.

Louise up on stage, behind the barbed wire, playing to the tough local crowd and winning them over, meeting his eye and winking, then standing perfectly still, stiffly upright, face impassive, guitar at eight-and-two, giving him the Luther Perkins stance, a private joke between them.

Jennifer Henderson had dreamed of finding refuge in the highlands of Tasmania, but the thought of the snow-dusted hills and stands of bracken beneath granite walls made Swann shiver. He reached for his orange juice and held it up to the light.

Acknowledgements

All characters in this novel are fictitious, and any resemblance to real people, living or dead, is entirely coincidental.

I'd like to thank by brother, Peter, and father, Tony, for their advice and stories, and Andrew Nette and Alan Carter for reading an early draft. Thanks always to my agent, Mary Cunnane, and to editors Meredith Rose and Janet Austin for their sound counsel, and to Ben Ball for his ongoing support.